Praise for *The Dreamers*

"*The Dreamers* is a startling, beautiful portrait of a community in peril. . . . This is an exquisite work of intimacy. Walker's sentences are smooth, emotionally arresting—of a true, ethereal beauty. . . . This book achieves [a] dazzling, aching humanity."

—*Entertainment Weekly*

"Walker offers a novel bursting with ideas, probing the scary and tantalizing possibilities at the edges of our existence."

—*USA Today*

"In *The Dreamers*, Karen Thompson Walker's second novel, dreams are . . . both more dangerous and more powerful than the Greeks could have ever imagined. . . . Walker uses evocative language to describe the almost bewitching nature of contagion."

—*The Washington Post*

"You'll be mesmerized by this well-constructed, vividly drawn exploration of loss and meditation on the concept of dreams versus reality."

—*Marie Claire*

"Walker writes beautifully about the things that define how a society either endures or collapses in crisis, a theme that may never have been more timely than it is now."

—Minneapolis *Star Tribune*

"Powerful and moving . . . [Walker] creates a symphonic voice."

—*The New York Times Book Review*

"Walker's roving fictive eye by turns probes characters' innermost feelings and zooms out to coolly parse topics like reality versus delusion . . . the perfect ambiguous frame for a tense and layered plot."

—*O: The Oprah Magazine*

"2019's first must-read novel . . . *The Dreamers* is overflowing with humanity."

—*Jezebel*

"[An] imaginative, disturbing, and ultimately spellbinding narrative, which asks provocative questions about our concepts of time and connection, and the bounds of possibility for life on earth."

—*Vogue*

"[Walker's] gripping, provocative novel should come with a warning: May cause insomnia."

—*People* (Book of the Week)

"And yet, we persevere, finding grace wherever we can, a case that Walker makes over and over in this moving novel that celebrates the marvelous resilience of the human spirit. Walker has explored these themes before in the mesmerizing, elegiac

The Age of Miracles. . . . She excels at wielding the storytelling power of cataclysm without ever losing sight of its effects on individuals."

—*Newsday*

"With mellifluous prose, Walker traces victims' experiences (awake and asleep), along with how their family members, friends, and doctors respond to the crisis."

—*Real Simple*

"Walker's prose is hauntingly beautiful . . . [*The Dreamers* is] a powerful examination of people doing their best to hold things together under extreme circumstances."

—*Paste*

"[*The Dreamers*] is a beautiful, heartbreaking reverie."

—*The Oregonian*

"*The Dreamers* does more than satisfy both the horror geek and the literary nerd. With clinical precision and psychological depth, Walker delivers a vivid embodiment of our ongoing national anxiety."

—*BookPage*

"*The Dreamers* is a beautifully written novel that is powerful, thoughtful, and entirely original."

—*PopSugar*

"A satisfying, suspenseful page-turner that leaves readers curious about the possibility of dreams . . . Recommended enthusiastically."

—*Library Journal*

"Readers will be drawn in by the telling as Walker manages to create spare prose that nonetheless conveys great detail, an approach that works well to add a bit of tension to this simultaneously languid and lush tale."

—*Booklist*

"Richly imaginative and quietly devastating . . . Walker jolts the narrative with surprising twists, ensuring it keeps its energy until the end. This is a skillful, complex, and thoroughly satisfying novel about a community in peril."

—*Publishers Weekly* (starred review)

"Within the spellbindingly measured narrative of the public health crisis are woven emotionally charged individual stories. . . . What is the nature of an epidemic? What is the nature of consciousness? What mix of loyalty and love binds individuals together? These are a few of the questions Walker raises in her provocative, hypnotic tale."

—*Kirkus Reviews* (starred review)

"*The Dreamers* is harrowing, riveting, profoundly moving, and beautifully written. In a word, this book is stunning."

—EMILY ST. JOHN MANDEL, author of *Station Eleven*

"Frighteningly powerful, beautiful, and uncanny, *The Dreamers* is a love story and also a horror story—a symphonic achievement, alternating intimate moments with a panoramic capture of a crisis in progress."

—KAREN RUSSELL, author of *Vampires in the Lemon Grove*

"A modern *Midsummer Night's Dream* . . . In this wonderful novel, Walker paints a haunting canvas exploring time, memory, consciousness, and youth."

—MARISHA PESSL, author of *Night Film*

"What a book! I read *The Dreamers* in a dream of sorts myself, entirely transported into Karen Thompson Walker's world of mysterious tragedy and infinite, if unexpected, compassion. This is a profound novel, and a deeply moving one. How she takes a terrifying situation and reveals it as a thing of beauty, a lesson in the human spirit, is a mystery to me, but she does exactly that, and fortunate readers will celebrate this extraordinary book."

—ROBIN BLACK, author of *Life Drawing*

BY KAREN THOMPSON WALKER

The Dreamers
The Age of Miracles

THE
DREAMERS

THE DREAMERS

A Novel

Karen Thompson Walker

RANDOM HOUSE
NEW YORK

2019 Random House Trade Paperback Edition

Copyright © 2019 by Karen Thompson Walker
Reading group guide copyright © 2019 by Penguin Random House LLC

Published in the United States by Random House,
an imprint and division of Penguin Random House LLC, New York.

RANDOM HOUSE and the HOUSE colophon are registered
trademarks of Penguin Random House LLC.

RANDOM HOUSE READER'S CIRCLE & Design is a
registered trademark of Penguin Random House LLC.

Originally published in hardcover in the United States by Random House,
an imprint and division of Penguin Random House LLC, in 2019.

LIBRARY OF CONGRESS CATALOGING-IN-PUBLICATION DATA
Names: Walker, Karen Thompson, author.
Title: The dreamers : a novel / Karen Thompson Walker.
Description: First edition. | New York : Random House, [2019]
Identifiers: LCCN 2017058603 | ISBN 9780812984668 |
ISBN 9780812994179 (ebook)
Subjects: | GSAFD: Science fiction
Classification: LCC PS3623.A4366 D74 2018 | DDC 813/.6—dc23
LC record available at lccn.loc.gov/2017058603

Printed in the United States of America on acid-free paper

randomhousebooks.com
randomhousereaderscircle.com

2 4 6 8 9 7 5 3 1

Book design by Elizabeth A. D. Eno

For my daughters,
Hazel and Penelope,
who were both born during
the years I was writing this book,
and who are everywhere
in these pages.

That night, the blind man dreamt that he was blind.

—JOSÉ SARAMAGO, *BLINDNESS*

THE
DREAMERS

1.

At first, they blame the air.

It's an old idea, a poison in the ether, a danger carried in by the wind. A strange haze is seen drifting through town on that first night, the night the trouble begins. It arrives like weather, or like smoke, some say later, but no one can locate any fire. Some blame the drought, which has been bleeding away the lake for years, and browning the air with dust.

Whatever this is, it comes over them quietly: a sudden drowsiness, a closing of the eyes. Most of the victims are found in their beds.

But there are some who will tell you that this sickness is not entirely new, that its cousins have sometimes visited ours. In certain letters from earlier centuries, you may find the occasional reference—decades apart—to a strange kind of slumber, a mysterious, persistent sleep.

In 1935, two children went to bed in a Dust Bowl cabin and did not wake for nine days. Some similar contagion once crept through a Mexican village—*El Niente,* they called it: "the Nothing." And three thousand years before that, a Greek poet described a string of strange deaths in a village near the sea: they died, he wrote, as if overcome by sleep—or, according to a second translation: as if drowned in a dream.

This time, it starts at the college.

It starts with a girl leaving a party. She feels sick, she tells her friends, like a fever, she says, like the flu. And tired, too, as tired as she has ever felt in her life.

2.

The girl's roommate, Mei, will later recall waking to the sound of the key turning in the lock. Mei will remember the squeak of the springs in the dark as her roommate—her name is Kara—climbs into the bunk above hers. She seems drunk, this girl, the way she moves so slowly from door to bed, but the room is dim, and—as usual—they do not speak.

In the morning, Mei sees that Kara has slept in her clothes. The narrow black heels of her boots are sticking out beneath the blankets of the upper bunk. But Mei has seen her do this once before. She is careful not to wake her as she dresses. She is quiet with her keys and with the door. Mei leaves only the lightest possible impression on this space—the comfort of not being seen.

This is California, Santa Lora, six weeks into Mei's freshman year.

Mei stays away from the room all day. She feels better this way, still stunned by how quickly it happened, how the friendships formed without her, a thick and sudden ice.

Each evening, Kara and the other girls on the floor stand in towels in the bathroom, blocking the sinks as they lean toward the mirrors to line their lips and eyes. Mei can hear them laughing from the desk in her room across the hall, their voices loud above the hum of the blow-dryers.

"It takes time to get to know people," her mother says over the phone. "Sometimes it takes years."

But there are certain stories that Mei has not told her mother. Like those boys who came to the door the first week of school. There was a bad smell in the hall, they'd said, and they'd tracked it to this room. "It's like something died in here," they'd said, walking in without asking, filling up the narrow room, flip-flops and board shorts, baseball caps low on their heads.

The boys got excited when they began to sniff around Mei's desk. "That's it," they'd said, pressing their hands to their noses. "It's gotta be something in there." They'd pointed to the bottom drawer. "What the hell do you have in there?"

It was her mother's dried cod, which had arrived in the company of three bars of dark chocolate and two lavender soaps.

"My mom makes it," she'd said. This is one of her mother's few inheritances from her own mother, Mei's grandmother, the only one in the family born in China and not San Diego. "It's fish."

She knows that these boys refer to her as *quiet girl,* as in *Hey, quiet girl, it's okay to talk.* She does not think of herself that way, as especially quiet, but there she was, as if under their sway: suddenly not talking.

"Jesus," said the one named Tom, who is taller than the others and plays basketball for the school team. He'd tied a red bandanna around his face, like a worker in a Civil War hospital. "That is foul," he said.

Every time she remembers it, that bandanna over his mouth, Mei's face turns hot with the shame of it.

In the end, she dropped the bag of cod down the trash chute at the end of the hall, ten floors down, the scrape of plastic on tin, while the boys gathered around her to make sure.

"I didn't know they'd be like that," Kara said later. This is how she learned that Kara was the one who told the boys about a smell in the room, though she'd said nothing at all to Mei.

This is one of the reasons that Mei spends her afternoons at a campus café, where, on this particular day in October, she waits until she is sure her roommate and the other girls will be gone from the floor, their hair dryers quiet, their flat-irons cool, and the girls themselves enmeshed by then in the complicated rituals of their sororities. The boys, she hopes, will be at dinner.

But when Mei gets back to the floor that night, nine hours after she left it, she finds a note, written in red, on the whiteboard that hangs on their door. "We're leaving," it says. "Where are you?" These words—it is obvious—are meant for her roommate.

When Mei unlocks the door, she finds Kara still lying where she left her that morning, her body curled toward the wall in the top bunk, her black boots still protruding from the sheets.

"Kara?" she says softly. Outside, the sun is sinking. The sky is clear and turning pink. Mei switches on the overhead light. "Kara?" she says again.

But Kara does not wake. Not to the sound of Mei's pleading, or to the louder voices of the two paramedics who soon detect—through her badly wrinkled dress—that she is breathing, at least, that she still has a pulse.

Kara sleeps through the screaming of the other girls as they see the way her head rolls back against the stretcher, the way her mouth hangs open, her brown hair falling loose across her face. She sleeps through the screeching of the crickets in the pine trees outside, and through the cool night air on her skin.

Mei stands barefoot on the sidewalk as the paramedics slide

the stretcher into the bright bubble of the ambulance, a little roughly, thinks Mei. Be careful, she wants to say. And then the doors swing shut without her, leaving Mei alone in the street.

The paramedics will later report that the girl sleeps through the wail of the siren, too, and the flashing of the lights. She sleeps through the bumps of the potholed streets as the ambulance rushes toward St. Mary's, where, after several attempts, two doctors find that they cannot wake her, either.

On the other floors of the hospital that night, women labor while the girl sleeps. Babies are born while she sleeps. She sleeps while an old man dies in a distant room, an expected death—his family gathered, a chaplain.

She sleeps through sunrise, and she sleeps through sunset.

And yet, in those first few hours, the doctors can find nothing else wrong. She looks like an ordinary girl sleeping ordinary sleep.

There will be some confusion, later, about what happened to her there, how her heart could have slowed so much without setting off the monitors. But this much is known to be true: over the course of many hours, her shallow breaths turn gradually shallower.

It is hard to say afterward why the final beats of her heart go unrecorded by those machines.

3.

The girls: they cry and cry, and they do not sleep. They sit around in their slippers and their sweats on the hard carpet of one another's rooms. They hold hands. They drink tea. If only they had checked on her sooner, they think. If only they had listened when she said she felt sick. They should have known, is the feeling. They should have done something. Maybe, they think, they could have saved her.

The boys turn quiet and they drink even more—cheap beer bought with fake IDs. They keep their hands in their pockets those first few days and just try to stay out of the way of the girls. It is as if the boys can sense it, even in those girls, in their easy closeness and their interlocking arms: the whole history of women and suffering, the generations of practice at grief.

To the girls, it feels wrong to get dressed. It feels wrong to wear makeup. Hair goes unwashed and legs go unshaven and contacts float untouched in solution. They wear glasses, it is then revealed to the boys. More than half of those girls wear glasses.

Her poor mother, the girls say to one another, their knees clutched tight to their chests, as if the shock has turned them even younger. They picture their own mothers. They imagine the phones ringing in their own kitchens, back home, in other towns in other states: Arizona, Nebraska, Illinois. *I can't imagine it,* the girls say to one another, *I just can't imagine.*

The funeral is in Kansas. It's too far to go.

"We should do something for her parents," says one of the girls. They are coming the next day, the girls have heard, to collect Kara's things. "We should order flowers."

The girls all agree right away. There is an intense desire to do the proper thing. This feels like their induction. Suddenly, here is life, cut right to its center. Here it is, dismantled to its bones.

They settle on lilies, two dozen, in white. Everyone signs the card.

They can think of nothing else useful to do, but a certain yearning persists. Meanwhile, a new generosity flows between them. How small their other concerns begin to seem, how meaningless, compared. Fights end, and slights are forgiven, and two of the girls reconcile by phone with the faraway boys who they loved so much in high school and who they had thought, until now, they'd outgrown.

But still, the girls want something more. They long to be of use.

When Mei walks down the hall, her arms crossed and her head down and her black hair pulled tight into a braid, the girls notice her as they have never noticed her before.

She shouldn't blame herself, they all agree. None are sure of her name, the Chinese girl, or maybe Japanese, who lived in the same room as Kara. There is no way she could have known that Kara needed help.

"We should tell her that it's not her fault," one of them whispers. "We should tell her that she shouldn't feel bad."

But they stay where they are.

"Does she speak English?" says another.

"Of course she does," says another one. "I think she's from here, right?"

Somewhere, from another room, there floats the smell of microwave popcorn. No one is going to class.

The basket of lilies arrives that afternoon, but it is less than the girls had hoped, unable, in the end, to accomplish what they had wanted, which is to convey what they can say in no other way, something essential for which they do not know the words.

Kara's parents: their faces are pale and hollowed. She is a woman in a gray sweater. She is Kara with different skin. The father wears a beard and a flannel shirt. He is a man who thirty years earlier might have been any one of those boys of the floor, slouching in a doorframe, his hands in his pockets like theirs, unaware of what is waiting up ahead.

Slowly, they begin to pack their daughter's things.

The girls grow shy at the sight of them. They hide out in their rooms, afraid to say the wrong thing. For a while, the only sound on the floor is the harsh crack of packing tape, torn from its dispenser, or sometimes the clinking of emptied hangers, the soft slip of dresses being packed into boxes.

Watching those parents from afar, the girls are quick to mistake all the ordinary signs of midlife—those wrinkles in his forehead, those dark circles beneath her eyes—for evidence of grief instead of age. And maybe, in a way, the girls are right: those faces are proof of the passage of years, and it is the passage of years that has led them right here to this task.

The voices of Kara's parents are hoarse and wispy, as if they were the ones who were sick. Once, a sudden gasp comes from the mother's throat, "Stop it, Richard," she says, and she begins to sob. "You're ripping it."

This is the moment when Mei peeks out at the parents, as if watching from a great distance, which, in a way, she is.

The father is struggling to roll up one of Kara's posters. It's Paris, black-and-white, tacked to the wall with pushpins, and bought, Mei knows, from the campus bookstore the first week of school. So familiar has the poster become to Mei that she has begun to associate Kara with the girls in the photograph, laughing and glamorous on a cobblestone street in the rain.

"Just stop touching it," the mother says to the father. "Please."

After that, the father is quiet.

Mei lingers in the hallway. She should introduce herself to these parents, that's what her mother would say.

But there is something unbearable about the way that man looks out the window, so like Mei's own father would, and how he doesn't seem to know where to put his hands. It is in the way he keeps touching his beard, the way he stands so silently in the corner of that room.

Mei hurries back to her new room without speaking to them.

Only Caleb is brave enough to approach Kara's parents. Caleb, tall and skinny, brown hair and freckles. Caleb, the English major, a little more serious than the other boys.

The girls watch him shake hands with Kara's father. They watch the way he holds his Cubs cap at his side while he speaks to Kara's mother. And the girls—every one of them—long to smooth his hair, which is sticking up on one side and sweaty from where the cap has been.

The girls love him right then for talking to those parents. They love him for knowing what to do.

Caleb helps the father carry the boxes out to the elevator, and any stranger who passes them might think they understand that scene—here is a father helping his son move out of a dorm.

Amanda: two doors down from Kara's room and the next girl to feel the symptoms. Dizziness, tiredness, a slowly spreading ache.

Her roommate has woken up with it, too. They both look pale and feverish. Their eyes are a little red.

"What if it's contagious?" says Amanda from her bed. "What if we have what Kara had?"

The other girls reassure them from the doorway, but they are too afraid to step inside the room.

"I'm sure you're fine," says one of them, barely breathing. Amazing how swiftly adrenaline spreads through the body, how soon the hands begin to shake. "But maybe you guys should see a doctor. Just to be safe."

The floor soon swells with panic as the news travels from room to room: there are two sick girls among them. It has not occurred to anyone until then that Kara's is a sickness that could spread.

Phone calls are made. The dorm director arrives. The sick girls are driven to Student Health. It is hard for the others not to wonder if they will ever see those girls again.

Hours pass.

The light slowly changes through the windows, but not one of them pays any attention to the weather out there, all that sun and no rain, and the land one day deeper into drought.

A gloom settles over the floor, and over one girl especially. She is known at home and at church as Rebecca, but here, for these past six weeks, as Becca or Becks or B.

Rebecca: a tiny redhead in borrowed jeans, now detecting a slight ringing in her ears. She wants to ignore it. No one has mentioned a ringing.

In the bathroom, she sets her glasses on the counter. She splashes water on her face. It's probably nothing. She is nervous, that's what this is. She is scared. But a dizziness is dawning in her head.

She leans on one of the sinks. They are the old porcelain kind, cracked and yellowed, and she can still see the stains from when she held her head upside down over that same sink, while two girls dyed her hair a thrilling auburn that first week of school, and all the other girls stood around her, advising. It was new to her then, that belonging, the sounds of ten girls laughing in a small space.

Rebecca has been to church only once so far, sneaking off the floor that first Sunday, ready to lie to anyone who asked. It's just that never before has she felt loved so quickly and never before by these kinds of girls.

These girls mixed her first drink. They've used their own rosy lipsticks on her inexperienced lips. These girls have plucked her eyebrows with their own tweezers and then shown her how to shape them herself. They've lent her their clothes and helped her buy a better bra, and she laughed right along with them, just the other day, when they discovered, all at once, that all their cycles were in synch.

But now Rebecca begins to worry. The dizziness is settling over her like a fog. She waits for it to pass, but it does not pass. A wild thought is blooming in her mind: maybe she is being punished—punished for the way she's been acting these weeks, skipping church and drinking so much, and lying to her parents about all of it.

There is a whining of hinges behind her as the door swings open. Kara's roommate, that quiet girl, walks into the bathroom. She holds a yellow towel under one arm, and a pink plastic bucket, inside of which a bottle of shampoo is rattling. She wears a sweatshirt and jeans, which is how she always arrives for a shower, Rebecca has noticed, instead of walking down the hall in a robe or a towel the way all the other girls do.

Rebecca feels a sudden urge to perform a kindness. "Hey," she says.

The girl does not look her way, and Rebecca recognizes the

habit as her own from earlier times, the surprise at being spoken to at all.

"Hey," says Rebecca again. "Sorry, but what was your name again?"

The girl looks up this time. She is pretty, in a way, dark eyes and good skin. But she should wear her hair down—Rebecca knows that's what the other girls would say—instead of tying it back all the time in that braid. And bangs, maybe. Bangs might make her look a little more fun.

"It's Mei," says the girl.

She sets her things down outside the shower stall farthest from Rebecca. She unravels her black braid with her fingers, but her hair holds the shape, crimped from roots to ends.

"I've been meaning to tell you something," says Rebecca.

She's been selfish lately. It's true. You were supposed to give people whatever they needed, and she has given nothing at all to this poor girl. If he asks for your shirt, her father would say, you should give him your coat, too.

Rebecca goes on: "I wanted to tell you that you shouldn't feel bad."

Mei looks suspicious.

"About what?" she says.

"There's just no way you could have known she needed help," says Rebecca.

Mei bites her lip and turns away. She steps into the shower stall and disappears from Rebecca's view.

"It's not my fault," says Mei from inside, her voice echoing against the tile. She seems to be speaking carefully now, each word a fragile object, pulled from a high shelf. "I didn't do anything wrong."

"Right," says Rebecca. "That's what I'm trying to say."

But the conversation is drifting away from her. She is screwing it up.

Mei closes the shower door behind her. There is the sound of the lock clicking into place. Through the gap beneath the door, Rebecca can see the sweatshirt and the jeans fall to the floor at Mei's feet, her hands reaching down to hang them up, and then there is a squeaking of fixtures, a rattling of pipes, the rush of water pooling on tile.

Rebecca tries to think of something else friendly to say through the door.

But something is happening to her vision. There is a flashing at the corner of her eye. There is some sort of distortion in her sight, like a ripple on the surface of water. She begins to shiver.

She tells no one, as if to speak the words aloud might make them more true, a kind of spell.

She goes back to her room and lies down in her bed. She has the idea that she needs to relax. She closes her eyes. It is four in the afternoon. A Bible verse comes into her mind: You will not know the hour or the day.

The first stage of sleep is the lightest, the brief letting go, like the skipping of a stone across water. This is the nodding of a head in a theater. This is the dropping of a book in bed.

Rebecca falls quickly into that first layer. Ten more minutes. She sinks further, just beginning the deep dive. This is when a sudden dream floats through her: She is at church with her parents. A baby is being baptized. But something is wrong. It's the minister's voice—in the dream, his words are somehow out of synch with the movement of his lips. And the noise of the water splashing the baby's forehead arrives a few seconds after the sight of it happening, like the pause between lightning and thunder. In the dream, Rebecca is the only one in the church who notices it.

But then the dream is interrupted—a bright voice rings out in the hall. Rebecca opens her eyes.

The voice that woke her is soon joined by other voices. Someone is laughing out there in the hall.

When she opens her door, she finds the hallway crowded with kids. There they are, at the center of the group, the two sick girls, back from Student Health, their ponytails bobbing, their laughing white teeth. In their hands bulge two burritos and two Cokes.

"I feel so stupid," says one of them, still in her sweats, as kids begin to gather around them.

"We both just have colds," says her roommate.

"Thank God," says Rebecca. The relief comes to her like a drug. "Thank God you're okay." Rebecca, too, begins to feel better. The ringing in her ears, at least, has stopped. The dizziness is floating away.

Whatever it is, they are fine. They are fine, the girls say, did you hear, they say, to anyone they pass in the hall. They are fine. They are fine. They are fine.

After that, something shifts. The fear breaks like a fever, and that night, the third night, the girls and the boys crowd together into Amanda's small room to get drunk, relief radiating from their cheeks.

There is Kahlúa and milk for the girls, and bags and bags of ice, and beer and tequila, and peach-flavored wine. There's the whir of the blender and the clinking of shot glasses and the music a little too loud.

There is talk of doing something for Kara, a plaque on the building, maybe, or the planting of a tree. Yes, they say, a tree, they say, or even a little garden of her favorite flowers. They toast their short friendship with her, these six good weeks. She was so sweet, they all agree, maybe the sweetest one among them.

They begin to get drunk, and there is no way around it: there is a giddiness in that room. They are young and they are healthy, and they have survived a terrible thing.

In a high corner of the room, Rebecca feels calm and brave,

her legs dangling from the top bunk. Somehow, Caleb is sitting beside her.

"What a shitty day," he says to her. He speaks softly—only she can hear.

She nods. She is aware of the warmth of his leg beside hers, the tilt of his head near the ceiling.

"It really was," she says.

She will try again tomorrow, she thinks through the buzz of the drinking, to make things right with Kara's roommate—what was her name again? Mei? No one, she realizes then, with another ping of guilt, has thought to invite Mei into this room.

Down below, the blender hums, a long clattering of ice.

Try this, they all say to one another, again and again, plastic cups passing from person to person, every mouth taking a sip. Shot glasses are used and reused.

The biology majors among them would someday come to learn this fact: certain parasites can bend the behavior of their hosts to serve their own purposes. If viruses could do it, here is how it would look: seventeen people crowded into one small room, seventeen pairs of lungs breathing the same air, seventeen mouths drinking from the same two shot glasses, again and again, for hours.

Finally, the party ends. It ends the way their parties always do, with a knock on the door and the voice of the R.A., just three years older than they are, and skilled at not actually seeing any alcohol.

"Okay, guys," he says through the door. "That's enough."

They drift, then, out into the hall, the fluorescent lights buzzing from the ceiling, as they sway toward their rooms, one by one, or two by two.

Rebecca is floating alone toward her room, a few steps behind the other girls, when she feels someone's breath in her ear.

"Come on," says Caleb. He takes her hand in his.

How surprising it is, the sudden intertwining of his fingers with hers, and the smell of him near her, his gum and his soap, the flat clear joy of getting picked.

"We can talk in here," says Caleb. He pushes open the fire door, and leads her into the stairwell.

The door swings shut behind them and slices away the light and the noise of the other kids, leaving just the two of them there, in the dark and the quiet, a boy and a girl sitting side by side on the same cold stair.

The other girls think Caleb is too skinny, but to Rebecca, he is tall and lean. There is something intelligent in the sharpness of his features, a kind of efficiency, like good design.

She waits for him to speak.

From his pocket, Caleb produces a bag of M&M's.

"Want some?" he says.

The stairwell is so quiet that even the crinkling of the bag of M&M's seems to echo against the walls. He pours some into her hand.

They sit this way for a while, not talking. She isn't sure how to do this. She can hear the crunch of M&M's against his teeth.

"I feel so bad that I didn't talk to her parents," she says, finally. "I didn't know what to say to them."

Caleb tosses an M&M down the center of the stairwell. Ten floors down, a satisfying ping.

"People never know what to say," he says.

She has heard a rumor that Caleb's brother died when he was young.

They talk awhile longer, drunk and dreamy. She can feel the Kahlúa in her head, a pleasant drifting. Everything around her, the dim lights and the rusted railings and the faraway sound of something dripping—all of it seems suffused with meaning, as if the whole night has been transformed already into memory.

There are things she wants to talk about, to tell him about all the rules she lived by back home, about no movies and no makeup and not going to regular school, about learning algebra with her brothers at a kitchen table, while her mother struggled with the home-school guides and her father tried and failed to start an orphanage. But she says none of these things in that stairwell. Instead, she leans silently against Caleb's shoulder, as if she can communicate her thoughts through different channels, like the warmth of her arm against his.

Caleb keeps dropping M&M's down the stairwell, as if they're sitting at the edge of a real well, wishing on stones.

"People don't know what to say," says Caleb, "because there's nothing you can say." She feels a telescoping into his past. "There's nothing to be said."

Already, she can hear her older self telling this story one day, years into the future, the terrible thing that happened when she was young, that girl Kara in the dorm, the second month of freshman year, her first glancing disaster. The whole event is racing away toward the past.

As they watch the last M&M fall through the air, they bump heads. When they look up, faces close and shadowed, they begin to laugh. Caleb touches her hair. It's happening. A kiss. His mouth tastes like chocolate. Their teeth touch; she never knows if she's doing it right. His hands rest on her hips. His fingers skim the skin of her waist, and she can feel him shaking slightly as he touches her, his nervousness more endearing than confidence. And this seems like a beginning, this here, the start of everything. She is warm with a furious hope, the elation available only to the very young.

The girls sleep late, heads hurting from Kahlúa. They wake, one by one, to pee or for water, or to swallow the Advil they keep beside their beds or only to pull the curtains shut against the morning light, squinting in the sunshine of yet one more cloudless day.

Then they climb back into their beds.

Soon, they are dreaming the vivid dreams of shallow sleep.

It is around noon, the girls later agree, that something extraordinary happens: their dreams begin to follow a similar plot, to swirl around the same subject, one distinct sound. All at once, the girls dream that someone, somewhere, is screaming.

It takes a few seconds for their eyes to open, for the noise to coalesce into a story: someone really is screaming.

In the hall, the girls find Caleb—in boxers, no shirt. They can see his ribs rising and falling beneath his skin as he shouts out into the hall. It is possible that none of these girls have ever seen true panic on a boy's face before.

It's Rebecca, he is saying. He is motioning toward his bed, where her curly red hair is spread out on his pillow. It's Rebecca, he says again, something is wrong with Rebecca.

4.

What a terrible thing going on at the college—this is the way the people of Santa Lora talk about it in the aisles of the hardware store and the supermarket, or as they walk their dogs in the woods. Have you heard what's happening at the college? they say to their neighbors over fences, and in the bleachers at the high school, as if the college were an island apart from the town, its gates impenetrable, even by germs.

A sleeping sickness. That's what the local reporters are calling it. One girl is dead, another unconscious, both from the same dorm floor.

There is a drought fanning out all across California. No rain in ninety days, and they are behind already from the year before. No one has ever seen the lake in Santa Lora sit so low or the sandbars rising in the middle like dunes, the old docks standing dry, fifty feet from the water's edge.

It's the worst drought in a hundred years. Or longer, some say. Five hundred, maybe, or more.

But the weather, this weather: it's glorious. Six weeks of sun-shine in a row.

It does not seem possible to suffer in weather like that, as if beauty were a spell that could ward off death, but they know the grapes are dying in the valley below, and their lawns are going browner by the day, parched by the same sun that is warming their porch swings long into October.

And yet, somehow, the disbelief holds: it does not seem possible in weather so pleasant for an eighteen-year-old girl to die.

But Santa Lora is a place that has suffered before.

This land is prone to shaking. These hills are liable to slide. And this forest is so fertile for fire that the cautious few among them keep their family photos packed in duffel bags at their front doors, in case of the sudden need to flee.

The tribe that once roamed these woods for game was rav-aged by smallpox from fur traders, and a party of pioneers once starved in these mountains. Ten years after that, the first wooden houses, built when the silver was found in the hills, were drowned with three feet of snowmelt that very first spring. You can still find the proof in the antiques store at the corner of Mariposa and Klein: photographs of women in dark dresses, the men in frayed coats, and those children, so serious, so spindly, standing knee-deep in the water, their eyes the eyes of those accustomed to tribulation.

A landslide later swallowed every bungalow on the east side of town, and the tiny city hall, with its dome and its bell, is only a replica of the first one—an earthquake cracked the walls of the original.

The first cemetery, long since closed to new arrivals, is packed with the dead of Spanish flu. Some say their ghosts still roam the mansions on Catalina Street, now shabby and subdivided for students. The people of Santa Lora had known it was coming, that flu. They'd heard word of it traveling west from town to town. They tried to block the one road into town, but the sickness got in anyway, and then it spread through the town like news. Twice as many people died of that flu here as in the next town over, leading some to suspect, back then, that Santa Lora was cursed.

The idea still sometimes surfaces in certain superstitious minds. Whenever a teenager drowns in the lake or a hiker goes missing in the woods, some in Santa Lora wonder if this is a land destined for catastrophe. What if misfortune can be drawn to a place, like lightning to a rod?

5.

If, on the fourth night of that first week, a stranger were to visit Santa Lora, and if that stranger were to go walking at the end of the day, at sunset, maybe, or just before, if he were to drift ten blocks east of the college, he might notice eventually a large yellow house, maybe a hundred years old, once grand but no longer, with a rusted rain gutter and a sagging porch swing and green beans growing out front. If he were to see that house, he might notice a girl. And he would wonder, as he walks, the way strangers sometimes do, what it is she is doing there, this girl at the window, so serious, so still, just standing, looking out.

She is twelve years old, this girl at the window. She is skinny in her cutoff jeans, dark hair. Glasses, bracelets, sunburn. Sara.

She has the feeling already that she will remember this night for a long time. But she feels this way often, a certain simmering. It is a habit of thinking she shares with her father—every ordinary moment holds a potential calamity, and you cannot know when one will rise.

Tonight, there is this: her father is late coming home.

From the window, she watches other cars slide into the other driveways on their street. She hears the opening and closing of her neighbors' doors. There's the crinkling of grocery sacks and the ringing of keys and the calm of their voices—other people are always so calm—as they speak to their children and their husbands and their dogs.

"He probably just stopped somewhere on the way home from work," says Libby, her sister, ten months younger, upstairs with the kittens. Five weeks old, they sleep in a box.

"You always freak out," her sister goes on. "But it's always fine."

"He's never this late," says Sara. She turns back to look at the street.

Outside, the birds are calling out from the trees, swallows, maybe, or chickadees. A pair of joggers fly by on the sidewalk. The college kids who share the big house on the corner are lighting a grill on their porch. Her father's blue pickup does not appear.

She can smell dinner cooking in the house next door, the gray one with the screened porch and the white trim, the house where the new neighbors live with their baby, those professors, as her father calls them, those professors who cut down the pine tree that stood between the two houses for so many years, for as long as their father can remember, since before he was born, which was thirty-five years before the girls were. It was our tree, her father is always saying. He stops often to inspect the stump. It was not their tree to kill.

The last of the light is draining from the sky. Insects have begun to bump against the screens.

When her chest tightens like this, it can be hard to tell if it's her asthma that's doing it, or her mood. She fishes her inhaler out of her backpack. Two quick puffs.

She checks the clock on the microwave again. He is an hour and ten minutes late.

———

But finally: the crunch of tires on gravel, the friendly rattle of the broken tailpipe.

She opens the front door. So many days seem likely to veer toward disaster, but so many turn the other way instead.

"We got hungry," she says to her father, hiding her gladness at the sight of him. His brown beard is going gray. His blue work shirt is wearing thin. "So I made sandwiches for Libby and me."

Her father slams the door of the truck.

"And we fed the cats, too," she says. She steps out onto the porch, bare feet on the splintering wood.

"Don't come out here," he says.

She stops where she is. He can get angry. It's true. But the reasons are usually clear. She waits for him to say why. He doesn't.

Instead of coming inside, he jogs around to the backyard, his work boots coming down hard on the gravel, his steps quick in the twilight.

Soon, he is uncoiling the garden hose. He is turning on the spigot.

Sara opens the back door.

"What are you doing?" she calls out into the dusk. She can hear the hose running in the dirt.

"Bring me some soap," he says. He begins to unbutton his shirt. "And a towel, too," he says. "Quick."

The buzz of adrenaline comes back quickly to her blood. There's a skinny bar of soap in the bathtub. She finds a towel in the dryer, where their clean clothes always wait instead of folded in drawers.

"What's he doing out there?" asks her sister. The tiniest kitten is curled in her hand, his mouth wide open, sharp teeth to the air. You have to really listen to hear that little cry.

"I don't know," says Sara. "I don't know what he's doing."

And then she's back downstairs, watching her father through the window.

It's hard to see through the screen and the low light, and he

has moved to the far corner of the yard by then, beyond the potatoes and the squash. But she looks again and knows that it is
true: her father is standing nearly naked in the backyard.

He is wearing only his boxers now, and he is holding the hose
over his head.

His chest looks bony beneath that stream of water, his beard
pasted flat to his chin. The rest of his clothes are scattered in the
dirt, like laundry fallen from a line.

Sara can see the new neighbors sitting in their kitchen next
door, wineglasses glittering on their table, the baby in the woman's arms. They can see you, she wants to say to her father. That
woman can see you. But she is too afraid to speak.

"I need that soap," he says. She can hear him shivering in the
dark against the screech of the crickets. A few fireflies blink
among the vegetables. "Don't come too close," he says. "Just toss
it to me."

The white of the soap as it sails through the air catches in the
glow of the neighbors' porch light. The woman is looking in their
direction.

"Now get back inside," says her father. "Now."

He scrubs his face hard with the soap. He scrubs his arms and
his legs and his hands, his hands more than anything else. She is
used to her father's ideas, how different they are from other people's, but a fresh fear is coming to her. Maybe he has done something wrong. Maybe that's why all the washing.

The floor creaks nearby—her sister's socked feet. "What the
hell?" says Libby.

How grateful Sara is for her sister right then, for the brown of
her eyes, for the clear of her voice, for those ladybug studs she
always wears in her ears—their mother's, they think, but aren't
sure. Even the smell of the pretzels on Libby's breath is a part of
it, just the truth of her sister beside her.

They stand together for a long time, not talking, watching
their father through the glass the way they sometimes watch

raccoons doing their evening washings—how strange the action of those miniature hands.

Libby keeps asking Sara what their father is doing out there. Sara keeps shaking her head. They are almost like twins. That's what people say, two sisters born so close together, less than a year apart—to a mother who was gone from this earth before either girl turned four.

Finally, their father turns off the hose. Finally, he picks up the towel from the dirt. The last thing he does is throw his clothes into the trash can out back. Their father, who never throws anything away, leaves his good brown belt in that trash can, still threaded through the loops of his jeans.

He won't talk about it. Not at first.

"Let me think," he says, raising his palm in the air, as if to hold back a crowd. He sits hunched at the kitchen table, the towel wrapped at his waist. His beard is dripping on the linoleum, that sound the same sound of every faucet in the house, every fixture slightly loose, the whole place disintegrating. "Just let me think for a minute," he says.

He shoos the girls out of the kitchen, and Libby goes upstairs to be with the kittens, but Sara stays near her father, one room over, waiting for some kind of news.

There is something about television that soothes her. Not the shows but the voices, the people, the knowing that she isn't watching *Wheel of Fortune* all alone, not really, because thousands of other people are watching it, too, an enormous web of people. She can feel them with her as she watches, as if, in a crisis, that link might work the other way, as if they could see her, send help.

Beneath the tick-tick of the Wheel of Fortune losing speed, her father's fingers thrum on the kitchen table. He opens a can of beer. From the living room, Sara searches the sounds for meaning, clues to the workings of a mind: the scrape of his chair, the sighing and the sips, the softening clink of the can as he drains it.

When the phone begins to ring, her father does not move. Sara lets it go, too, but her sister answers it and then runs downstairs to whisper into Sara's ear: "There's a boy on the phone for you."

With the scratch of that whisper comes a sudden tensing of her body. She does not get many phone calls—and never once from a boy.

Her voice, she can tell, is shaking as she picks up the phone: "Hello?"

"Sara?" says the boy. "This is Akil."

Akil: a surge of surprise and happiness comes into her. Akil, a new boy at school. He plays Sara's husband in the play: *Our Town*.

"Hey," she says, but she is breathing too hard. She is not sure how conversations like this should go.

"Is this your cell phone?" he says. He has a formal way of speaking, this boy, the slightest accent, almost British, but his family is from Egypt, she has heard him say, his father some kind of professor. "I meant to call your cell phone," he says.

"Oh," she says. "I don't have one."

She regrets it immediately—why draw so much attention to it, how strange she must seem to other kids?

"Oh," he says.

Libby is watching her, straining to hear what is being said on the other end.

"Anyway," he says. He clears his throat. In the space of that pause blooms an immense feeling of longing. "Do you know," he says, "what time rehearsal is tomorrow?"

Her face flushes with embarrassment—this is only a practical call.

"I forgot to write it down," he says.

The call is over in less than two minutes. And then the world of the house comes flooding back: her father in that towel at the table, that look in his eyes, his refusal to explain what is wrong.

Wheel of Fortune goes on and on. One puzzle is solved, another presented. She becomes aware eventually of an ache at the back of her jaw. Only then does she know how hard she's been clenching her teeth.

Finally, her father speaks.

"Sara," he calls from the kitchen. Here is a wisp of hope. An explanation is coming, an arranging of parts into a whole.

"I want you to go downstairs," he says, "and count how many gallons of water we have."

That's when she knows. Something awful has happened.

The basement: she hates the basement. The basement is proof of everything that could ever go wrong. Here is where they keep the cans of food they will eat if there comes a nuclear winter. Here is the water they will drink when everyone else runs out. Here are the bullets they will use as barter, if one day money loses its meaning. And here are the guns her father will use to guard all that food and that water and those bullets when other people come to steal it all away.

It is hard to picture sleeping down there, with the bare bulbs and the spiders, the smell of dirt hanging always in the air, the one small window, boarded up. But they keep blankets and pillows in the corner, in case. Three cots wait in a stack.

By the time she reaches the jugs of water on the far side of the basement, her hands are shaking. She counts slowly. She counts twice.

The weather is changing, her father is always saying. The seas are rising. The oil and the water are draining away. And asteroids. Asteroids are what worry her most. From her bed at night, she can see the stars, and she sometimes senses them moving closer, always at bedtime, on the lookout for the star that might not be a star.

"But maybe none of it will happen, right?" she says often to her father. No one can see the future. He cannot know for sure. "Things might be fine for a while, right?"

"Maybe," he always says, shaking his head like he means to say no. "But sooner or later, something big is going to change. Things can't go on as they've been."

This is why they grow the vegetables in the yard. This is why, when their squash ripens, they jar it, and when their potatoes come up, they will freeze-dry them. This is why they keep a two-year supply of her asthma medication in a box on the highest shelf of the basement.

No one else knows what they keep in there. Not even her father's brother, Joe, who was born in this house like her father and who came to visit the summer before, after being away for so many years, on drugs, her father said, in Arizona. For that whole visit, two weeks, they kept the door to the basement locked because the most important thing about the basement is that the contents of the basement stay secret.

A small sound comes from the stairs behind her. She looks up. It's only Daisy in the doorway, staring down at her, one white paw outstretched in the air, her shadow huge on the stairs.

Sara remembers then what her father has said about the cats. When it happens, he has said, they'll have to get rid of them. There won't be enough food and water to share. He will do it humanely, he's said. But he might have to shoot them. That might be the least painful way. She thinks of when the kittens were born, the needle-prick points of those teeth, the small eyes, still sealed, and the way Daisy carried them around with her mouth, how she knew right away how to do that, knew right where to hold them—by the loose bit of skin at the backs of their necks.

Sara's throat grows tight. They are only babies. She and her sister will have to convince him not to do it.

In the kitchen, her father is staring out the window at nothing. People notice his eyes, an uncommon green. There is more gray than she remembers in the hairs of his bare chest.

"So?" he says.

"Fifty gallons," she says. "We have fifty gallons of water."

"Okay," he says, standing up from the table, still pinching the towel at his waist. "Okay."

Little by little, the situation turns clearer. He doesn't tell the story in order. The facts surface slowly, like the invisible lemon-juice notes that her sister learned to write that summer in the yard—you have to heat them in the sun to make the letters show. That's the way his story comes out of him that night, demanding of patience and in need of deciphering, the simplest parts left out.

Something happened to him at work.

"They didn't tell us anything," he says. He is a janitor at the college. "They didn't tell us one goddamn thing."

The girls stand listening in the kitchen, quiet.

"They should have told us why we were cleaning those rooms with bleach," he says.

His voice is rising to a shout, and the more he talks, the less the girls do, as if volume were like oxygen, a thing that runs out.

"I would've worn a mask," he says. "I would've worn gloves."

It takes a long time to understand the crux of the story.

A sleeping sickness—that's what he keeps calling it. A strange sleeping sickness has broken out at the college.

"But they're not admitting it," he says. "They're trying to keep it quiet."

Also this: it is spreading.

"Have people died?" Libby asks. She is the calm one, the balm, easy with a faith in the goodness of things. She isn't quick to get scared, but here she is, scared.

"Listen to me," says their father, squeezing their shoulders hard, too hard. They step back. "I don't want you girls going outside," he says. "Not for a few days, at least. Okay? We're all going to stay right here in the house."

Then he stands up fast, like he's just remembered something else. He rushes down the stairs to the basement. They can hear him down there, an urgent sorting and shuffling.

"What about school?" Libby whispers, and Sara feels suddenly much older than her sister, just the year but it matters, and she can hear it, the difference, in that question. School is the least of their worries. Whatever needs doing, Sara thinks, it will be Sara, and not her sister, who will do it.

Their father returns to the kitchen with three white pills in his hand.

"Take this," he says, dropping one into Sara's hand. He goes to the counter to cut Libby's in half. She can't swallow big pills.

"What are they?" asks Sara.

"Antibiotics," he says. "Now go to bed."

Bedtime: they can hear the mice moving in the attic. The sounds upset the kittens, who wander the floor in circles, heads turned up to the ceiling, white throats exposed as they cry.

The sounds upset the girls, too.

"Dad," they call down from their bedroom.

No answer. They can hear the clicks of his fingers on a keyboard, the beep and shudder of their old computer connecting to the Internet.

If you bang on the ceiling with the butt of a broomstick, the mice quiet down for a while. This is their father's trick, and you can see the proof of it on the ceiling, the marks of the broomstick, moons and half-moons, stamped into the plaster from all those nights before this one, a time-lapse map of a small migration, from one side of the room to the other.

"Dad," Libby calls again. "Dad, come up here."

Sara can see him without looking, his eyes in the blue light of that ancient monitor, the waiting and the waiting as webpages load through the telephone line.

"What is it?" he says finally, his voice far away.

"The mice," the girls shout together.

In the silence that follows, Sara can picture his face, going tight with the effort of patience.

"You're just going to have to live with it for tonight," he says.

It's a scratching sound, like the scrape of a fingernail digging into a wall, like a tiny prisoner, trapped somewhere in the house, as if a thousand days of scratching will finally break him out.

"Let's leave the lights on," says Libby. She is curled beneath a yellow quilt, handmade—by their mother, maybe, or maybe not. They are always on the lookout for things that might have been hers.

Most of what they do know comes from a newspaper article they once found folded in their father's desk drawer: one morning in June, a jogger came across a three-year-old girl, crying in the front yard of a house. An even younger girl was standing in the doorway, her diaper overfull. Sara has memorized every detail: how this jogger found an uneaten lunch in the kitchen, macaroni and cheese in three bowls, and a woman lying unconscious on the floor. Asthma is the one thing Sara knows for sure that she has inherited from her mother.

They stay awake a long time on this night, listening to the workings of the mice. Sometimes a big fear can magnify the smaller ones.

Soon the morning will come, but they will not get dressed for school. They will not walk to the bus stop. When their teachers call attendance, no one will answer to their names. Sara will not speak her lines in the dress rehearsal for *Our Town*, or practice—in that last scene—taking Akil's arm in hers and walking off the stage.

Sara is used to not sleeping. She is a dreamer of bad dreams, dreams that keep her mind moving for hours—an afterglow. But it's weird to see her sister awake, too, so late. Libby is staring at the ceiling, eyes wide.

Something needs to be said in that room, but there is no one to say it. Sara finally does it herself.

"Don't worry," she says to her sister. Her voice doesn't feel like her voice, the tremor that comes before a lie: "It'll be okay," she says. "I think everything's going to be fine."

6.

Infectious disease is not the only thing that can spread. On the fifth day, a specialist in psychiatric disorders is called in from Los Angeles.

She has seen this kind of thing before—how one girl can sometimes feel the feelings of another, a different kind of contagion, the way a yawn sometimes jumps from mouth to mouth. A certain kind of empathy. A hundred cheerleaders once fainted this way on a football field in Dallas—and only one of them turned out to be ill.

It's a two-hour drive from the neuropsychiatric hospital downtown, in her five-year-old Volvo, Goldfish crumbs crunched into the leather, her daughter's Legos rolling back and forth across the backseat.

She is Catherine to her colleagues, Katie to her family, Dr. Cohen when she walks the halls of her locked ward.

The city gives way to the suburbs as she drives toward Santa Lora, the suburbs to miles of lemon groves. A long succession of switchbacks finally delivers her up into the mountains and the shade of a thick pine forest.

The radio stations fall away. Her cell phone goes silent. And then the road twists through forty more miles of uninterrupted woods.

What a relief it is when a motel appears beside the road. But the windows are boarded up. A faded sign still advertises COLOR TVS.

But finally, a lake glitters through the trees. The woods crack open. A campus comes into view, college kids spread out on lawns, the grass browned to the color of wheat. Santa Lora.

The hospital, when she gets there, is no bigger than the motel.

The patient is asleep on her back, one arm resting on her stomach. The room is dim. The blinds are drawn. Catherine knows from the chart that her name is Rebecca. She has been asleep for sixty hours.

The girl's mother—she must be the mother—is sitting beside the bed, her eyes bloodshot, overwide. Mothers: talking to the mothers is the worst part of her job.

"Can I open these?" Catherine asks, but she does not wait for an answer. She pulls the cord, and sunlight fills the room.

This mother seems relieved to have heard that this affliction might be psychological, as if the failings of the mind are any less destructive than those of the body.

"You mean she might not have a real sickness?" says the mother.

"That's not what I'm saying," says Catherine.

The girl's blood pressure, the internists have told her, is normal. Her pulse, too. It was the same with the first girl, they say, the one who died. No symptoms beyond the deep sleep. This girl looks as if the slightest noise might wake her, or the faintest feather of a touch.

Catherine has seen patients rendered similarly lifeless by catatonic depression or by sudden traumatic news. When one's life seems broken beyond repair, there remains one last move: a person can at least shut her eyes.

Catherine has forgotten this girl's name, but it feels too late to ask. "Does she have any history of anxiety?" she asks. "Or depression?"

The mother shakes her head hard. But the parents, Catherine has learned, never know what is really going on.

A Bible has been pressed into the crook of the girl's left arm, as if its messages can be transmitted to the soul through the skin.

A tiny sound comes from the girl's mouth.

The mother jumps up. "Rebecca?" she says.

The girl's eyelids begin to flutter.

In a healthy human being, Catherine knows, this motion of the eyes beneath the lids would indicate REM sleep, the state most conducive to dreaming. But Catherine cannot say for sure without tests what is happening inside this girl's brain.

She orders an MRI. She will be back in two days, she says.

Catherine's daughter is asleep by the time she gets back to Los Angeles, the babysitter reading on the couch. But that night, like every night for the past month, her daughter wakes screaming after midnight. Nightmares are common at her age.

It takes a while to calm her.

"Mama," she whispers into Catherine's ear, her cheeks lit by a night-light shaped like the moon. "I think there's something wrong with my eyes."

"What do you mean?" she says.

Her three-year-old arms are wrapped tight around Catherine's neck.

"When I close my eyes," says her daughter, "I see something scary."

"Those are dreams," says Catherine. "Like we talked about."

What a crazy thing to do, her own mother had said: to have a baby on her own—and on purpose. Every one of her days hums with the possibility that she might be doing it wrong.

But also there is this: the secret pleasure in these minutes right here, that warm little body pressed into her chest, her hot breath on her neck, and the simplicity of the cure—a talk and a hug in the dark.

"This time," says her daughter, "I dreamed there were snakes coming out of my skin."

"Wow," says Catherine. "That would scare me, too."

One of her patients used to see that same image, but while she was awake. On an MRI, the dreaming brain looks almost identical to the brain of a schizophrenic.

It strikes her again, how many of a child's fears are just rational responses to the facts of everyday experience.

Two songs and a back rub—and then her daughter is asleep again.

Catherine is back in her own bed when she hears a new message ping on her phone: a third girl from the same dorm floor has lost consciousness in Santa Lora.

7.

At sunrise, a professor of biology takes a walk in the woods of Santa Lora.

His white hair is cut close to his head. He wears a ten-year-old jacket. Hiking boots. Nathaniel—that's his name.

No dog. No phone. Just a thermos full of coffee and an empty plastic bag.

The sky is clear. The air is cool. The woods are ringing with birdsong: blue jays and Steller's jays and chickadees.

At a certain bend in the trail, a log has been carved into a bench. Here is where, a few hours from now, Nathaniel will bring his freshman biology seminar, to point out certain features and phenomena of trees: the intricate root structures of pines, how the bark beetle has worked with the drought to kill so many here, and then, the highlight, the zombie tree.

He calls it that for the kids, this ancient stump. No trunk, no branches, no leaves, just a hollowed-out stump, and yet, somehow, this stump lives on. The bursts of green in the grain of its wood—chlorophyll—are proof of ongoing life, as if this remnant of a tree is at once alive and also dead. "How can that be?"

the kids will want to know, or the bright ones will, the few really interested ones. He has been bringing his classes here for years. It comes as a surprise to most of them, that trees have certain ways of communicating with one another, that they send chemical messages through the air, and that they sometimes help their neighboring trees survive. "This stump's relatives are keeping it alive," he will say. "They're delivering nutrients to its roots."

On this day, Nathaniel also comes across a familiar scattering of dark glass in this spot. Beer bottles. This is what he has brought the plastic bag for.

He doesn't blame the kids for the drinking. Or for wanting to do it out here in these woods—among the ponderosas and the manzanitas, the white firs and the cedars, instead of sitting around on the particleboard furniture of their dorm rooms. He gets it: the mountains, the stars. There is a privacy in wilderness. But the trash—come on, these kids are old enough to pick up their own trash.

He is bending down to pick the glass from the dirt when he notices someone lying a few feet off the trail. A boy in an army jacket, dark jeans, tennis shoes, is nestled, facedown, in dried leaves.

"Hey," says Nathaniel. "Hey, kid."

He crouches down. He shakes the boy's shoulder. The smell of alcohol is floating off the boy's skin, accompanied by the loud snores of drunken sleep. He zips up the kid's jacket. He turns the kid's head to the side—at least he won't choke if he vomits in his sleep.

At home, he calls the police: "There's a kid passed out drunk in the woods," he says. He tells the operator exactly where to find the boy. "Probably just needs to sleep it off, but thought you guys should know."

A bowl of oatmeal. A glass of orange juice. The rattle of pills against plastic: high blood pressure. It might be stress-related—that's what Nathaniel's daughter thinks. Grief, she says over the phone from San Francisco, is a kind of stress. So is age, he argues. Decay comes eventually for every living thing.

He opens a small notebook. Someone else might call it a journal, but not Nathaniel. It is slim and small in his hands, a line-a-day diary, the kind that stretches five years: one line reserved for each day. *What is the point of that?* Henry used to say to him. *What can you say in one sentence?* But it is a comfort to do it, a mysterious distillation, like gleaning salt from the sea, like the perfection of the simplest chemical equation. He writes quickly, without too much thought—that's the point, the habit, the doing: "Went to see Henry yesterday. His cough seems better."

A shower, a sports coat, a pair of dark socks.

His car keys are rattling in his hand and his lecture notes packed in his bag when he finally stops to look at his email.

Now is when he opens a message marked urgent: a student in his freshman seminar, Kara Sanders, has died of an unknown illness, possibly contagious, and two other students are exhibiting the same symptoms. More details to follow.

Her name brings no face to his mind. He feels a little guilty for it, but it is early in the year. He doesn't know them yet. There is something familiar about it, though, the feeling of waste. Things are always happening to these kids: suicides, overdoses, drunk driving. It seems worse than it used to be. Is it worse?

His inbox is filling up with a series of campus-wide alerts about precautions and symptoms. Classes are canceled, one says. Campus is closed until further notice. They tend to overreact to these things, to see a larger pattern where there isn't one. A shooter on campus last fall turned out to be someone holding a water gun. The smell of gas is almost always just someone boiling water in a dorm kitchen. A freak case of meningitis is often the only one. But okay, he's not in charge of these things, so he sends his students an email reiterating: today's class is canceled.

After that, the house is quiet, too quiet, the echoing scuff of his shoes on the wood. A brief disorientation: what to do, now, with the day.

But soon he is standing quietly in line at the bakery, where no one is yet talking about the sickness, and then he's driving the two miles to the nursing home, with an almond croissant wrapped up on the passenger seat for Henry.

It has a certain grandness to it, this place, Restoration Villa, with its fountains and its porticos, and the way it overlooks the lake. It was once a sanitarium for the wealthy and tubercular, a history that in other circumstances would have appealed to Nathaniel, and to Henry. But a point comes in every visit when Nathaniel begins to read in the small movements of Henry's face a coded message aimed at him: *How could you leave me in this depressing fucking place?*

On this morning, nothing here will seem amiss: the metallic slide and click of the patients' walkers in the hallway, the low laughter of the nurses, the televisions running like ventilators in the other rooms. He will spend the morning reading to Henry from Henry's favorite sections of *The New York Times* while Henry sucks on small pieces of the croissant like lozenges. In this way, Nathaniel will come across a small news story in the back pages, a little surprised, to see that this event in Santa Lora, like a pebble, is making traces in distant waters. People love a tragedy when it's happening far away: an odd sickness has surfaced on a campus in a small California town.

"She was one of my students," he will say to Henry.

And Henry will turn his head at this news. He will aim an unreadable expression at Nathaniel. His mind is like a school of fish, obscured by dark water. Once in a while, though, something tugs on the line.

————

That night, Nathaniel's daughter will call from San Francisco. He will let the call go to voicemail. "It's me, Dad. I saw the news and just wanted to make sure you're okay." He will send her an email: "Yes, all fine here. Love, Dad."

8.

Rebecca: still sleeping, five days deep, one arm strung with an IV of saline.

If her eyes were to blink open on this particular day, she would find a heart monitor beside her and four white walls, and two baskets of flowers and one Mylar balloon, and the crosses, so many crosses, brought here by her parents, along with the Bible. In the chair beside the bed, she would find her mother, her mouth covered by a paper mask, her eyes tired, forehead wrinkled. She might hear the faint clicking of knitting needles as her mother busies her hands, or else the soft sound of her voice, so weary, on the phone: "No, not yet, they still don't know what it is."

But on this day, like the others, Rebecca's eyes stay shut.

For days, her blood has been leaving her veins in vials, drawn again and again by the nurses—more tests. Doctors come and go with no news, while in other rooms, a few other mothers huddle over their own sleeping children, just watching them breathe, as if they are newborns again with lungs still new to the task. They look so healthy, these kids, their young bodies so sturdy in their beds, pink color in their cheeks, their chests rising and falling, as steady as metronomes.

Five now lie sick.

For now, they are alive, but the future is receding farther from them every second, time itself rushing forward without them.

On this afternoon, a minister arrives in Rebecca's room. He and her family hold her hands in theirs, while the sound of prayer floats through the room. A laying on of hands.

Does she feel it in a dream, the pressure of their palms on her shoulders, her forehead? Can she sense their hopes in that touch? Who can say? She sleeps right through it all.

No one knows then that something else, too, more ordinary, is also brewing in Rebecca's body, an invader of a different sort. Only later will anyone discover that a secret cluster of cells is already floating free inside her—too small yet to be called an embryo, but multiplying quickly—as it prepares to anchor in her womb.

9.

In an earlier time, they would have burned everything they owned, but chemicals now do the cleansing work of fire. Bleach: the usual smells of the dorm must have survived somewhere beneath it, all that cologne and the popcorn, the spilled beer and the cigarettes, but Mei can smell only this one thing from her room, the bleach, as clear and harsh as fluorescence.

With the bleach come new rules for everyone on Mei's floor. No leaving. This is the main thing. Just for now, they say, just to be safe. No visitors, either. And no class.

No work, either. The dean Mei babysits for sounds annoyed on the phone. Who will watch her daughter? Mei is not explaining this right. She is not being clear. This dean makes her nervous, with her big house and her shelves full of books, and it seems somehow embarrassing to mention the sickness. When she tries again, the dean softens: Wait, you live on *that* floor?

Mei can tell that the college is not sure what to do. An uneasy feeling: to discover that the adults are no more prepared than the kids are.

No one says where the students from the other floors will go. But Mei can see what is happening from her window. They stream from the dorm like ants, the unexposed, ten floors down, burdened by huge loads. All day, the skid of suitcases on pavement. All day, the distant voices drifting in through the screens, a line of buses waiting at the curb. It is what it looks like: an evacuation.

Some of those leaving look up at the tenth floor as they go, but most keep their heads low, their eyes averted, as if what is happening up on that floor is too intimate for the others to see.

No one is using the word *quarantine*, but Mei looks it up. From the Italian, *quaranta giorni*, forty days. Forty days: the period that ships were once required to wait before entering the port of Venice—time enough, they hoped, for a contagious disease to burn itself out.

On the first day of the confinement, two men from the dining hall bring a cart full of sandwiches for dinner. They wear white paper masks, these men, their voices muffled like surgeons', and Mei can tell what they're thinking, from the way the one holds the elevator while the other sets the boxes on the carpet, as if they have planned this maneuver in advance: how to spend the fewest possible seconds in contaminated air.

Already the floor feels smaller than before, too small. And it seems to Mei that the kids are multiplying. Their hands on the doorknobs. Their fingers flicking the light switches. Their bare feet on the carpet, their spit in the sinks, stray hairs floating everywhere in the air.

It is hard to feel hungry. Mei concentrates on the chewing, the cold lettuce of the sandwich against her teeth, while the other girls chat and complain.

It obsesses them immediately: what they cannot do and whom they cannot see. "It would be easier if we were used to being apart," says one girl, whose boyfriend, she is saying, lives in a different dorm.

Already the days seem longer than before, only twenty-four hours deep, as if the passage of time requires some movement through space and here they all are, stopped in one place.

Mei's mother calls again.

"You're calling too much," says Mei. She covers her mouth while she chews, as if there is anyone with her to see.

"I'm just worried," says her mother. "I'm so worried."

But her voice, like that, so urgent, so thin, brings the opposite of comfort, like the constant touching of a tooth when it's sore.

"I'm fine," says Mei.

She is aware of her voice as she speaks, the way it echoes against the bare walls, as if amplified. She's been allowed to bring only one bag from her old room to this one; the old room, where Kara got sick, is now sealed shut with yellow tape. There is nothing here to soften the sound, those lonely acoustics of an empty room.

"Do they know yet what it is?" her mother asks again.

Out in the hall, Mei can hear one of the boys, a runner, jogging from one end of the floor to the other, again and again, an improvised track. Weird Matthew, the others call him, to distinguish him from the other Matthew. But running seems as good a use of time as any other.

"I told you," says Mei. "I don't know."

She can hear her mother breathing into the phone.

"I love you," says her mother, but there is a stiffness to it. They are not the kind of family who says it out loud. The words feel extreme between them, a registering of danger more than tenderness.

"Me too," says Mei.

After that, she listens for a while to the sound of the boy running in the hall. He is training for a marathon, she overheard him say once. He likes to run barefoot, like the Kenyans, he says, like the ancient Greeks, like humans were meant to do. Now his footsteps land on the carpet. There's a moment's shadow each time he passes her door, coming close, fading, then coming back again, like the intermittent ticking of a clock.

On the second day of the quarantine, a message appears in the parking lot, ten floors down from the window of the study lounge. In giant white letters, made of chalk or flour, someone has spelled out the name of a girl, Ayanna, and something else, too, a code, maybe, or an abbreviation, stark and bright against the asphalt. A boy is squinting in the sunshine nearby, waiting for his work to be seen.

Mei can feel the hours in those letters, the planning and the labor, the bending of that boy's back. No back has ever bent that way for Mei.

"What a waste of time," says Weird Matthew, the runner. He is standing at the window, too, barefoot and sweaty, gulping water from a thermos. "Right?" he says.

A nearby window scrapes open in its frame. Ayanna in pajamas, the girl from Barbados, is waving wildly at the boy. Ayanna in V-necks and jeans, pink toenails in flip-flops, white teeth and smooth skin, that simple, effortless beauty. The sweet, appealing lilt of her accent. All the boys are in love with her, and maybe so are the girls, who forgive her for her loveliness—because what makes her so radiant is not only her looks but her warmth, the plain kindness that seems to glow from her cheeks. She is the only girl who is friendly to Mei in the hall.

When he sees Ayanna, the boy in the parking lot stands up and waves back with two hands, like a man in need of rescue by a helicopter. Ayanna shouts something down to him, but he can't hear it. He cups his hand to his ear. Soon they are talking on their phones instead but still waving, as if two tin cans have been strung between them.

Mei watches them from the window until a sadness comes into her, as quick as adrenaline. She closes the curtains.

She calls her old friend Katrina. She should have gone to Berkeley, with Katrina, she sees now. Or else CalArts, like she wanted to, where she could have majored in what she really wanted to: drawing or painting or both. What a bummer, Katrina says, when Mei tells her about Kara and the others, and Mei feels right then that her old friend is floating away. It doesn't sound like her, this word, *bummer*. Everyone is floating away.

That same day, two new doctors arrive on the floor. One is some kind of specialist, in from the East Coast. She wears green scrubs and green gloves and a thick, cream-colored mask that looks fresh from a package, crisp and clean.

She studies their eyes. She looks at their throats. She listens to the beating of their hearts. She does not seem at all relieved by the fact that everyone on the floor has woken up well.

"The incubation period could be long," she says, as if their bodies are instruments for the measurement of time, which, in a way, they are. "The longer it takes to present itself," she says, "the farther it could spread."

When it is Mei's turn to be examined, the doctor hands her a mask like her own, elastic loops dangling.

"From now on," she says, "wear this at all times." Her manner is lab-like, as if she is handling hazardous chemicals instead of people.

Mei is watching her face the way she watches flight attendants during turbulence: if they keep pouring the coffee, she knows things are fine—some kinds of tumult frighten only the unaccustomed or the untrained. But this doctor's face, so tense and so tight, suggests that expertise is having the opposite effect.

"And there should be no physical contact of any kind," says the doctor. "No kissing," she adds. "And no sex."

A heat comes into Mei's cheeks. Sometimes she still feels like a child.

A second doctor follows the first, a different kind, a psychiatrist, maybe, or something like it.

This doctor asks questions about Kara's mood before she died. "Do you know," she says, "if your roommate had recently received any upsetting news?"

"I didn't know her very well," says Mei.

"Did she ever express any dark thoughts?"

"Not to me," says Mei.

And what about the others? this doctor wants to know.

Mei shakes her head.

"I didn't know them either," Mei says.

After that, they all look more like patients than before, with masks stretched tight across their faces. The paper feels hot against Mei's cheeks. You can feel yourself breathing, and it's hard not to think about it, how precarious that rhythm, as if those masks have made the sickness more likely, instead of less.

Meanwhile, a new affliction begins to spread in the dorm—a boredom like Mei has never known.

She spends a long time staring out the window of the study lounge, at the lake shimmering in the distance as it shrinks away in the sun. The receding water has left the sand littered with fragments of a hundred lost things: sailboats from earlier decades, sunken for years, an ancient truck, rusted down to a silhouette. There is something suddenly unsettling about this landscape, which seemed so romantic to her before, how the woods that line the slopes around the lake are diseased and dried out, and how the trees stay standing long after death, branches blackened by fire or their trunks eaten away from the inside by beetles, as her biology professor has explained. But they go on standing, like headstones.

She thinks suddenly of Kara, of the girl's body—her bones. How ludicrous it seems in this time that the troubles of a body can still shut off a mind.

"What are you looking at?" asks one of the other girls, after a while, as if Mei has found some secret diversion that should be shared and not hoarded.

"Nothing," says Mei.

She watches, bit by bit, as a wind rises and blows the chalk letters of Ayanna's name all away.

This is when a boy's voice floats up behind her.

"Imagine a runaway train," he says. That's it—no other introduction.

"What?" she says.

It's Matthew, Weird Matthew, in red running shorts, bare feet. His mask is hanging lopsided on his face.

"Imagine there are five people tied to the tracks," he says.

"Oh God," says the other girl in the study lounge. "Not this stupid train thing again."

Mei has seen it from a distance, an odd quickness in the way this boy speaks, the way he moves, as if his body must run every day in order, sometimes, to be still.

"The train is going straight for the people," he says.

He's still sweaty from all his running in the hall. She can see it in the curls of his hair, dark and clumped, and in the spots on his shirt. She can smell it.

"Why are they tied to the tracks?" she asks.

"That's not the point," he says. He is staring at her while he talks. She can't quite look into his eyes. She notices then that there are holes in the armpits of his shirt.

"Now imagine there's a lever near the tracks," he says. "If you pull that lever, you can save the people by diverting the train to another track."

But here is the catch: someone is tied to the other track, too.

"If you flip the switch," he says, "you save five people. But you kill one."

Matthew's whole body is vibrating, as if with a kind of energy he cannot contain. It's coming out in this way: a stream of words to a girl he's never spoken to before.

"Do you pull the lever?" he wants to know.

It feels good to sink into a problem so distant. This might already be the longest conversation Mei has ever had on this floor.

"Do I know the people?" she asks.

The question seems important, but Matthew shakes his head like it isn't, like it isn't important at all.

"I guess I'd have to flip the switch," she says.

"Right?" he says. He looks like her answer—this agreement—has given him some kind of release.

A commotion is suddenly rising in the hall. The nurses have arrived to take their temperatures again.

Matthew keeps talking.

"But what if there's no lever?" he says. "What if the only way to stop the train is by throwing something heavy onto the tracks? And what if the only heavy thing that's nearby is a really fat man?"

She can see where this is going.

"Do you push the man onto the tracks?" he asks.

This one is easy.

"No," she says. "No way."

"But isn't it the same as pushing the lever?" he says. "Either way, you're killing one person to save five."

"I don't think it's the same at all," says Mei.

One of the nurses rushes into the study lounge: "Hey," she says through her mask, her green scrubs swishing as she walks, her green-gloved finger wagging. "That's too close, you two. Five feet apart at all times."

Mei steps back but Matthew stays where he is, as if he hasn't heard her or he doesn't care.

The other kids lie around all day in the halls, waiting for something to happen, to change, or at least for the next meal to come. After only a few days, they have turned sleepy and sluggish, but who can say what is causing it: the sickness or the stillness?

They talk endlessly of the weather. The sky is enormous, and the sun so appealing, and the leaves translucent in the afternoon light. They pop the screens from the windows, no matter the flies. They hang their arms out over the sills, just for the feel of the outdoors on their skin.

Mei can imagine what it must look like from the outside, all those heads in the windows, like victims of a fire. But then again, there's no need to imagine it—two news vans have set up in the parking lot and are showing the footage live on national television. Kids crowd around their flat-screens to see. That's us, they say, pointing. That's us. We're on TV.

But the excitement does not last. The boredom returns faster every time. How swiftly it comes over them, the feeling that this containment will never end.

On the third day, one of the boys finally breaks the monotony. It is the guitarist, this time, Drunk Todd, they call him. He is a late sleeper anyway. No one notices until noon.

They can hear him breathing from the stretcher as he floats down the hall on his back, those paramedics like rowers, and his eyelids as pink as a child's. He is the first to leave the floor in three days.

The others take the news quietly this time, as if they have lived their whole lives with this kind of peril. They are seventeen or they are eighteen, but some skills come fast, like a universal grammar, just waiting to be put to use.

The study lounge that same afternoon: Mei is reading in there when Ayanna puts her head down on the table. It is just the two of them in the room, that quiet camaraderie of two readers in one space. And it is such a subtle thing, the way Ayanna sets her book down beside her, taking time to mark her place, the way she rests her head on her arms, slowly, carefully. There is no fainting. No collapse. Her mask remains in place, white and neat on her face.

"Are you okay?" asks Mei, from across the room, her heart beginning to pound.

It seems such a violation to wake someone you barely know. Mei touches her shoulder. She whispers her name. A square of sunlight shines on Ayanna's back.

"Are you okay?" Mei asks again. This is when Ayanna mumbles reassuringly. She nods slightly. She does. It is the nod that Mei will remember, and the relief.

Mei goes back to her chair by the window.

The door to the study lounge swings open. It's Matthew. She is aware of a brief burst of gladness at the sight of him, this strange boy. Maybe he has another question for her. Maybe he wants to know what she thinks.

And he does arrive with a question. It's this:

"What the hell?" he says, his words dampened by his mask. "Ayanna?"

"She's okay," says Mei, her book in her lap. "I think she's just tired."

"Ayanna," he says. "Ayanna."

This time, Ayanna stays quiet. When Matthew begins to shake her, one of her arms falls out from under her. There is the soft smack of her cheek making contact with the table, the slight rolling of her head, and her arm dangling below.

Matthew turns to Mei.

"You're just sitting there doing nothing?" he says.

The room begins to fill with other kids, their voices like magnets to the others. "Ayanna," they keep saying through their masks. Some are afraid to go near her. "Ayanna," they call from a distance. "Ayanna."

Somewhere, in another dorm, the boy who loves this girl is making popcorn or doing laundry—maybe he is thinking of her right at that moment.

"She said she was okay," Mei tells them, but they are not listening. Her cheeks are turning hot beneath the mask. Her eyes are starting to burn. "She said she was fine just a minute ago."

Ayanna's head now lies heavy on the table. You have to look closely to see the faint rising and falling of her back as she breathes. It's an unsettling milestone: two cases in one day.

"And this one," says Matthew, pointing at Mei. "She's just sitting there reading like nothing's wrong."

By the time the paramedics come for Ayanna, Mei has escaped to her room, where she lies curled on her bed for a long time, on those bright green sheets, chosen so carefully in August, the sheets of the girl she had hoped to be at college, not so serious as before, a little whimsical, maybe, a little bolder.

She can feel a tightening in her throat. Tears. Through the wall next door, there comes the faint throbbing of a television—is there any lonelier sound?

After that, she stays so long alone in her room that she does not hear the news until late the next day: two more girls have fallen sick.

10.

The eyelids flutter. The breathing is irregular. The muscle tone is visibly slack. With each new patient, Catherine notes it again—these signs that the sleepers might be dreaming.

What weird cases. Curiosity is part of what keeps her coming back all this way.

By her third visit to Santa Lora, a sleep specialist has confirmed it: the mapping of brain activity shows that these sleepers are, indeed, dreaming.

Dreams have never much interested Catherine. The field of psychiatry has moved on to different territory. Most of her colleagues would argue that dreams are entirely meaningless, a kind of mental junk, randomly generated by the electrical impulses of the brain. Or at best, some might say, dreams are like religion—a force that exists outside the realm of science.

But on her long drive home that night, it is hard not to wonder what it is those kids are dreaming of.

Maybe they dream of the lost and the departed, the once known and the dead. They dream of lovers, certainly, the real and the imagined, that girl at the bar, that boy they used to know. Or else they dream, as Catherine sometimes does, the mundane dreams of cluttered desks and computer screens, the loading of laundry, the clatter of dishes, the mowing of over-grown lawns. They dream they can fly. Or they dream they can kill. Maybe they dream they are pregnant and feel elated. Or they dream they are pregnant and are devastated. Or maybe, one or two of them, dream the answers to the problems they've been struggling with for years—like the nineteenth-century German chemist who insisted that the undiscovered structure of the chemical compound benzene came to him in the form of a dream.

If any of those kids dream of falling from great heights, they do not—for the first time in their lives—wake up before their bodies hit the ground. Instead, they dream right through these impacts and then go on dreaming after that.

The true contents of these dreams go unrecorded, of course, but in some patients, the accompanying brain waves are cap-tured with electrodes and projected on screens, like silhouettes of the hereafter. Catherine is as shocked as the sleep specialists are by what she sees on those screens. These are not the brains of ordinary sleepers. These are not the brains of the comatose. These brains are extraordinarily busy.

By the time Catherine is pulling into her driveway back home, the news has leaked to the media and is streaming through the speakers of her car radio: there is more activity in these minds than has ever been recorded in any human brain—awake or asleep.

11.

That same night, in the kitchen of a large gray house ten blocks away from the college, a mother is singing to her newborn baby. A father is cooking dinner.

Of course they've heard the news. Of course. But at this point, just ten days in, it is still possible to enjoy the smell of onions browning in a pan, and the warmth of the baby's head against his hand, and to say to Annie, as he opens the wine: "See? It's getting easier, isn't it?"

The baby is seventeen days old.

They are new to Santa Lora, Ben and Annie, visiting professors, their boxes still spread on the pinewood floors, their books stacked like firewood in the dining room, and the disassembled shelves, waiting for screws, and her prints in brown paper, leaning everywhere, unhung, against the walls. Also a soccer ball, clean and white and bought on impulse along with the grill—a backyard, can you imagine? A separate room for the baby. A whole house. They are delirious with space. They are young but not that young, these the last years in their lives when they can still be thought of that way.

Annie is sitting at the kitchen table in a T-shirt and boxers, the pajamas she's been wearing for days and days, her breasts hanging loose beneath the cotton—so changed they seem like someone else's, so much larger than before, and the centers gone wide and dark.

Grace is asleep in her arms. Those little pink feet, one crossed over the other.

"Can you defrost another bottle?" says Annie.

Her milk has been slow to come in. For a while, the baby was lighter every time they set her on the scale, as if she might soon float away, which is how it felt to them as they waited, like two animals, waiting for their baby to thrive. She's a skinny little thing, said one of the nurses that first week, which made Annie cry right there in the hospital, from hormones, maybe, or from exhaustion, or from something much simpler: love.

But they've had a good day. The baby is finally gaining weight, thanks mostly to the milk of other women, donated to the hospital by mothers with too much supply. How weird this would have seemed to Ben before—milk pumped from other women's breasts—but now, there is only urgency. There is only getting his daughter whatever she needs.

He has learned to bathe the baby while Annie's incision healed. He taught himself to change a diaper. And there is all the other washing, too, the cleaning of dishes and sheets and clothes, always the sound of bottles clicking in the sink, so much work and no sex and the days so often ending before he has ever showered. For seventeen days, they've been sleeping different sleep: short and sudden, and like sipping salt water for thirst—they wake more in need than before they closed their eyes. Every hour is needed, every moment put to use. It is exactly what he has always feared would happen with a baby. But what he didn't understand before, what he failed to imagine in advance, is how much pleasure there is in being so consumed.

These minutes, though, this evening, they form a sudden

pause, an unexpected quiet, during which they have realized, for the first time in weeks—and with a flush of joy—that there might be time enough to make a salad, to cook a piece of fish.

Here I am with my wife, thinks Ben, as he washes the lettuce at the sink, here we are with our daughter, Grace—there is a delight in just saying her name. What pleasure there is in some statements of fact, such simplicity, such calm.

To say they are ignoring what is happening at the college would be not quite true, or not quite fair. A few sick strangers—those poor kids, but none from the classes they teach—is only one of a hundred bad stories that must be overlooked every day. To close one's eyes can be an act of survival.

Annie turns her head toward the back door. She is saying something that he cannot quite hear.

"What did you say?" says Ben. He turns off the water to listen.

"Can you hear that?" she says, standing up with the baby, who stretches and stirs in response—the baby has a way of arching her back like a fish, her whole face turning red with the strain of it. "The birds," says Annie. "They're going crazy out there."

From the backyard, there come the urgent cries of the swallows who live beneath the air conditioner, their nest wedged against the windowsill. That nest was one of their earliest discoveries here, even more endearing than the goslings who float on the lake at dusk, as if they had come to a place so bursting with life that even the air conditioners could engender it.

Annie's is a temporary position at the college, two years in a physics lab, and his is only part-time, teaching literature. But there is a charm in the modesty of it, like the warped floors beneath their feet, a pleasant shabbiness.

"Maybe there's a hawk somewhere?" says Annie. With Grace curled against one arm, she creaks open the screen door. She moves slowly, still sore from the cesarean. "Maybe that's what's bothering them? A hawk?"

She stands barefoot in the yard, squinting through the lenses of her glasses. Her dark hair, like his, is unwashed, curled in a loose knot at the nape of her neck.

She is scanning the sky, which is pale and blue, the light just starting to fade. Behind their fence lie the woods, pine trees packed tight on a slope, at the top of which, a mile or so in the distance, is a large blackened patch, the bare branches proof of the last wildfire.

In their yard, the two swallows are skittering back and forth between the nest and the olive tree. The yellow house next door looks deserted.

"Hey, birds," Ben says for Annie's enjoyment. "What's wrong with you guys?"

He likes the shape of her mouth when she smiles, her small teeth, not quite straight, her lips waxy with ChapStick.

"Yeah," she says. "What's wrong with you guys?"

Their birds continue screaming. This is the way they think of them, as *theirs*.

Grace suddenly opens her eyes. Her little arms shoot out from her sides as if startled.

"Do you hear that, Gracie?" says Ben. "Those are birds. Birds are the only animals that can fly."

They've been advised to talk to her as much as possible, but they did not need to be told. It is an immediate urge: to tell her everything they know.

Just three months removed, their apartment in Brooklyn feels already like a cage from which they've finally been sprung. That apartment, three hundred square feet, and the site of so much unhappiness. And what luck to be released right here, to this place, these mountains, bordered on three sides by state forest, a place where the smell of pine sap floats over fences, where they sit evenings outside in Adirondack chairs, bought for ten dollars at a yard sale, and where they listen to the crickets buzzing in the trees and to the voices of children playing in the woods. And the stars—you can actually see the stars. And the cabins—some people actually live in log cabins here. And the strawberries and the tomatoes and the avocados and the corn, all of it sold at the produce stand on the road into town, stocked each day with the fruits of the valley below. Here is where they've waited these months for the baby to come. California.

A second sound now surfaces, just as urgent or more so, the doorbell. Someone is ringing it again and again. Surprise jumps between Annie's eyes and his, no words needed. So much can be said without saying it, the efficiency of marriage.

Ben is the one who answers the door, and so he is the one who finds her: one of the girls from next door, the younger one, is standing in sandals on their front porch. She looks as upset as the birds.

"Excuse me," she says, her voice breaking, her dark eyes blinking with tears, pink cheeks.

She is maybe ten years old, or eleven, sucking on a strand of her hair. He is not used to speaking with children.

"Are you okay?" he says.

Suddenly his wife is beside him, taking over.

"My God," says Annie, one hand over her mouth. "What is it?"

"It's an emergency," says the girl. In her ears, tiny studs, the color and shape of ladybugs.

Annie reaches out toward her shoulder, but the girl steps away.

"I'm not supposed to touch anyone," she says.

Annie's eyes flash at Ben's.

"What do you mean?" asks Annie, but the girl doesn't say.

They've been watching these sisters for a while. They have seen them walk to the bus stop in the mornings and water the vegetables at night. They know they sit reading sometimes in the windowsills or in the widow's walk at the top of that big, old house. The quiet ways of these girls seem so different from their father, who came over shouting one day, something about a tree. He and Annie could not make him believe they were only renting this house, and that it was the owners who must have cut down that fir.

"Just tell us what you need," says Annie to the girl.

Right then, a window scrapes open next door. The girl's older sister calls out to her from their house. "Libby!" she shouts. How startling to hear that quiet girl yell. "Get back here," she says. "Get in here. I'm serious."

These girls are afraid—Ben can see it in their faces.

Across the street, a nurse is just arriving home in blue scrubs. Ben knows her name, Barbara, and nothing else. She glances in their direction, in curiosity or in judgment, but she keeps moving. She goes inside.

"Please," says the girl on the porch. "I just need to get into your backyard for a minute."

He cannot understand what is happening, but whatever this girl needs, he wants to provide it. This girl is his daughter in ten years. He has begun a running narration to that older Grace, mouthing to himself as she sleeps on his chest: *When you were a baby*, he likes to say, *we lived in California*.

"Come on, then," he says to the girl.

She refuses to come into the house, so they walk the long way instead, around the side, all three, he, Annie, with the baby, and the girl. He unlatches the gate in the side yard. He throws it open. The girl runs through.

They have stopped asking her questions.

Soon the girl is crouching over something in the grass behind the oak tree. This is when they finally see it: a white kitten is huddled in the corner of their yard. In its mouth, it holds a tiny swallow, fresh wings hanging from its teeth.

"Let it go, Chloe," she is saying. "Let it go right now."

Later, Ben will think of this moment as the *arche kakon*, the start of the bad times, as he would say of Greek tragedy, as he has written so often on whiteboards for his students, as if that kitten were an omen of every rupture that will follow. But Annie would laugh at this kind of thinking. She is a scientist, his wife, a scholar of physics. You're too superstitious, she would say. But isn't her physics just as much like magic as anything else?

The girl squeezes the kitten's jaw until it drops the bird on the grass. It's one of the babies. Dead.

"There's a hole in our screen door," says the girl, holding the kitten with two hands. "This one keeps getting out."

She runs from the yard, and soon they hear the slamming of her front door.

Ben crouches over the bird. The small wings, those miniature feet. He can see the wounds where the cat's teeth have punched through the feathers and the flesh.

Their birds continue crying out from above. How much do they know? he wonders. How much can they feel?

"Do you think they're okay?" says Annie. There are tears in her eyes. This is something that has been happening since the baby, a change in hormones or in outlook—who can say? "Those girls?"

Annie is looking at the house next door. She is chewing at her fingers. It's a habit of hers, the reason her skin is so raw and so red around the nail beds. He touches her wrist; she stops.

"I don't know," he says. A moroseness is creeping into his head, heavy and familiar. "I hope they're okay."

But you never know for certain what goes on in other people's houses. Their neighbors in Brooklyn never would have guessed how close Annie came last year to moving out.

They try to go back to their meal, but the onions have charred by then. And soon the baby is awake, her cries filling the kitchen.

Ben has forgotten to defrost a bottle of breast milk, so he works on that now, turning it over in warm water at the sink, while Annie tries to feed Grace with her body, from which only a few drops of milk ever flow. Grace looks more and more desperate—she keeps pulling her head away from Annie's breasts.

"I can't believe you forgot to warm the bottle," she says. She takes it from his hands and holds it under the tap, as if the slush inside will melt more quickly under her watch than his. He knows what she is not saying, how his mind is always drifting in a thousand directions. "We have a child now," she says. "You can't be so flaky all the time."

He has seen it already, how a child can unite them but also divide.

After that, Annie disappears upstairs with the baby. Ben drinks a glass of wine, quicker than he means to. Something has turned. The mood has spoiled. How often that used to happen in Brooklyn: a nice night slipping from their grasp. He drinks another glass.

That night, he dreams the same dream he's been dreaming for two years: Annie leaves him for her dissertation advisor. Certain tied knots come loose in the night. This time, she takes the baby with her. And there is something else new: at the end of the dream, his teeth begin to loosen from his gums.

To those who believe in the fixed meanings of dreams, the loss of teeth is significant, symbolic of anxiety or fear. They would say that the dream presaged what will happen in the morning and maybe everything that happens after that. But he is always trying to lure his students away from those kinds of readings, asking them to be more expansive in their thinking, less obvious, less easy, more true. All they want are the answers, those kids, a grand order of things, as if every story were only code for something else.

He is awake at the time of the accident, as he will later tell the police, in bed but not asleep. The baby's breathing is slow and steady in her crib, and Annie lies beside him, one bare leg stretched out on the sheet.

Six in the morning, everything quiet, that earliest, faintest light.

Into this silence there comes a sudden boom, as loud as thunder but nearer. It rattles the windows in their frames. Some sounds trigger a kind of vision. An image comes to mind.

"What was that?" says Annie, sitting up fast in the dimness. He can tell she isn't sure whether she dreamed it or really heard it. Car alarms are ringing outside.

He reaches for the light, but no light comes. The power is out. His hands are shaking. Grace begins to cry.

He goes to the window in his boxers. Something has happened across the street, where the nurse lives. It is hard to see through the smoke.

"What is it?" Annie asks again.

Through the drifts of smoke, he can see that the house no longer stands. The walls have caved in, leaving a pile of blackened wood in which small fires burn. The lawn is scattered with debris.

"It's the house across the street," he says. "It looks like there was some kind of explosion."

Already, neighbors are coming out into the street, hands over their mouths, a few running toward the lot with garden hoses, water streaming. In the air, scraps of paper are fluttering away in the breeze.

"An explosion?" says Annie.

The utility pole on the corner has snapped. Electrical wires are hanging like garland in the trees. They hear sirens in the distance.

Later, while the firefighters do what they can, and the police keep the people away, Ben and Annie stand around with the other neighbors in bathrobes, Ben with the baby in his arms, her eyes wide and serious, as if she, too, senses the mood. The sun is rising around them, while every dog on the street is barking and speculation is spreading through the crowd. A faulty hot water heater, maybe, or a stove left on too long. "That could do it," says one of the older men. "A gas stove left on for many hours."

Everyone hopes that the nurse was not at home. Maybe she was at work, they say, the overnight shift. But they can all see her car right there in the driveway, the windshield cracked and smudged black.

"First those college kids getting sick," says one of the older women. "And now this."

Some try to look for luck in the situation: "At least the fire didn't spread to the other houses," they are saying, the way people sometimes do. There is a comfort in thinking up something worse than what is.

Through all of this, the two girls next door stay inside. Ben can see them up in the widow's walk, watching the street from above, their faces faintly red from the flashing of the fire trucks across the street.

At the same time, their father is doing some kind of work on the exterior of the house. He is standing up on a ladder, thick beard, no shirt, the sound of hammer and nail.

Annie is the first to notice him. "My God," she says. "I think he's boarding up the windows."

He looks like a man at sea up there, closing the hatches of a ship, as if preparing for a storm that no one else can see.

12.

The tenth victim is found in his bed with the eleventh: two boys, roommates, sleeping secretly on one twin mattress. These boys in their boxers, long-limbed and pale, who pretended so much interest in the girls of the tenth floor, now sleep through the lesson made so instantly clear to the others: how disease sometimes exposes what is otherwise hidden. How carelessly it reveals a person's private self.

The twelfth is discovered slumped in one of the showers, warm water streaming over her bare skin. Her body is blocking the drain, and this is what the others notice first, a tide of water pooling on the carpet in the hall. She is lucky, they say, that she didn't drown in that sleep. But as she is carried away, under cover of a towel, she does not look lucky. Her dark hair drips down the hall as she sleeps, fingers pruned, the checked pattern of the bathroom tile imprinted on the pale skin of her thigh.

But the girls—the ones who are left—notice something else about her, too, a small flickering of her eyelids. The idea spreads quickly: like the others, she is dreaming. It seems important, this dreaming, as if these girls live in some other time, when what you saw in your sleep could still be taken for some kind of truth.

By now, experts in contagious disease have begun to fill the rooms of the bed-and-breakfasts of Santa Lora.

These are scientists who have floated down the Congo to reach villages hot with hemorrhagic fever or swabbed the saliva of bats in the remotest caves of southern China. They have suffered their own bouts of malaria while finishing their doctorates in the jungles of Zaire, and they know how it feels to breathe like an astronaut in a full-body biohazard suit. It is with some surprise that these travelers now turn their attention to a patch of earth they have not been watching, the soft belly of America, the small town of Santa Lora, California, population 12,106.

They do not, these experts, believe the cause of the sickness could be psychological.

Instead they suspect meningitis, which is not so rare a flower in the halls of college dormitories, where it travels in kisses and the steam of hot showers. Or encephalitis lethargica, another strange sleeping sickness that haunted the early twentieth century. But the symptoms don't quite fit.

It isn't bird flu or swine flu or SARS. It is not mononucleosis.

What they do know is that this sickness is unusually contagious, like measles: you can catch measles if you walk through a room ten minutes after an infected person has coughed a single cough.

Meanwhile, the afflicted go on sleeping a deep and steady sleep, their bodies now fed by plastic tubes taped into their noses, their skin kept clean by the gloved hands of strangers.

No one wants to say so right away, but already an idea is creeping into the minds of some of these scientists, like a premonition coming true: this sickness might be something new.

13.

On the twelfth day, Halloween, the weather finally turns, the first rain in three months. Big fat drops in the woods, a murmur in the trees, the unfamiliar smell of it soaking the pavement. And the California ground—it's too dry to absorb it.

So rare is rain that it seems somehow ominous to Sara as she watches it from the widow's walk of their house, the way it pools in that nurse's bathtub across the street, which stands oddly intact amid the wreckage of the explosion, exposed to the air and the sky, the yellow caution tape glistening in the wind.

Sara has added to her worries this new one: a house can spontaneously blow up. "That nurse probably had the sickness," her father keeps saying. She and Libby watched the firefighters pull her body, beneath a sheet, from what was left of the house. "She probably had the stove on when she fell asleep."

But no one else is talking about the sickness.

Outside, life on the street flows on. A woman in a blue windbreaker is walking her poodle. The man next door, the one with the baby, is dragging his trash cans across the driveway. Sara's school bus has already drifted past her window without her, packed with kids in costumes, like any other Halloween.

"Put this pot up in your room," says her father, in the red flannel shirt he's been wearing for three days, his old jeans, no shoes. Their house is full of leaks.

In their bedroom, Libby is hunched over the floor. A wet spot is blooming in the ceiling above her head. She slides the pot beneath the leak.

"It's dripping all over your script," says Libby.

Already the pages of *Our Town* are sticking together with rain, the yellow highlighter bleeding across the front page. Sara had been spending her lunch periods at rehearsal instead of sitting alone on the quad.

Libby helps her spread the pages of the script out to dry.

The phone begins to ring

A face comes into Sara's mind: Akil. But it's stupid to think of him calling her now. It is ten in the morning on a Tuesday. She knows right where Akil will be—she can see him without being there: chewing on his pencil in pre-algebra, one foot bouncing on the carpet beneath his desk, three rows over from hers, always finished with his work before anyone else.

The phone rings again. She answers it.

"Is this Sara?" says a woman on the line. Voices like this make her nervous. That crispness.

"Who's calling?" she says.

Libby is watching her from the doorway, mouthing to her: *Who is it?*

"Is your mother or father at home?" says the voice on the phone. It's the attendance office from school.

"Dad," she calls. "You forgot to call the school."

She can feel it like a heartbeat, the distant buzz of the school bell ringing through the day. She senses her shadow self moving through her school hours: the daily quizzes in pre-algebra, the shouting in the cafeteria line, the hiding out in the bathroom during the break between classes. Three rehearsals of *Our Town* have taken place without her.

It bothers her to think of Amelia, the understudy, speaking the lines that Sara has memorized. "Her?" Amelia had said when they found out Sara had gotten the part. "Seriously?" she said out loud to her friends. A terrible thought had flashed in Sara's mind at that moment—that Mrs. Campbell might have given Sara the part because she felt sorry for her.

Downstairs, she can hear her father talking to the woman on the phone.

"I don't have to explain myself to you," he says.

He is not allowed on campus anymore because of a misunderstanding the year before. It's not illegal to carry a gun, he always says, but it's not allowed on school grounds. Mrs. Chu noticed it beneath his coat during a parent-teacher conference. From the slip of that gun into her teacher's view grew a sequence of visits from a social worker.

"You should all watch out," her father is saying now to the woman on the phone, his voice louder than before. "You're going to be lucky if you survive this thing."

After that, Sara hears the phone click into its cradle.

"No one in this town knows a goddamn thing about what's coming," he says to himself or maybe to the girls. His mind is like that: always mired in a terrible future.

He has laid them out like laundry: the three gas masks that usually hang in the basement. One for each of them—Sara, Libby, and their father. They haven't left the house in a week.

A germ, their father has told them, can float free in the air. It could be anywhere. All you have to do is breathe it in.

"What if this is like last time?" Libby whispers to Sara.

Last time: the solar flares, six months earlier. Those flares, their father said, would cause a geomagnetic storm that would knock out power all over the world for weeks or months, or maybe forever, and no one knew about it, he said, because the media was under some kind of gag order, which is a thing that happens all the time in this country, and if you don't believe that, you're just being naïve. He had kept the girls home on that day, in case of violence or looting. Sara was too scared to eat, as they waited for the radio to snap silent, for the auroras to streak the California sky. But the lightbulbs went on glowing, steady as stars, and the sky kept clear and quiet. "We got lucky today," their father finally said, as they climbed the stairs to their bedrooms that night, the danger apparently past. "But it's good to be cautious."

They are eating peanut butter sandwiches at the kitchen table when they hear a knock at the door.

"Don't open it," says their father, his chair scraping hard on the linoleum. He reaches for his gas mask. They've had them for a while, these masks, but there has never been a reason to wear them. Hers and Libby's are smaller than his, specially made for kids, and he let the girls decorate them, so that their names shine in puffy paint, gold glitter against the dark green rubber of the masks.

"Get upstairs," he says to the girls. The knock comes again, louder this time.

They watch from the stairs as their father fits the mask to his face, tightening the straps before getting close to the door.

He opens it, but only a crack, the chain snapping taut across the opening. Sara feels a rush of embarrassment for her father in that mask, the way the strands of his beard hang below it, like a plant, overgrown. These are their private preparations on view to a stranger.

On the doorstep, it turns out, is a policeman, and Sara is sure she sees the future in his uniform: he will take her father away.

"Is everything okay in here?" says the policeman.

From the bedroom window, the girls can see the top of his hat, his tan shirt spotted with rain, his car parked out front.

A strange sound is coming from the house next door, drowning out what her father is saying to him. Some kind of sawing. Sara looks out the window—it's the professor, on his porch, cutting off the top of a pumpkin.

Her father's voice is rising now, echoey through the mask: "I didn't threaten anyone," he says to the policeman.

"Well," says the policeman, his words slow and careful, a pair of handcuffs clinking on his belt. "This woman from the school felt concerned by what you said."

The sawing next door slows to a stop. The professor is watching the policeman. His wife is out there, too, with the baby. Stop staring, Sara wants to say.

"This is bullshit," says her father, and Sara wishes she could go down there and calm him, drain all that sharpness from his voice. He does things a hard way when usually there are easier ways. But she could translate, maybe, like the children of immigrants, explain what he really means. "I was trying to warn her," he says. "Do you even know what's going on?"

The policeman nods. His face is as calm as snow. Yes, he says, he is aware of the situation at the college.

Libby picks at the wallpaper while they listen. You can see the different layers of it, like tree rings, the velvety green paisley from when this house was new, and then all the later sheets on top of that, each one less ornate than the last, their family's money fading away through the years, all those layers leading somehow down to this: a policeman standing on their doorstep and saying these words: "Are your children here? I'd like to speak with them, too."

"You don't have any right," says her father.

But she and Libby are already peeking down the stairs.

"Are you girls okay in here?" the policeman calls when he sees them.

"We're fine," says Libby.

"Yeah," says Sara. "We're fine."

The rain is getting heavy, the ringing of drips in the pots around the house.

"You should be careful what you say to people," says the policeman. A sudden surge of hope comes to Sara. "Okay?" he says.

What a relief it is to see the slow turn of that man's shoulder, and then the back of his uniform as he walks across the yard in the rain, the beautiful rumble of his engine starting up.

And then her father is back inside, the door locked again, his gas mask lying flat on the table, his lungs breathing the safe air of the house.

At dusk, like fireflies, the trick-or-treaters start to fill the sidewalks, first the younger ones, pressed into parkas and trailed by their parents, wet leaves clinging to shoes and capes, and then the older ones, quick as burglars, pillowcases slung over their shoulders.

"Jesus," says their father, looking out through the boards on the windows. "This thing is going to spread through the whole town tonight."

She can almost picture it as it happens, the disease jumping from one person to the next, through the grazing of hands in a candy bowl. She once watched a show about a murder, where the police used a special kind of light to make invisible traces of blood glow green in the dark. A seemingly clean room proved suddenly streaked. She pictures the sickness like that, too, a trail of green snaking through the town.

When their doorbell rings, there's no question of answering it. "They'll go away," says their father. "Turn out those lights."

Anyway, they have no candy to give.

From her bedroom window, Sara can see two boys from her class on her porch. They are dressed like skeletons, one with a knife sticking out of his chest. The boys always dress up like that, she has learned, as if they don't know that the scariest things are invisible.

If she and Libby had been allowed to go trick-or-treating this year, they would have gone as they always do, as fancy ladies from another time, wearing their relatives' dresses from the attic, pinned up to fit them, the hems dirtier every year.

The boys ring the bell again. Sara hopes they don't know that this is where she lives. Finally, the boys give up and move on to the new neighbors' house, where two jack-o'-lanterns glow against the night and where the front door swings open again and again, the woman standing in the doorway with the baby in her arms—they've dressed her up as a pumpkin.

"I told you to turn off that porch light," says their father.

Sara spends the rest of the evening up in the widow's walk, practicing her lines from *Our Town,* coming back again and again to that part near the end, when she's dead and speaking from some sort of heaven, and telling Emily, the pretty one, freshly dead from childbirth, not to try to revisit her life. "When you've been here longer," she says now to her reflection, slow and deep the way Mrs. Campbell has taught her, "you'll see that our life here is to forget all that." She looks out over the lights of the neighborhood as she speaks, the pumpkins glowing on the porches, the college buildings in dark silhouette, and the bulk of the hospital in the distance, where the sick kids lie sleeping their strange sleep. She likes the way Mrs. Campbell has explained the meaning of her last line, how the living can't see the good in life while they're living it. She says the line slowly now, as if she herself possesses all the wisdom in its words: "No, dear," she says softly, buzzing with a vague nostalgia. "They don't understand."

She does not see who it is who picks the squash from their front yard and smashes it on the side of their house, or who writes in shaving cream on their driveway: WEIRDOS.

When the doorbell stops ringing and a quiet falls over the neighborhood, she finds her father hunched over the old computer, waiting, as always, for a page to load.

That computer is too slow for the girls to use it the way the other kids do. The other kids are always mentioning events that have transpired online, the flirtations and the fights, a vast second society that echoes mysteriously through the one she knows.

"I was wondering," she says to her father. "What about the play?"

"What play?" he says.

From behind, he looks older than he is, his shoulders bony through his T-shirt, the balding spot on the top of his head.

"At school," she says. "The one I've been telling you about."

He's typing now. He works slowly at it, as always, using only one finger and spending long seconds searching the keyboard between words, as if the letters get reshuffled each time he looks away.

"This is the first I've heard of it," he says.

"It's this Friday," says Sara. "Remember?"

He stops typing.

"A theater full of people?" he says. "Are you kidding? Do you know how fast this thing would spread in a room like that?"

The sting of tears surprises her. It's just a stupid play. And hers isn't even the best part. She wipes her eyes fast. She bites down hard on her lip. The slow tap of her father's typing resumes. Then, suddenly, Daisy the cat is beside her, rubbing her face against her shin—it seems the cats can sense it in Sara, the sadness that sometimes comes into her.

Later, Libby will do her the favor of not commenting on her tears.

"No way," says her father. "The only safe place is right here."

14.

On her fourth visit to Santa Lora, as she is leaving the hospital parking lot, Catherine gets a call from one of the nurses inside.

"It's one of those sick college kids," the nurse is saying again and again. She is out of breath. "One of those kids," she says. Catherine can hear a commotion in the background. "One of them—he woke up."

The boy is found wandering the hall in his hospital gown, IVs trailing behind him. He is barefoot on the linoleum, eyes squinting in the fluorescent lights, while in the rooms around him, the other sick go on sleeping.

But the parents: the parents jump up from their chairs and crowd out into the hall, to watch this boy walk, as if he has risen from the dead. Catherine can feel the hope radiating out of their bodies.

But he doesn't look right, this boy. He is eighteen years old, but he is walking like an old man. His gait is slow, his limbs stiff. There's a slight stoop in his posture.

He keeps shaking his head, as if trying to figure something out. When he speaks, his voice comes out in a whisper.

"This doesn't make sense," he says. He is looking around. He fingers the stubble on his chin.

"You're in the hospital," says Catherine, the one psychiatrist in the building. "You've been unconscious for four days."

A skepticism flashes on the boy's face.

"It's been a lot longer than that," he says.

You have to be gentle with delusions. It can be better not to argue.

It's natural, she tells him, to feel confused. But confusion—this is not quite the right word. This boy's words hum with a strange confidence.

"It's been a long time since I was here," he says. There's a weariness in his face.

"What do you mean?" says Catherine.

But he stops talking. She has the feeling as he speaks that he is only thinking out loud. An odd sensation comes to her: he is treating her as if she is a hallucination, some figment of a dream.

She guides him back to his room. He asks for water. One of the nurses brings a cup.

For now, he sits calmly on his bed.

Catherine steps out of the room to call home. A change of plans: she won't be home tonight, she tells the babysitter, who is accustomed to this kind of thing, Catherine's overnight shifts a part of their arrangement. Her daughter gets on the phone: "When are you coming home, Mama?" Her voice is so sweet and so clear. A surge of longing comes into Catherine, her eyes blurring with unexpected tears. This boy's parents, she remembers—someone should call his parents.

The other doctors are conferring in a cluster down the hall.

When she comes back, the boy's room is empty.

"I asked you to watch the door," she says to the orderly at the nursing station. She is used to the protocols of the psychiatric ward, but this is a regular hospital, not set up for supervision.

"I did," says the orderly. "He didn't come out of that room."

In the boy's room, a sudden breeze is rustling the blinds—the window is open. This room, she remembers, is on the third floor.

A terrible certainty comes into her mind, as the other doctors flood into the room behind her: whatever was happening inside that boy's mind will remain locked forever beyond anyone else's reach.

She pauses at the window, afraid of what she will see, knowing without knowing: and there he is, three floors below, facedown on the sidewalk, his hospital gown pooling out around his body.

The soles of his bare feet are as white as the moon. His blood shines beneath the streetlight. And his neck—obvious even from this height—is broken.

15.

Some will say later that the official response was too slow. But certain procedures *are* being followed. Lists are being made. Calculations. There is, after all, a mathematics of disease: how one case grows to three or four, and each of those four to four more.

A quiet arithmetic, a naming of names—this is how it comes to be that thirteen days after the first girl fell sick a nurse's gloved finger is pressing the doorbell at the house where Annie and Ben and their baby live.

Have they heard, the nurse wants to know, about the sick kids at the college?

A burst of adrenaline comes into Ben's blood.

She seems nervous, standing there, this young nurse in green scrubs and fresh gloves.

She is holding a clipboard under one arm. She is asking about their baby.

"Is she here?" she says. "Your daughter?"

"Why?" he says, but the details are rushing into his mind, all those reports he has only half heard. An infant can do that: shrink the world to the circumference of her throat.

"We're taking every precaution," the nurse says. "We're monitoring everyone who's had contact with the sick." She speaks as if reciting the words of a script, newly learned.

"But who do we know who's sick?" asks Ben. There's a sudden tightness in his throat.

The nurse looks away, as if the truth embarrasses her.

"No one called you?" she says. She is tugging at the chain of her necklace; a tiny silver cross catches the light.

He's been having nightmares about losing the baby. He wakes with a physical sensation, a terrible emptiness in his arms.

It's the milk, says the nurse. It's the donated milk from the hospital.

"Jesus," says Ben. They have a freezer full of it, rows and rows of bottles, pumped from the bodies of other women. And a bag full of old bottles that Grace has already drunk.

"One of the donors," says the nurse. "One of them might have been exposed."

He will remember, later, the look on Annie's face as she walks down the stairs, that last moment before she knows to be worried—that open look, flat, smooth-cheeked.

She is holding Grace in her arms, one hand on the back of her little head—that head. You can still feel the soft spots between the plates in her skull, not yet fused. Fear feels different, so much sharper, with a baby.

"Has she been feeling all right?" asks the nurse.

"Oh my God," says Annie, bringing her hand to her mouth. "Oh my God."

She is so sorry to bother them, says the nurse, and she's never done this before. Her charm bracelet is clinking against the clipboard. But they're just trying to be really careful.

"I'm supposed to ask if she's been sleeping more than usual?" the nurse says.

"What do you mean?" asks Annie. She tries to say more, but already she is crying, this new silent cry she's been doing so much of lately and has almost never done before—she is usually the sane one between them. She is the even keel. But now, Ben is the one who keeps having to take over, like a translator.

"She sleeps a lot," he says.

Even then, the baby is dozing in a sunsuit, mouth open, in Annie's arms.

"I need to take her temperature," says the nurse.

She does not have children, this woman—he is sure of it. It's in the way she speaks to them so carefully, as if from some great distance. He's been seeing everyone that way, lately, sensing who has had children and who has not, as if he can suddenly see all the strings that bind one person to another.

Soon the nurse is holding a wand a few inches from Grace's forehead, no contact. It's the same kind of thermometer they used in the hospital in those first few hours of her life when her body was still learning to regulate its own temperature, and her limbs, so accustomed to life underwater, were squirming slowly, like a jellyfish moving in a current.

"They said it was sterilized," says Ben. "I thought the milk was supposed to be sterilized."

The nurse's hands are shaking as she holds the thermometer over Grace's head. She is standing as far away as she can. She keeps having to start over.

"There was some kind of mistake," she says. "I'm sorry."

Behind her, the porch swing is rocking lightly in the wind. A dog is barking somewhere. Grace begins to open and close her lips like a fish.

Finally the beeping: no fever. A tiny ping of relief.

But someone will be back to do it again in the morning, says the nurse. They'll have to do it twice a day.

In the meantime, they should stop using the milk. They should throw out whatever they have left, and switch to formula.

And there is one more thing: "We have to ask that you keep

her at home for now," she says. She is peeling off her gloves. She is already backing away. "And also," she says, "please don't leave town."

For weeks, they've been learning to coax Grace to sleep. There is a certain way to swaddle her, a certain rhythm at which she likes to be rocked. They have a turtle that projects lights through its shell and a seahorse that plays soothing music. But she sleeps best to the beating of their hearts, which is why they've spent so many hours, both of them, with the tiny heft of her head pressed against their chests, her back curved, her fists clenched, the one bringing the other water or coffee or a few bites of grilled cheese, while the other moves as little as possible for fear of waking Grace up.

But now, they are afraid to let her close her eyes.

Ben skims in an hour all the stories they haven't read, the two weeks of coverage of the sickness so far. The reports conflict, how serious it is or not. He can't figure out how many have died. It is hard to find the real facts.

But the warmth of Grace's body in his lap—this is a fact. And the way her eyes drift between his face and the glow of his laptop—this is a fact, too. The rising and falling of her chest is a fact, and the knowing every second that air is moving in and out of her lungs.

"It's my fault," says Annie. "This is my fault."

"It's the hospital's fault," says Ben.

He is reading the directions on the formula they've been keeping in the cupboard, just in case they ever ran out of the donor milk.

Annie is trying to nurse her. There is magic in human milk— that's what they've been told. Antibodies and hormones, secret messages, even. Any drop Annie can give is a drop she should give. But her milk, as usual, runs out quickly, and Grace is soon pulling away from her chest, rooting around for some other source.

She soon sucks down the formula, and there is an animal comfort in knowing that their baby's belly is full.

She is a quiet baby. Everyone says so. But is she quieter than usual tonight? Maybe this thing is already hiding in her bloodstream. Maybe it's slipping into her little brain, even now.

They do not wear gloves when they touch her. They do not keep a distance from her breaths. They do not even think of it that night: that their baby might be a threat to them. Why say it, this truth that is implicit between them after only three weeks: that if anything ever happened to her, well, what would it matter what happened to them after that?

In the morning, Annie takes Grace's temperature right away: normal. She looks normal, too. Eyes wide, cheeks pink. Her legs wag as usual on the changing table. What a perfect little being—in knit cap and footed pajamas, and those miniature fingers perched in her mouth. How is it possible that their bodies knew how to make her?

But soon Grace is screaming in Ben's ear. It's a mood that sometimes rolls through her, and only Annie can soothe her when she gets like this.

After a while—and he feels guilty thinking it—he wants to get away. Here is what he has learned about loving a baby: the time away from her is vital to the pleasure of being with her.

"How about I go get her more formula," he says to Annie. His keys are already jingling in his hand.

Annie is examining her little forehead. "Did they say anything about a rash?"

"She's always had that," says Ben. He remembers those dots from the first time he held her, in the white light of the operating room, that startled look on her face, Annie's blood on the linoleum.

There's an urgency in the way he is tying his shoes, in the way he is searching for a hat to cover the hair he hasn't washed in a week. He hasn't left the house in two days.

But then the door is closing behind him, and he's out. And there it is: the rush of those first minutes alone, the smooth glide of the car backing out of the driveway—even that is a part of it, the satisfaction of something moving according to his will. How quiet it is out in the world—that's what he's noticed since the baby was born—and how orderly. A flock of black birds is drifting over the mountains in formation. A serene voice on public radio is introducing a piece of jazz. A lightness comes into him as he drives, like a first sip of whisky numbing his throat, a quickly spreading calm.

This town, these neighbors walking their dogs on the streets— this does not look like a place where a plague is right now unfolding. You can draw a lot of comfort from the normalcy of others—if this thing were really spreading, would the neighbors be raking their lawns? Would the mailman be delivering catalogues?

He takes the long way, along the lake. He stops for a coffee and feels the wonder of it, this thing he hasn't done since Grace was born: to drink a whole cup while it's hot.

But by the time he is standing in the baby aisle of the drugstore, he is starting to worry again. He is beginning to miss her. At three weeks old, their book has said, her mind cannot grasp the idea that an object continues to exist even after it leaves her sight. But Ben feels that way, too, as if whenever his daughter is out of his view, she might easily slip out of the world.

16.

By now, certain alternate theories are beginning to circulate online. It's the government, they say. Or it's Big Pharma. Some kind of germ must have gotten loose from a lab at the college.

Think about it, they say: Do you really believe that a completely new virus could show up in the most powerful country on earth without scientists knowing exactly what it is? They probably engineered it themselves. They might be spreading this thing on purpose, testing out a biological weapon. They might be withholding the cure.

Or maybe there's no sickness at all—that's what some have begun posting online. Isn't Santa Lora the perfect location for a hoax? An isolated town, surrounded by forest, only one road in and one road out. And those people you see on TV? Those could be hired victims. Those could be crisis actors paid to play their parts. And the supposedly sick? Come on, how hard is it to pretend you're asleep?

Maybe, a few begin to say, Santa Lora is not even a real town. Has anyone ever heard of this place? And look it up: there's no such saint as Santa Lora. It's made-up. The whole damn place is probably just a set on some back lot in Culver City. Don't those houses look a little too quaint?

Don't be naïve, say others—they don't need a set. All that footage is probably just streaming out of some editing room in the valley. If you look closely, you can tell that some of those houses repeat.

Now just ask yourself, they say, who stands to benefit from all this. It always comes back to money, right? The medical-industrial complex. And who do you think pays the salaries of these so-called journalists reporting all this fake news? Just watch: in a few months, Big Pharma will be selling the vaccine.

17.

It is hard to tell who is in charge—beyond the campus police who take turns standing near the elevators—but someone somewhere has decided that it is time for Mei and the others to leave the dorm. Rumors zoom: the germ is in the water, they say, or the ventilation system, or there's poison in the carpet or the paint.

In just a few days, Mei has grown numb to the chill of the stethoscope on her chest each morning, and those gloved hands that read the glands of her neck like braille, the spearmint breath of the nurses. Even the skin behind her ears has begun to adjust, chapped by the elastic that holds the mask to her face. And something similar, maybe, is happening to her mind.

A weariness has come over the whole floor, a quiet, as they rush back and forth past the emptied rooms, each one sealed shut with yellow tape.

But now: they are told to pack a bag.

Once outside, Mei stands blinking in the sunlight, as if she's been kept all these days underground. The campus is empty of students. Dried leaves skid across wide lawns, where so recently Frisbees sailed instead, and where, in a different time, these same freshmen lounged in tank tops, bare feet.

She is alert to the smallest sensations, the fall breeze moving the fine hairs on her wrists, the seesaw call of a bird she cannot name, the sun, hot and fresh on her face. A sudden coming-to.

Also there is this: a new profusion of police. Their cruisers are parked on the sidewalks. Their belt buckles flash in the sun.

A row of news vans is waiting, too, satellite dishes pointed to the sky. Soon her parents will see these pictures: Mei, small and thin, on the evening news, walking like a hostage among the other masked kids.

They walk as instructed, single file, a few feet apart, a chain of kids slowly snaking across an abandoned campus.

From somewhere behind her there comes a sudden thud, the sound of a duffel bag landing on the pavement. The crunch of quick footsteps. A sprint.

She has an idea who it is before looking: Matthew. There he is, sprinting away from the line. The sound of his footsteps is immediately drowned out by the shouting of two dozen police officers, now running, too. The other kids stop to watch as Matthew's faded baseball cap flies off his head. There's a kind of glory in it, or desperation—who can say?—in that boy's legs pumping so quickly in the sunshine, the way he tears off his mask and how it floats to the ground behind him, as slowly as a petal.

A burst of envy comes into Mei as Matthew shrinks away in the distance. This is the kind of thing she would never do.

Matthew is young, and he is fast, and the rooflines of town are visible, just beyond the chapel and the library. He keeps running. What does it matter whether he has a destination in mind or not? A sense of possibility—that's what they've been missing, and so they cheer for him, Mei and the others, as he runs.

But the police finally cut him off, surprising him from behind the dining hall. A synchronized gasp floats up from the throat of every kid in the line as they watch the police tackle Matthew to the pavement.

When they return him to the line, there is a long red scrape on his cheek. And in that scrape, and in the bits of asphalt that linger in the cut, something only suspected has been proven true: these kids have no say at all.

One of the boys behind Mei is talking.

"So?" he says. "Why don't you?"

She realizes then that he is talking to her.

"What did you say?" she says.

"Why don't you ever leave your room?" he says through his mask.

"I do leave my room," she says. Her pulse is beginning to pound.

He looks at her, skeptical, as if she has told some kind of lie. At the edges of his mask there grow the beginnings of a mustache—some of the boys have stopped shaving.

"No offense," he says, "but I forgot you even lived with us."

She has heard somewhere of the bonds people sometimes form in times of crisis, but somehow she has gone the opposite way. A friendly face flashes in her mind: Jennifer from her English class—if only Jennifer were here with her now. She doesn't know her that well, but they've had lunch a few times after class. The thought embarrasses her: this Jennifer is maybe her only friend at college.

She shifts her duffel bag from one shoulder to the other. It is something for her hands to do.

It's a short walk to where they are going, and when they get there, a disappointment.

"The gym?" say the girls. "We have to live in the gym now?"

It's only temporary, say the nurses, who seem newly jittery, in their latex gloves and green scrubs. The ventilation system in the dorm, it was decided, might have been contaminated.

The doors to the gym have been propped open so that no hand need touch the metal of the handle. Bacteria, they've been told, can live for up to five days on a surface. A virus, even longer.

"Maybe they're not telling us the truth," Matthew shouts as the police release him into the gym. "Maybe all the others from our floor are dead."

"You're not helping," say the girls.

But Mei has wondered that same thing. It is hard to know what is happening. It is hard to know what is true.

Inside, green cots have been arranged on the basketball court in a configuration familiar from news coverage of hurricanes. The cots stretch from one basketball net to the other. A blue blanket, rolled tight, waits on each one.

"Are you okay?" Mei asks Matthew as he passes.

But he says nothing. He keeps walking.

As the others claim cots with their bags, voices echoing in that vast space, shoes squeaking on the polished floor, Mei climbs the bleachers until she reaches the top bench. From that high perch, she calls her mother.

"I've been calling you all morning," says her mother. "I'm so scared I can't eat."

Mei is resting her feet on her duffel bag, the purple nylon thinning from years of tennis lessons. She speaks softly into the phone.

"I've been thinking," says Mei.

She pauses. It is a hard thing to say. It was a big deal to come here, the scholarship and all, this expensive school. From where she sits, ten rows above the floor, the movements of the other kids look as mysterious as the scurrying of mice.

"Well," Mei starts again. "When all this is over, I've been thinking about moving back home."

Just the idea is a relief, like crawling back into her own bed.

But her mother is quiet. It's a way she has of showing disapproval, a silence for when she doesn't like what she is hearing.

"Maybe," says Mei, "I could reapply to CalArts."

Far below, there is a squeal of laughter from one of the girls. Things like that are still possible, bursts of laughter.

"Mom?" she says now. More silence.

She looks down at her phone: it's dead.

And now someone is yelling. "Hey, you," calls a voice from below. It's one of the campus guards. "You, up in the bleachers." The faces of the others all turn in Mei's direction. "Get down from there," he calls. "Everyone needs to stay down here on the floor."

All the electrical outlets in the gym, she soon discovers, are already choked with other people's phones.

It is hard to say whose idea it is. It seems somehow to rise spontaneously from the group, buoyed in part by the vodka that one of the boys has snuck in from the dorm. A certain excitement attaches itself to the idea right away, a bubbling up of three words: Truth or Dare.

Mei overhears all of this from her cot, where she lies curled with her sketchbook. She is good at it, this listening without seeming to listen. The soft slide of her pencil on paper. She is drawing a series of birds.

A shadow falls across her page. The baseball player, Ryan or Rob—she can't remember his name—is standing over her. She can see the dark outline of his mouth through his mask.

"You have to play, too," he says.

A mechanical breeze floats through the gym, some by-product of the ventilation system, rustling the banners that hang from the ceiling and spreading the smell of the pizza that has arrived from the dining hall for dinner.

"No thanks," she says.

"You're going to hear all our secrets," he says. "So we should get to hear yours."

From behind him comes the scrape of metal against wood—already the others are dragging their cots to the sides of the room so that they can sit in one wide circle at midcourt. She feels it immediately: the impossibility of saying no.

But someone else seems immune to it: Matthew. There he is, reading some kind of philosophy book in the corner. "You're not seriously reading for class?" says the baseball player. Matthew says nothing. He now wears a butterfly bandage to the right of his mask.

One of the girls goes first.

"Truth or dare," says the baseball player.

"Truth," she says.

That first question from that boy's mouth comes as slowly as a smoke ring, the enjoyment spreading across his face in advance of the words: "Have you ever kissed a girl?"

The group likes this question. Mei can feel it all around her, the way the boys shift in their places and the girls laugh softly behind their masks, the expectation. Touch of all kinds has turned hazardous. There is a kind of electricity in that room, a wanting.

"No," the girl says, finally, smiling through her mask. "I've never kissed a girl."

Next up is Caleb. He chooses dare.

"I dare you to moon us," says the first girl.

There is the immediate jingling of his belt buckle as it comes undone, and then the flash of pale skin as he pulls his jeans down and then up again in one swift motion, as if this were a trick he has performed many times before. What variety there is in what human beings will do if asked.

One by one, the secrets tumble out: who is a virgin and who

is not, who has done what with whom. One of the girls, beloved by some for the size of her chest, is dared to take off her shirt, which she does, standing for a moment in the center of the circle, shivering in a white lace bra, arms crossed tight against her stomach.

A certain boy is dared to kiss a certain girl. "Without your masks," calls the baseball player, which releases a round of protest from the group, a crossing into real risk.

"You guys, this is not right," say a few of the girls. "It's not safe."

But they want to do it, this boy and this girl. Mei can tell from the way the girl slips a fresh stick of gum onto her tongue, and how the boy drops his mask on the floor while she folds hers quickly into squares and stuffs it into her jeans.

Even the brushing of one hand against another might be enough to spread this thing between them, just the breathing of the same recycled air. And yet, here they are, lips against lips, as if the danger is increasing the delight, like the pleasure of a diver as his feet leave the cliff. The kiss goes on and on, and it seems it is adding to their enjoyment, too, to be watched like this by the others, who cheer with such force that the campus guard comes rushing into the gym from outside, just missing the sudden parting of those lips, and then the clumsy return of the masks to their faces like two teenagers caught undressed in someone's basement.

"Settle down in here," says the guard. "Lights out in half an hour."

Mei sits sweating all this time in her spot on the floor as they move around the circle, coming closer and closer to her. It's a stupid game. They are too old for it, anyway. An idea, crisp and clean, floats into her head: to get up and go back to her cot.

But she stays right where she is.

When she is asked to choose between truth and dare, she sits quietly, holding her knees, picturing the motions of her legs, the straightening out of her knees, the standing up, the walking away from the circle. Instead, she says, finally: "Truth."

"Okay," says the baseball player. "If you had to hook up with someone in this room, who would it be?"

The room bubbles with laughter. Her face turns hot. She has lived side by side with these people for eight weeks, but they remain as they were at the start, a roomful of strangers.

She keeps quiet, head down.

The other kids are all watching now, waiting for her to speak.

Through the masks, it is hard to read faces, but she can detect the amusement simmering in the room. In the distance, Matthew does not look up from his reading.

"Wait," she says. "I change my mind. Dare," she says. "I choose dare."

"Fine," says the baseball player. "Then I dare you to sneak outside."

She is a follower of rules, a fearer of consequences, and yet, how much safer it seems to take this risk and not the other. What relief there is in these words.

She feels a tiny thrill as she walks toward the exit sign, which glows green above her head. Maybe she really will leave here, escape and not come back. The other kids crowd behind her and wait.

She checks behind her—the guard is out front, not watching.

Her hands shake as she reaches out and pulls the metal handle. But something in the door resists. There is a faint rattling of what sounds like a chain.

She pulls harder, a panic rising in her chest.

"It's locked," she says. "We're locked in."

The others don't seem to believe her. The boys push past her to try it themselves, the smell of alcohol and sweat rising up from their bodies.

Matthew, too, comes suddenly charging over from his bed.

"This is fucked up," he says as he rattles the handle, the veins in his wrist visible beneath his skin. The bandage on his cheek has come loose and is dangling from his face, the scrape beginning to scab.

"Isn't this a fire hazard?" says one of the girls.

This is how the game ends, and the mood sours in the gym, and soon—in one more stroke of lost autonomy—they are told to turn off the lights.

Later, Mei falls asleep to the small noises of her neighbors, the ones who kissed, now moving around in one cot.

She wakes sometime later to the sound of screaming in the dark. She does not remember, at first, where she is, her mind rising slowly from the deep. There is a clanging of metal against wood. Many voices.

"Stop!" someone is shouting, the word echoing across a vast space. "Caleb, stop it."

It comes back to her suddenly: the gym.

It is too dark to see, but the sounds soon arrange themselves into a picture—cots sliding on the floor, banging one against another, like boats in a storm.

"Stop," the voices shout in the dark. "Stop."

Finally, someone finds the lights, and the buzz of that fluorescence reveals a cluster of cots lying crooked and overturned, sheets tangled on the floor. Everyone is squinting now, except Caleb, Caleb who is wide-eyed and walking slowly through all of these obstacles as if none of them were there, tripping again and again.

"He's asleep," says his roommate. "He does this sometimes. He sleepwalks."

Caleb's eyes are open—but like the eyes of the blind. He is walking toward the bleachers on the far side of the gym.

"But this is different," says the roommate. Caleb is saying something they cannot understand. "He usually wakes up right away," says the roommate. No one needs to say it, that this must be the sickness. "He's never stayed this way so long."

Caleb Ericksen, eighteen years old, a farmer's son, an English major, and now this new distinction: the first of the sleepwalkers to be reported in Santa Lora, California.

As the paramedics tie his wrists to the stretcher, he kicks and he shouts, and the others wonder what parallel plot might be taking place in his dream.

But they soon make another discovery, even worse: two others among them are still sound asleep in their cots. They have slept through what no normal sleeper could.

And soon they, too, are carried away like the others.

18.

They sleep like children, mouths open, cheeks flushed. Breathing as rhythmic as swells on a sea.

No longer allowed in the rooms, their mothers and fathers watch them through double-paned glass. Isolation—that's what the doctors call it: the separation of the sick from the well. But isn't every sleep a kind of isolation? When else are we so alone?

They do not, these sleepers, lie perpetually still. The slow sweep of an arm across a sheet, the occasional wiggling of toes—these motions excite the parents, as do the rare moments when their children seem to speak in their sleep, the way a dreamer of a terrible dream might speak out in the night, her voice echoey in her throat, as if trapped at the bottom of a well.

Caleb arrives at the hospital still sleeping his wide-eyed sleep. He arches his back against the restraints of the stretcher. A doctor leans over him like an exorcist.

In that somnambulant state, Caleb has been wheeled through a thicket of camera crews, who called out questions to the paramedics as they passed. The flailing of Caleb's arms and that glazed stare on his face will soon travel the world via satellite.

When finally his sleep turns quiet, he is placed in isolation with the others. He lies just a few feet away from Rebecca, whom he has known for only a few weeks but in whose body a small part of him has secretly remained.

In the days since Rebecca arrived at the hospital, the doctors have come no closer to understanding her condition, but in another realm, more ordinary, a complex progress has been made: that cluster of cells has burrowed into the wall of her womb and is hooking itself up to her bloodstream. The nutrients that are right then sliding into her stomach through a tube in her nose are now feeding not one being but two. No bigger than a poppy seed, and yet, so much is already decided—the brown eyes, the freckles, the slightly crooked teeth. Her sense of adventure, maybe, her affinity for language. A girl. It is all of it packed into those cells, like a portrait painted on a grain of rice.

Meanwhile, on the other side of the glass, Rebecca's family hold their Bibles to their chests and watch the soft movement of her eyelids, that delicate flutter. A few feet away, Caleb's foot twitches slightly beneath the sheets. For now, their secret sleeps with them.

That same night, a sudden breaking of glass is heard in the hospital hallway. A dull thud. One of the nurses has collapsed on the floor. The linoleum where she landed is streaked with dark blood. So are her scrubs. It takes some time to locate the source of all that spatter: the vials she was carrying when she fell.

In the end, it's just like the others—the sleep has spread to her.

19.

The lake: now muddy and shrinking in the sun, but once a glittering, uncanny blue. It was Little Pine Lake in the language of the tribe that once used these waters for healing rituals. It was Lake Restoration when it was printed in cursive blue letters on the brochures for the sanitarium, now repurposed as a nursing home. The lake was renamed again, along with the whole fledgling town, by a later developer, who longed for a Spanish-sounding name and who built the whole downtown in mission style to match his invented saint: Santa Lora.

Most of the tourists and the weekenders have always stopped thirty miles before they get to Santa Lora Lake—they swim and they boat in the larger, more famous lake down the road.

But this small lake, along with the mountains around it, dominates the logo of Santa Lora College, inscribed on signs, imprinted on T-shirts, embroidered on jackets and hats.

Nathaniel first looked out on these waters thirty years ago, as a young biology professor, his daughter squirming in the arms of his wife, their marriage already foundering, only one year in. This was supposed to be a temporary job, a stopping place. He would have left years ago if it were not for Henry, the surprise of falling in love in middle age. The unexpected simplicity of focus: him. And this lake is where they liked to walk together, he and Henry, in the three decades that followed.

This lake is where Sara and Libby learned to swim, in the shallow waters marked off by buoys each summer, and patrolled by teenage lifeguards. It is this lake that shimmers in the background of one of the few photographs these girls have ever seen of their mother: her dark hair blowing across her face, a bouquet of daisies in her hand, her wedding dress, cream-colored, knee-length. In the picture, she is clutching a pair of heeled sandals with one finger, while their father stands beside her in a simple gray suit, both of them barefoot and smiling in the sand, as if their whole lives, as they say, are ahead.

There is less of this lake than there used to be. Every year it recedes, revealing more of what it has swallowed over the decades: cans as abundant as seashells, pieces of beach chairs and coolers, a skeletal, half-buried Model T.

But this lake, and the families of ducks that glide across its surface every spring, still charmed Ben and Annie on their very first day in Santa Lora, and Mei, too, and her parents, at the end of their campus tour.

This lake has put out forest fires, its water scooped up, pelican-like, by specially designed helicopters and then dropped on the flames in the hills.

And this lake still provides a quarter of the water that runs through the pipes of Santa Lora. This is the source of the rumors that now begin to spread through town: maybe that water is contaminated.

But the facts are these: on the fourteenth day, a researcher at a government lab in Los Angeles isolates the Santa Lora pathogen in a petri dish. The source of the troubles, it turns out, is not madness or poison or bacteria. Santa Lora is being haunted by a force neither alive nor dead: a virus. One previously unknown to science. And this virus does not swim in the waters of the evaporating lake. Instead, this bug travels like measles and smallpox and flu. This thing—it flies.

Airborne: at the hospital, this news confirms what the staff has suspected for days. Two doctors and four nurses now lie sleeping alongside their patients. The ventilation system has been turned off.

And on this, the fourteenth day, the hospital closes its doors. A quarantine.

Locked inside are twenty-two sleepers, sixty-two other patients, forty-five visiting family members, thirty-eight doctors, nurses, and other staff, and one psychiatrist from Los Angeles: Catherine, trapped with all the others, a hundred miles from where her daughter sleeps.

20.

That same night, a cloud of smoke is spotted wafting from the woods outside of town. It is windy this night. It is dry. Santa Ana winds are pushing west from the desert: fire weather.

As on so many nights before this one, the flashes of fire trucks light up the streets of Santa Lora. Emergency radios crackle with the news of yet one more wildfire burning these ancient drought-dried woods. In a town already worried, the crack of sirens wakes the healthy from their dreams.

But not the baby, who is snoring, by then, in her crib, an hour past when she usually wakes up to eat. And not Ben, either, who has fallen asleep on the rug while watching her breathe through the slats of her crib. And not Annie, who joined him there sometime later, draping a blanket over his body before closing her eyes beside him.

Ben and Annie: in how many places these two have lain side by side. On various twin beds all through college—legs tangled as they breathed each other's breath. On that basement air mattress at her parents' house, where she used to sneak down to join him, after her parents went to bed. In those sleeping bags in Mexico, the summer after college, when they were so young and so serious that they spent their evenings like this: Annie trying again and again to explain to him string theory, Ben reading aloud from Proust. Together, they have slept the sleep of too much whisky and too much wine, the jetlag sleep of their first afternoon in that hostel in Rome, the daytime dozing in hammocks, years later, on her family's back porch in Maine, and the naked napping of so many Sundays in Brooklyn. There was the restless, jealous sleep the year before last, when Annie started working late with her advisor. There was the going-to-bed-mad sleep when she insisted that nothing had happened, but that she needed time to figure things out. There was the lonely insomniac sleep of the two weeks she then spent at her parents' house without calling, Ben alone and sleepless in their studio, and then the hard sleep of grief and relief when she decided she wanted to come back, and asked, could he forgive her? They've slept the brief shoulder sleep of so many car rides and train rides and planes, the beach sleep in Mexico, those sunburns on their honeymoon, the sleep of bad dreams and good dreams, the dreams they've shared and the dreams they haven't, and all the dreams they never remembered and never would, so many of which have traveled through their minds while their two heads have lain not more than a few inches apart.

And now, for the past three weeks, they've been sleeping this new kind of sleep, clipped but deep—such steep efficiency— because who knew when the baby might open her eyes and call out?

But on this night, in spite of the sirens, the baby does not wake. On this night, the baby does not cry.

Instead, all three remain as they are, deep in their separate sleeps, lights off in the baby's room, minds speeding off in distant directions, even Grace's, whose unknowable dreams send her eyelids fluttering and her lips shuddering and one arm quivering lightly in her crib.

One house over, Sara and Libby wake up fast. So do the cats.

"Dad," the girls call out in the dark, while the sirens scream outside.

But they know what to do. They know where to go. This is something that happens a few times a year. Fire season. Soon they'll be waiting out in the truck while their father hoses down the roof. A single ember can travel for a mile on the wind and set a house like theirs on fire.

"We can't leave the kittens," says Libby.

She is trying to gather the kittens up, but they overflow her skinny arms. Two have already squirreled beneath her bed, the hairs on their backs sticking up, their white tails inflated like dusters, tiny eyes flashing in the darkness.

Sara rushes to her father's room at the end of the hall. He sleeps with his window open, no matter the season—his whole room is vibrating with the wail of the sirens and with the staticky voices of the police radio he keeps always by his bed.

"Dad," she says. She is suddenly shy in the doorway.

By the low glow of the streetlight, she can see his silhouette, the way he's lying on his side in that wide old bed, how quiet he is in the dimness.

A gust of dry wind sends the curtains whipping into the room.

"Daddy?" she says.

She switches on the lights: his eyes are closed, his face is slack. With two fingers, she pulls back the sheets. She pokes him on the shoulder, which is bare and a little bony. He has grown so skinny these last few years.

"Wake up," she whispers.

How strange to touch his face, to smell the old sweat on his skin, the staleness of his breath as he snores.

Libby runs in behind her, wiping her hair from her face. "You guys have to help me get all the cats," she says. "They're running everywhere."

"He's not waking up," says Sara.

It is Libby who shouts into his ear—no response. It is Libby who pinches his arm.

"Be careful," says Sara. "Don't hurt him."

But his face registers no pain.

And it is Libby who leans up close to his face, her curls falling across his forehead as she bends to make sure he is breathing.

"It's the sickness, isn't it?" says Libby. Her eyes are already watering.

By now, they should be downstairs with their bags, shoes on. At the earliest sign of a fire in those woods, their father likes to get out of town—it's a dangerous corridor, what with only the one road out. The safest place to be is away, and the safest time to go is before anyone else thinks they should.

They are starting to smell the smoke.

This bedroom is the wrong place to be in a fire. The third floor, the most dangerous place.

"We can't leave him up here alone," says Libby.

The sirens cry on. Sara looks out the window. It's too dark to see where the smoke is coming from or how near or far its source.

A terrible calmness is descending on her. A series of decisions needs to be made. He would want them to leave and get somewhere safe—she is sure. Downstairs, at least, ready to run if they need to. But she will not do it.

"We're not going to leave him," she says. "We're gonna stay right here, no matter what."

Outside, the eucalyptus trees are bending hard in the wind, their branches scratching against the roof as if for ballast.

"Think of how many wildfires there have been since this house was built," says Sara, leaning close to her sister. "Think of how long it's been here and stayed standing."

And so they sit that way in their nightgowns, holding their father's slack hands, waiting for whatever will come.

Three streets over, the sirens wake Nathaniel from a troubling dream.

In the dream, he and Henry are thirty years younger—they have only recently met, two young professors. Nathaniel's daughter is a two-year-old girl, stacking blocks on the rug in that tiny apartment that Nathaniel rented after the divorce. In the dream, Henry is looking for something. He is searching the apartment. Frantic. Nathaniel understands without it being said what Henry is searching for: some kind of poison. And what Henry wants to do with the poison is drink it. What Nathaniel cannot understand is why. Henry is begging for Nathaniel's help, begging. He can't live like this, Henry keeps saying, but Nathaniel cannot follow the thinking: live like what? He cannot, in the dream, understand the source of Henry's suffering. Eventually, he follows Henry through a doorway that leads, somehow, to the living room of Nathaniel's grandmother's house in Michigan, and Nathaniel has a sudden certainty that the poison is hidden inside the grandfather clock that ticks in the corner. But he will not tell Henry where it is. Why not? Henry keeps asking. His face is young but his eyes are pained like an old man's. Why won't you do this for me?

When Nathaniel wakes, his whole body is tense. He is sweaty in his sheets.

Had he dreamed this dream in a different time, he might have considered it prophecy. Or perhaps, at certain moments in history, he would have taken it as a message from God.

If he had dreamed it fifty or a hundred years ago, the era of Freud, the leading experts might have argued that the dream is not about Henry at all, not really, but about Nathaniel's own childhood, some repressed sexual desire from infancy, the dream's true meaning concealed from his conscious mind, and in need of analysis.

And yet, those who favored Jung in that same era might have read it differently still, insisting that a dream cannot be so simply reduced. Not everything is about desire. And as Henry liked to say to his literature students, the poem is the poem—you can't translate it. They might point out, too, the presence in the dream of certain archetypes from the collective unconscious: the father figure, the child, the clock.

But these are ideas from a different time.

These days, science doesn't take much interest in dreams.

For Nathaniel, professor of biology, this dream of Henry is merely an upsetting distraction. It will remain unexamined. He rushes to think of something else.

On this night, the night of the fire, it is easy to find a different focus. It is almost a relief: the smell of smoke in the air, the scream of the sirens, the fact that there is work to be done.

He is soon standing out in the yard, spraying his roof with the hose.

At the hospital, the smell of smoke goes undetected. Twelve hours into the quarantine, a more pressing danger is floating through these fluorescent halls. A fifth nurse goes under. And an old man, admitted for pneumonia, now sleeps with the others in the isolation wing.

There are not enough beds for the families trapped in the hospital, so they sleep on the floor in the halls. At this late hour, no one can tell by looking who among them might be sick and who well.

Certain small problems are already threatening to grow larger: two toilets have stopped flushing, and the usual shipment of cafeteria food has not arrived—the truck driver too spooked by the news to approach the building.

Inside, Catherine keeps her mask tight, her hands in double gloves, her psychiatric training leaving her only slightly more prepared than the others. One thought keeps beating in her mind: if this sickness takes her away, her daughter will not remember even one wisp of her days with her mother. It seems suddenly selfish to have brought her into this world alone.

She tries to write a note to her, in case—to read when she's older. But she is unable to put down on that page anything more than the biggest, most obvious thing: *You were loved.*

In the gym, no one is sleeping. Twenty-six kids are awake in the dark, four fewer than the day before. A belief has spread among some of them that sleep itself is the poison, the cause and not the effect. How can you catch it if you never close your eyes? Mei is lying in her cot, shaking beneath her blanket. They are stiff, those blankets, as rough as old coats. She is holding her phone to her chest like a cross. Someone is whispering in one corner. Someone is crunching candy in the dark.

Into this wide space, the sirens rise quietly, muffled by the windowless walls. But the faint scent of smoke soon slips into the gym.

"Do you smell that?" says the voice of one of the boys on the other side of the room. Mei can see his silhouette against the green glow of the exit sign. He is pressing his hands to the door, feeling for heat.

There is a rising of voices as the word travels through the room: *fire.* The smack of bare feet hitting the polished wood floor.

"We need to get out of here," someone is saying.

The voice of the guard out front calls into the room: "Everyone stay calm," he says, as always, from a great distance. Those guards are afraid to breathe the same air as the kids. "The fire is way up in the woods, but we're keeping an eye on it."

A tide of protest goes up in the gym. They can hear the wind growing outside. There's a need to see what is happening out there, how near or far that fire might be.

Some of the kids begin to crowd near the front door. The guard backs away. "You need to obey the perimeter," he says.

But the smell of the smoke is getting stronger.

"What do they care if we burn alive?" says Matthew, as Mei slips her shoes on, her backpack.

Matthew tries it first. He walks quickly toward the guard.

"Stop," says the guard, but it is suddenly obvious to everyone watching: that guard is afraid to touch him. Matthew keeps going—he walks right out the front door.

And then the crowd realizes it, too. Never before has Mei felt so connected to these other kids, to the force of them all walking out the door, quick and firm, on only the strength of their minds, as if crossing hot coals. There is a terror and a thrill, that sudden sense of purpose. She can hear the guard calling for help on his radio.

When the wind hits their faces, some tear off their masks right away, let them float off behind them like freed birds. Who knows how many of these kids carry the sickness already, the thing multiplying in their bloodstreams, even now, awaiting its moment to bloom?

But for now, on this night, they feel fine—fine!—and what they do is they run. All of them. Even Mei, her backpack pounding against her spine, and the air, slightly smoky, rushing into her throat. The wind is so violent it swallows her breath—a Santa Ana.

If the guard is calling after them, not one of them can hear his voice, too loud is the weather in their ears.

Matthew will know what to do next—this is the idea that

propels her toward him in the dark. She stops where he stops, which is in the shadows of the back entrance to the library, a boy, tall and skinny, a stranger, really, leaning against a wall.

"Where can we go?" she says. Her breaths are coming fast from the sprint.

The fire is more distant than she had imagined: a slight glow, tended by helicopters, way up high in the woods. It seems suddenly clear that the fire is not what is making them run.

"I don't know," says Matthew. He keeps looking around. His face is half hidden in the shadows cast by the streetlights. "I don't know."

The other kids are streaming past, footsteps crunching quickly in the dark.

"This was stupid," says Matthew. He is rubbing his hands together. "They'll send a SWAT team here any second."

But a surprising idea is forming in Mei's head. The start of a whisper is coming up from her throat: "I think I know a place," she says.

"What?" he calls in the wind.

Louder this time: "I know where we can go."

She will never know the meaning of that flash of surprise on his face—the same way the boys sometimes looked at her as a child, when she revealed how fast she could run across a soccer field.

He asks no questions.

The two of them just go.

What a rush it is to provide this boy with the exact thing that is needed.

The lawn, when they get there, is wet beneath their shoes; this grass always so much healthier than the grass in other yards, no matter the drought. A row of white roses is blowing in the wind, the petals a confetti on the grass.

"I babysit here," says Mei. The Mercedes is gone from the driveway, but the porch light is on. "They're out of town."

It is surprising how easy this is: as easy as turning that key, as quick as one finger punching the code for the alarm system.

Inside, the air smells like clean laundry—and like safety, too, as if no trouble can come to a home so well kept. The feeling is in the marble countertops of that enormous white kitchen, the abundance of copper pots. It's in the miniature succulents arranged in mason jars, one in each windowsill. It's the way the wood floors shine beneath the overhead lights, which run on a timer to make it look like the house is occupied, which, for now, it is.

"We have to take off our shoes," says Mei.

Matthew looks skeptical, but he kicks off his sandals, one held together by tape—none of the other boys wear sandals like his. She tries not to notice how dirty his feet are as they sink into the creamy white rug in the living room.

"Where are they, anyway?" he says, while she sets his sandals on a rack in the closet, as if to say in tableau: At least we kept our shoes in the proper place. "Maybe they knew something we didn't."

"They're just on a cruise," says Mei.

Matthew laughs a private laugh. His mask now gone from his face, it's the first time that she has really noticed his mouth, the thin lips, the beginnings of a mustache, his teeth packed tight as tile, the overcorrection of braces.

"Do you ever wonder why they need such a huge house?" he says. "I mean, what do they do with all these things?"

He lifts a small sculpture of a bird from its spot on the piano. He flies it around like a kid.

"Be careful," she says.

Maybe they shouldn't have come here.

Over the fireplace hangs a gleaming honey-colored guitar, someone's signature laced across the belly. It's not for touching—this is what she's been telling the little girl who lives here, two years old, just beginning to understand what you can and cannot do. No touching, repeats the girl whenever she passes that guitar, no touching. But here is Matthew, reaching up for a strum.

"Oh," says Mei. "Um, can you leave that alone?"

It's the wrong thing to say. How embarrassing, this concern for material objects, but also: the way her voice goes up at the end, like a question, like maybe he shouldn't be touching it?

"Relax," he says. "Aren't they in the middle of the ocean?"

His whole body is moving. His fingers are snapping. His feet are tapping. There is a feeling of adventure in the way he pauses to play drums on the coffee table like it's a dashboard, the way he climbs onto the little girl's rocking horse, the absurd bend of his long legs at the sides. And it's a little contagious—it is—his wildness.

"I just want to close the curtains," says Mei. "So the neighbors won't see us."

There are a lot of windows.

Afterward, she finds Matthew in the kitchen—with a bottle of wine in one hand, a corkscrew in the other.

"You really can't do that," she says.

But a moment later comes the soft pop of cork leaving bottle. A tenseness spreads through her—who knows what else this boy will do?

"It isn't right that they have so much when some people have so little," says Matthew. "We could pour all this down the drain as a protest."

Instead, he pours the wine into two coffee mugs and slides one across the counter toward Mei.

"No thanks," she says.

He laughs. It was a mistake, she knows now, to bring him here.

"Come on," he says.

He is just standing there, staring, so she takes a tiny sip. The taste is a surprise: fresh and cool in her mouth, not at all like the heavy red wine she has tried once or twice at Katrina's, never enough to feel more than a slight warmth on her tongue—it seemed so important, back then, not to mess with her mind. But it sounds juvenile now, like bullshit—that would be Matthew's word.

"We have to remember to take the bottle with us when we leave," she says. "So they don't know we drank it."

"That's the least of our worries," he says.

She takes a few more sips. Maybe she doesn't want to be this girl anymore, this girl who follows the rules.

Now and then, the call of sirens in the distance. The chop of helicopters.

Matthew turns on the television. They sink into the couch, the cool of real leather beneath her palms.

"Look," says Matthew. "We're on TV."

On the screen is the campus, as seen from a helicopter, ringed with the flashing of police cars. Unconfirmed reports, says the reporter, suggest that as many as twenty students have left quarantine.

From this couch, the situation seems less and less urgent. It seems a little funny, actually. Matthew keeps refilling her mug.

He is saying something about American history. He is saying something about the fucked-up ethics of quarantine, civil liberties.

At a certain point, she has the urge to close her eyes. A few seconds later comes the sound of strumming. The autographed guitar from the mantel is now stretched across Matthew's lap.

"I think that's just for decoration," Mei says, but she is melting into the couch.

The bottle of wine stands nearly empty on the coffee table.

"This thing is totally out of tune," says Matthew.

Somewhere in that room is the idea that he should not be playing that guitar, but it is a concept and not a feeling, like something theoretical and not at all connected to her.

She's getting tired, too, so tired—maybe she's never felt so sleepy in her life. A flicker of fear makes her wince: What if this is it, the sickness finally taking over her body? But this concern quickly floats away. Something is dulling every possibility but this one: the cool calm of the leather couch beneath her palms, the softness of the cushion beneath her head.

"Hey, wait," Matthew says. "Maybe you should drink some water before you go to sleep."

But it's too late. She falls asleep right there, sitting up on the couch beside Matthew. It's a dark, oceanic sleep: deep and still, and empty of dreams.

21.

The girls: from the gym, some sprint to the parking lot, barefoot or in flip-flops, hair flying in the wind. They pack into their cars, in threes and fours, zooming toward the main road. One car is stopped by the police right away. One is found parked outside a boyfriend's house, the girls eating pizza inside. But one car makes it through, flies right out of town, undetected. Inside that car buzzes a familiar exhilaration, a free-floating fun bubbling beneath everything. It's in the sound of their voices, singing loud to the radio, the flashes of forest in the headlights as the road turns and turns at high speed. What a story they'll be telling someday. The high of the near miss. They zip past cabins and campsites until there is nothing but woods in all directions. They swerve to miss a deer, headlights gleaming in its eyes. How they feel is invincible. And also, suddenly: in love—with each other, with themselves, with life! Everything is a part of it. The stars. The woods. The smell of smoke in the air. The proximity of danger—or the idea of it, anyway—is only heightening the plea-sure of being eighteen years old in a fast car on a dark road on this particular night.

They make it twenty miles to the next town over, a tiny roadside place, population 250. They stop at a gas station, buy gum. One girl uses a fake ID to buy a six-pack of vodka lemonade. Money slides from her bare hands to the bare hands of the clerk. One of the other girls whispers something flirtatious into a stranger's ear, her breath mixing with his. Their palms glide across the counter. Their hands touch the handles of the coolers as they pull out the ice cream and the wine. They finger the key chains that hang near the register.

They cannot at this moment conceive of it—the danger they present. It is impossible (impossible!) on this night and in this mood to imagine that just one day later, they will all succumb to the sleep in a room in the retro motel they will soon find down the road, or that, a few days after that, the clerk will be found slumped on this same counter late in the graveyard shift. The sleep will come for that stranger, too, who, after a few days backpacking alone, will fall asleep in his sleeping bag, deep in a remote part of these woods, and will lie there, undiscovered, for two years.

22.

You never know at the start how much damage a wildfire will do, but the following sunrise reveals only a few acres of dead trees, black and stark against the sky, the branches stripped of needles, as if winter has finally come for the evergreens.

Much later, officials will trace the spread of the sickness to this night, to the tainted exhalations of those twenty-six students as they poured down the hill through the woods into town.

But here the timeline grows murky, the chain of transmission unclear. Always, there are gaps in these narratives. A limit to what can be known. In some kinds of cracks, speculation is the one thing that takes root.

In the first minutes of morning, on the day after the fire, Sara is stretched out on a wooden floor, her head turning slightly in her sleep.

One of the kittens is licking up something from the floor. That's what she wakes to, the white of those paws at eye level, the ticking of eager claws. Otherwise, the house is quiet. Sunlight.

Their father, in his bed, seems the same as before, still deep and silent in sleep.

"Dad," she whispers. No answer.

The panic from the night before comes back in a different form: congealed. Her father has the sickness—he must.

Sara feels a swell of something else, too: that she has seen all this coming in advance, has been expecting it for years, not this disaster exactly, but some inevitable loss, some sudden coming apart, as if all those nights she lay awake worrying were all of them rehearsal for this.

Their father looks calm in his bed, and young, or younger than usual, anyway, his forehead as smooth as a sheet. How rare it is to catch that body at rest, those eyes closed.

His eyelids, Sara notices, are fluttering.

She wonders what it is he dreams of in that head. Of catastrophe, or its absence? Of a different life, or their own?

When they pull the covers back from his body, the smell of urine wafts up from his sheets.

"I think we should call someone," says Sara. "Maybe 911."

"No," says Libby. "He wouldn't want that."

And it's true. They know what he would say: the police are a bunch of liars, the doctors are just in it for the money, the whole system is rigged against them.

"And they'll take us away," says Libby. "We'll be foster kids and never get to see each other."

These visions have been deposited into their heads by their father. How many times has he warned them what would happen if social services took them away?

There is no grandmother to call. No aunt. There is no friend of the family who would know what to do. Always it has been just the three of them in this house, and in life. And now, in a way, it's just the two.

In the end, it comes back to water. His body needs water, doesn't it? They have no way of getting it into him.

Sara is the one who finally calls for help. She is the one who tells the lies that need telling. She is calling from Minnesota, she says, from her grandmother's house, she tells the dispatcher. Her dad, back home, he might be sick, she says into the phone, with that thing, she says, that sleeping sickness. Could someone go check on him?

Later, the girls watch their house from the woods, the little hill at the edge of the street, knees pressed tight to their chests, as if they are only the neighbors sitting there in that dry dirt, picking at pinecones while they wait, just someone else's girls. Sara sees now how their house must look to the neighbors, those windows boarded up, those rain gutters rusting away.

"So what," says Libby. She is squinting in the late afternoon sun. "I don't care what they think."

A breeze comes up from the lake. It is colder out there than they thought, after so many days inside.

In the air: the scent of pine sap, the buzz of insects, the cries of the baby who lives next door. The mother is out front with her, pacing the porch. She has put her face up close to the baby's cheek. Her mouth is moving, like singing.

"That's the smallest baby I've ever seen," says Libby.

The baby's face is red. Her eyes are squinty. She is bundled in a white knit blanket.

Before leaving the house, the girls corralled the cats down into the basement and locked it. They left the front door open for the rescuers. Their plan stretches only a few hours into the future. They will hide outside for a while. Tomorrow is a darkness. The next day unknown.

When a siren finally calls out in the distance, Sara squeezes her sister's hand—help has come for their father. But when the double doors of the ambulance swing open, it looks like something else.

Libby gasps: four figures are descending from the van in full-body blue suits. Like astronauts, thinks Sara. Men or women—the girls can't say which, not with those goggles and those masks, the hoods that cover their heads. They wear green rubber gloves that stretch over their hands and all the way up past their elbows. Even their shoes are encased in plastic. And aprons—each one wears a clear plastic apron over his or her suit, as if these people are butchers, here to cut up some meat.

"What are they going to do to him?" Libby asks.

"They'll help him," says Sara, but she isn't so sure. Their father's fears suddenly flower in her own mind. A surge of guilt tightens her stomach.

"I told you," says Libby. "You shouldn't have called."

But it is too late. Already, these strangers in suits are crossing through the front door, soon to reappear as flashes of blue in the upstairs windows, their suits just visible above the boards on the glass.

The baby is crying again next door, but the mother has stopped rocking her. Instead, she is standing perfectly still, staring at what is happening at the girls' house. She is holding one hand over her mouth, like someone receiving bad news. Or a shock. She has let the baby's blanket fall loose, little pink feet sticking out in the air.

When the girls' front door swings open again, there he is—their father—spread out on a stretcher, which swings like a coffin in the arms of the workers.

He looks so exposed on that stretcher, his bare chest and his boxers. She doesn't like the way his head bobs as they carry the stretcher down to the sidewalk.

Not everything that happens in a life can be digested. Some events stay forever whole. Some images never leave the mind.

"He wouldn't want this," says Libby. She throws a pinecone into the woods. Her boyish little arms. "He would hate this."

"What else could we have done?" says Sara. But a tenseness is moving through her body, regret traveling the length of it, one muscle at a time.

The soles of their father's feet are dirty as usual and callused, and now disappearing into the white of the ambulance. One of the workers is spraying the other workers down with some kind of mist.

The woman next door has disappeared with the baby.

Before the van leaves, one of the suits returns to the porch with a can of something in his hand. The girls can hear the metallic rattle as he shakes the can in the air, and then the long shush-shush of spray paint gushing through a nozzle.

"Hey," Libby whispers. "What are they doing to our house?"

A giant black X is now dripping down the splintered wood of the front door. They hear the rattling again, more spraying, as the worker draws a second X, this time on the side of the house.

It takes the girls a long time to know that they are hungry. Once the sun sets over the hill, and the crickets begin to call to one another and the street is almost dark, the girls creep back into their house, quiet as criminals, and afraid to turn on the lights. They are eleven and twelve years old. They are all alone in a big house.

23.

Ben is waiting in the drive-through line, the car full of diapers and groceries, when he thinks to check his phone. Maybe he senses, somehow, the trouble he will find there: two missed calls from Annie, a message. "It's me," she says in the recording. "Come home right now."

He calls her from the parking lot. No answer.

He drives home fast, baby toys rolling around in the backseat. A sensation of floating.

The night before this day, he dreamed that he was floating in the ocean with the baby. No raft. No land. He was holding her with one arm, paddling with the other. Her head kept slumping forward into the water. That's what the dream was about: the keeping of her nose above the swells. But she soon fell away, and the rest of the dream was just the thrashing of his arms in search of her in that dark, cold water. It went on for hours, this thrashing, but what do we know about the physics of dreams? Perhaps, in the room where he was sleeping on the floor beside her crib, only a few seconds ticked by on the baby's whale-shaped clock.

He speeds through town, hugging the lake.

At a stoplight, he calls Annie again. Nothing.

When he finally reaches his driveway, he leaves the groceries in the trunk, the car unlocked. He rushes up the stairs.

He hears his wife's voice before he sees her: urgent and curt. He doesn't notice the markings on the house next door.

"Finally," she says from upstairs. "I've been calling and calling."

"Where is she?" he says. But the baby is right there as usual, lying on her side in her crib: blue eyes open, alive. He holds her warm head to his face. "Is she okay?" he says. She is still so small that her hands keep disappearing inside her sleeves.

It scares him, sometimes, to remember that he did not want to have a child, as if time can sometimes run backward toward a reckoning, in which whatever *is* will be revoked and replaced with whatever might otherwise have been.

"The neighbors have it," says Annie. "They have the sickness."

A tenseness comes into his stomach.

"What do you mean?" he says. But he knows what she means.

"They brought the father out on a stretcher, just now," she says. "Unconscious."

Could it waft through the air through one open window and into another? Or could it float up from the throat of a girl who so recently stood on their porch, only a few feet away from the baby?

"And the men who came were wearing those suits," says Annie. "You know, all plastic, no skin showing. The kind they wear for Ebola."

"Jesus," he says.

On any other day, he might have worried more for the daughters of that man, but today he can think only of his own, who right then is squirming against his chest, her immune system not yet fully formed. What an adult's body would quickly discard might flower in the body of a newborn. He rocks her in his arms, as if she is the one who needs comfort.

"Let's leave," says Annie. "Let's just get in the car and go."

Maybe she won't get it from the milk, she keeps saying, but if they stay in this town, she is sure to catch it some other way.

She is stacking Grace's clothes in a little pile on the bed, packing.

"But they said we're not supposed to leave town," he says.

Annie sighs, hard and deliberate, as if she's been arguing with him all day.

"I knew you would say that," she says.

There is something mean in her voice, something new.

"Stay if you want to," she says. "But I'm taking her away from here."

Only Annie can say a thing like that, as if she and the baby are still housed together inside one body.

She is pulling a suitcase down from the top of the closet.

"Let me do that," he says. She isn't supposed to be lifting anything yet. "If we're going to go," says Ben, "we better do it soon." There is only an hour before the nurse will be back to take the baby's temperature.

But it takes a long time to gather up what they need. By the time the bassinet and the diapers, the clean bottles and the formula, the swaddle blankets and the pacifiers and the pump—by the time they are all lodged together in the trunk of the car, it's time to feed her again, which means the doorbell is ringing just as Grace is finishing a bottle of formula, her eyes going droopy with the last of it, then to sleep in Annie's arms.

Ben feels his face radiating with the secret of their leaving.

"Just be normal," whispers Annie as the doorbell rings again.

The lie is in the way Ben makes sure to take off his shoes before opening the door so that he answers it barefoot, like a man who is in for the night.

On the doorstep stands the same nurse as before, but she's wearing more gear: full green scrubs and a paper mask, blue gloves that stretch to her elbows.

"The procedures keep changing," she says through the muffle of the mask. With the back of her wrist, she nudges a strand of hair from her eyes. "Ready?" she says.

When she sees their daughter, still dozing in Annie's arms, a little gasp comes up from her throat.

"How long has she been sleeping?" she says.

"She always does this after she eats," says Annie.

The nurse writes something on her clipboard.

Annie starts to get up from the couch.

"Just stay there," says the nurse. She holds her hand out in the air, firm, like a push. "I can take her temperature from here."

None of them speak while she holds the thermometer out toward Grace's forehead. The only sound is the wind blowing through the trees, and, much closer, in parallel: the air moving in and out of their daughter's lungs.

Finally, the wand beeps. "No fever yet," says the nurse.

Ben doesn't like the way she says it, that one word, *yet,* as if she can see the future in that thermometer.

"And still no other symptoms?" says the nurse.

Already she's moving toward the door, her scrubs swishing as she moves. Even with the gloves, she uses as few fingers as possible to touch the doorknob, as if grasping it with pincers.

"I'll be back tomorrow at nine," she says.

"Of course," they say, and they nod. "See you then."

But by tomorrow, they'll be a hundred miles away, in San Diego with Annie's sister.

Annie rides beside the baby, in the backseat—that's the way they've been doing it since the start. More than anything else, these two agree on this one thing: for their daughter to ever feel alone in the world seems the worst possible thing.

"I think she'd be sick by now if she were going to get it from the milk," says Annie. It sounds true as she says it, as certain as science. You can't always distinguish between reason and hope.

She is looking for Ben's eyes in the rearview. She is holding their baby's hand. His little family.

"Don't you think?" she says.

By the time they pass the college, Grace is asleep again. They see now, for the first time, the news vans that have been lined up on College Avenue for a week, their broad sides turning pink in the sunset while grim news flies invisibly up from their spires, some of it pouring out through the speakers in Ben and Annie's car: thirty-nine cases, a local reporter is saying, which is almost twice the total of the day before, and still no word on what is causing it.

Ben turns off the radio.

They leave town the only way you can, on the road that twists up over the mountains and then down again to the valley on the other side. The houses are fewer and fewer as the road rises. And for a few minutes, in the shade of those old woods, they feel free of this thing.

"We'll be in San Diego by eight," says Ben, as if the danger comes from the land itself, and all they need is a geographic cure.

But a turn in the road reveals a long line of brake lights. A trail of cars is waiting in the dusky light.

"I don't see an accident," says Ben. His hands begin to sweat on the steering wheel.

"Let's not get paranoid," says Annie.

The possibility floats between them for a moment, a quiet whiff of hope: that this is an ordinary calamity, one that can be cleared away with tow trucks while the drivers trade insurance information.

Yes, they agree, an accident.

But they've never seen so much traffic on this road.

Ten minutes pass. Twenty. Their wheels roll so rarely that the speedometer detects no movement at all. Some of the other drivers have turned their engines off.

The sun is sinking fast. Grace is snoring her little snores.

In sleep, she always looks lifeless. And he is just as likely as Annie is to drop his head down close to her chest and listen for the workings of her lungs. Don't bug her, they say to one another as she sleeps, don't bug her, don't bug her, but then they do it anyway, one or the other, a compulsion they have shared since her birth.

"I want to wake her up," says Annie. "Just to make sure. Can I wake her up?"

Many cars ahead, two doors swing open. A man and a small boy emerge and begin to walk together along the side of the road. They stop near Ben's car and the man points at the woods, and then the boy is walking into the woods alone. You can tell what is happening, the boy pausing to unzip his pants near a tree, his back turned to the road.

The father, arms crossed, nods at Ben. "He couldn't hold it," he says, a small smile.

There's a camaraderie among parents that Ben didn't recognize before. Strangers with children are not so much like strangers—he doesn't need to know them to know a lot about their lives.

Ben calls to the man: "Can you tell what's going on up there?"

The man comes a few steps closer, the sound of his shoes crunching on the dirt.

"There's a checkpoint up there," he says. "They're searching for those kids. The ones they had in quarantine or whatever at the college. The ones that got out."

They're probably hiding in the woods, says the man, looking around, as if they might be watching. But he doesn't blame them, he says. "We're trying to get out ourselves."

The man notices Grace in the backseat.

"How old?" he says.

"Three weeks," says Ben.

The man shakes his head, as if Ben has said something painful.

"Enjoy it," he says, glancing back at his son. "You won't believe how fast it goes."

Ben nods. A polite smile. But he rolls up his window—it doesn't need to be said, how efficiently an infant proves the relentlessness of time.

When finally they can see the front of the line, it's dark. Real darkness, a deep sea, not like the nights they knew in New York. They can see the constellations in this black sky, but the glow of the stars is not as bright as the klieg lights that shine from the tops of the police cars, or as the flashlights that wave in their hands.

A group of college students is standing around on the side of the road, while a police officer points a flashlight into their trunk.

"Do you think that's them?" says Ben. "Those kids?"

But the backseat has gone quiet. He turns. That's when he sees her: his wife's head is slumped against the window, eyes closed.

"Annie," he says.

Nothing.

"Annie!" he says again. "Wake up."

Then he's out of the car, and he's swinging the back door open. He is shouting her name in the dark. A clarity of focus. He shakes her and shakes her. Her head falls forward against her seatbelt.

The people in the car behind him are watching him now, a man and a woman. Does he need help, they are asking, but he does not hear them, and he does not see them. He sees only Annie, her face slack, her eyes closed—and their baby still sleeping in the car seat beside her.

"Annie!" he shouts again.

Now the baby wakes up and begins to cry—and it is her voice, and not his, that finally wakes his wife.

"What?" she says. "What's wrong?"

Relief comes to him in the form of his heart beating too fast. A difficulty speaking.

"Why are you looking at me like that?" says Annie, but a sudden understanding flashes across her face. "I'm fine," she says. She's yawning. "I'm just exhausted."

It's true that for weeks her sleep has been landing like this— sudden and unannounced, no matter the hour. Sleep when your baby sleeps—that's what all the books advise. But right now, Ben is not thinking of all those times these past weeks when Annie has fallen asleep sitting up in a chair or when he himself has dozed off in his clothes and his shoes and without eating any dinner.

His movements are angry as he goes back to the driver's seat. He has an urge to slam the door—a feeling more than a thought.

"I couldn't do this without you," he says, facing forward. He doesn't need to explain what he means.

In the rearview, he sees Annie holding a bottle up to Grace's mouth.

"Yes, you could," she says, their daughter's lips smacking against the plastic of the bottle. "You'd have to," she says. "So you would."

At the front of the line, a policeman asks for their driver's licenses.

"What about the baby?" he says.

Ben feels his face flush.

"She's only three weeks old," he says.

"I need every passenger's name," says the policeman, and so

Ben gives him her name—first name, middle name, last, which still sounds new in his mouth, and weird, like something invented, which, in a way, it is.

"Wait here," says the policeman.

When he looks down at his clipboard, something changes. He steps away from their car. He puts on a paper mask.

Ben is not prepared for this. The feeling of getting caught. He wants to apologize or explain, like a teenager trying to buy beer. But Annie touches his shoulder from behind. Don't say anything, says her hand.

The next time the policeman speaks, he is talking through a mask: "She's on this list," he says, nodding in the baby's direction.

Annie takes over, leaning out the passenger window.

"What list?" she says. "She's fine. See?"

At that moment, Grace is staring at the warning label on the inside cushion of her car seat: a diagram of an infant's head flying forward in response to the force of an airbag—you are never allowed to forget all the terrible things that can happen to a child if you make some kind of mistake.

"You need to turn around, sir," he says, as if speaking to criminals. He points to the other lane, eastbound. "You need to go home."

They've seen no other car turn around in this way, but here they are, Ben twisting the wheel, hard to the left, backing up and twisting it again. He can feel the other drivers watching him.

"I told you we shouldn't leave," he says, as they ease back down the hill in the dark. "We should have stayed home."

A slice of moon has appeared on the horizon, but it's not enough to light the woods.

"If it had been up to me," says Annie, rigid in her seat, "we wouldn't be here at all."

And there it is: the thing unsaid for all these months.

He does not speak right away, afraid of what he might say.

She had a job offer in New York, but it had seemed so vital to get away from the place where things had gone wrong between them.

Now she is talking to the baby.

"Daddy wanted to punish me," she says.

This is the opening of a jar. Months of restraint give way: it turns out that all the things they haven't said—whether from kindness or fear or something else—are still sitting there, just waiting to jump from their throats.

But haven't they been happy here?

"We were so sick of New York," he says.

"You were," she says.

He is suddenly furious.

"I'm not the one who wanted to use the donor milk," says Ben. "I always thought it was weird using milk from strangers—who knows what they put in their bodies?"

It means something to Annie, breast milk, something profound that he does not understand and that does not include him.

In her silence, he goes further.

"You could have tried harder to feed her," he says, which, even as he says it, seems not true at all, a thing he has never thought before until now. "Maybe if you could just commit to something for once."

Maybe then, he says, we wouldn't be in this situation. But regret is pooling in his mind already. He is afraid to finish the thought, which is a substitute, anyway, for the thing he really means: I am afraid for our baby girl.

"Fuck you," says Annie.

These words are followed by a silence that lasts the rest of the night.

He wishes she would yell, but she does not yell. And it feels as if he cannot speak, either.

Later, Annie goes to sleep in Grace's room. Ben wants to sleep there, too, beside his wife and his baby, but the door is closed. He cannot imagine turning that knob.

This has always been her harshest punishment: to make him sleep alone. He lies awake for a long time before sleep and then wakes quickly, after only a few minutes, to the intense smell of the tea she drinks at night—mint and eucalyptus—the smell of his wife coming to bed. But the scent fades too quickly to be real, an olfactory hallucination, a doctor once called it—he has had them all his life. This is the truth: Annie is not in the room. Here he is, alone in their bed.

Meanwhile, on that same night, in another part of town, the swirling sounds of an organ are streaming out into the street. A row of bridesmaids stands shivering outside a church. Every wedding after this one will be canceled or postponed. But this one goes through, the last vows to be said in this town.

The bride has been feeling woozy all day. It's normal, her mother says. Just nerves. And anyway, she was up so late the night before, finalizing the seating arrangements, after a long day of work—a nurse in a doctor's office. No wonder she feels so tired. She does look a little pale, the bridesmaids agree, but two smears of blush put the color back into her face, and an extra layer of concealer hides the gray beneath her eyes.

But whoever shares her lipstick that day, whoever borrows her eyeliner, whoever kisses her cheek that night or dances too close or clinks her flute of champagne, whoever touches her hand to admire the ring, whoever catches the bouquet at the end of the night—all of them, every one, is exposed.

This is how the sickness travels best: through all the same channels as do fondness and friendship and love.

24.

In the annals of infectious disease, there is a phenomenon known as a super-spreader: a person who, by some accident of biochemistry or fate, infects many more people than the other victims do.

Rebecca, it turns out, still suspended in sleep, holds exactly this kind of sway.

Unlike the other families, Rebecca's relatives remain at her side: her mother sleeps in the bed beside hers, and her father lies unconscious as well. Over there in the corner rest her two teenage brothers, curled like children in their beds. All of them, now, are snaked through with tubes.

If they were awake, this family—keepers of so many memorized verses—they might think of Matthew, Chapter 9, when a father whose daughter has just died comes to Jesus and asks for his help, and how, before healing her body, Jesus says to the mourners around the daughter, "Go away. The girl is not dead but asleep."

Meanwhile, in that same room, there swims one more, too young yet to dream. A sesame seed—that's what the books would say if Rebecca were reading them. Already the cells are organizing themselves into layers. Soon the organs will begin to form. In a week, that speck of a heart will divide into chambers. In two weeks, the contours of the face will begin to emerge. In three, the first sprouts of hands and feet.

Only one thing is needed now: time.

25.

And then everything accelerates, as if the increase in cases has caused a quickening of time.

All of this in one day:

A man in a wrinkled suit slips out of consciousness during the sermon at Santa Lora Lutheran, but a few always doze in those pews, so it is only afterward that anyone realizes what is wrong.

A woman who cleans houses discovers two bodies in the master bedroom of a renovated Victorian on Alameda. "They're dead," she whispers into the phone, but they are soon reclassified, this dean and his wife: joined not yet in death but in sleep.

A florist's van speeds into the lake at midday, no brakes. The driver makes no attempt to escape. Ten dozen roses drift for hours on the water before gradually washing up on the beach.

The stories soon multiply, as stories often do: the jogger found splayed on a sidewalk while his infant wails in a stroller, the park ranger, curled and hypothermic, in the woods on a rarely used trail, and the story, perhaps apocryphal, of the fisherman who falls asleep at the wheel of his boat, way out in the middle of the lake, his dog barking in the moonlight while the boat drifts farther and farther from the shore, never to be seen again.

The sickness wafts through the ventilation systems of the YMCA and the high school. And it spreads through the intensive care unit of the hospital.

Certain connections are being made: how the florist delivered bouquets to the wedding of a nurse, how the dean might have bought an orchid from the florist that week.

The story now begins to blaze across the national broadcasts. Now is when the details surge to the tops of home pages, crackling through millions of news feeds all over the world. The headline is posted and reposted and commented upon: "Mysterious Sickness Continues to Spread Rapidly Through California Town."

The appetite for information exceeds what information there is.

Politicians—from mayors to the president—rush to fill the vacuum with press conferences, while talk show hosts devote whole hours to the subject. There is something like thrill beating hard in their voices. Hear the click-click of a roller coaster inching up an incline. Already, the arguments are starting. How to handle this thing, what to do. Questions are being raised: Why didn't the CDC respond sooner? Are the health workers wearing the right protective gear? And how could the authorities lose track of twenty-six kids being held in quarantine?

26.

O n the afternoon of the seventeenth day, in the lakeside
sunroom of the nursing home, where Nathaniel has spent
so many hours sitting beside Henry, a ninety-year-old woman
dozes off in her wheelchair. The noise of her breathing, wheezy
as usual, but strong and steady, keeps the staff from disturbing
her. Why not let an old woman sleep? The television runs all
afternoon. The bougainvillea scrapes against a hundred-year-old
window. The sun drifts across the lake. She is still asleep at dusk,
her head against her shoulder, as the dinner plates begin to clink
in the cafeteria. She seems to awaken slightly when the nurses
lift her into her bed. She says something about her children. And
this rousing, this brief opening of the eyes, delays the call to a
doctor. Even much later, when she fails to wake in the morning,
it takes a few hours for anyone to realize that it's the sickness.
This is a place where to die in one's sleep is considered the best
way to go.

After that, new procedures are put in place: the nursing home
is closed to visitors.

Nathaniel receives this news that same afternoon, from a security guard, stationed in the parking lot.

"It's only one case," says the guard. He seems to want to console. "But just to be safe."

Nathaniel writes Henry's name on the white paper bag in which an almond croissant is cooling. "Can you make sure he gets this?" he says, and hands the bag to the guard.

As he drives out through the front gates, he feels only the tiniest ping of worry. To him, this thing still seems overblown. Didn't they put the campus on lockdown twice last year, and both times were false alarms? Hysteria—that's the real disease of this era.

His walks in the woods grow longer each day, the dry crunch of boots on pine needles. These trees, too, are going to sleep, in a way—sent there by drought and bark beetle. It's been happening for years, he tells his students, this ravaging, but no one talks about it, this other, slower wasting. These trees live and die on glacial time, their journeys so slow as to be almost imperceptible to humans. While one root creeps across the soil beneath a field, our history unfolds at high speed.

His classes have been canceled for two weeks. There is a lot of day to fill.

But on this afternoon, an idea comes to Nathaniel with a gust of relief: there is a pipe under the bathroom sink that needs fixing. Here is something that needs doing.

At the hardware store, the man behind the counter wears a white hospital mask, blue latex gloves.

"We're out of masks," he calls to Nathaniel as soon as he steps inside. "No more gloves, either."

He can feel it everywhere in town, this buzz of panic and gloom. They almost want it, don't they, the drama and the thrill?

"I'm just looking for a stop valve," he says. It's the tiniest part, seven dollars apiece, but without it, one leak in one sink could drown a whole house in water.

The man behind the counter is surprised, and disappointed, maybe, that anyone, at a time like this, would be working on a problem so ordinary.

It was Henry's house, this house, before it was theirs, the kind of place Nathaniel never would have picked out for himself, all these small rooms, one leading to another, and each one packed tight with furniture: wingback chairs and grandfather clocks, mahogany bureaus filled with tablecloths. Persian rugs. Victorian wallpaper. Candlesticks.

They used to argue about the streams of newspapers that flowed into the house, and the travel magazines, the journals of poetry from France and Italy, the boxes of sheet music and the fountain pens, found at estate sales and garage sales and antiques stores. Henry kept a cocktail glass for every kind of drink, and always more and more books, stacked geologically on the dining table and the living room floor and on the landing at the top of the stairs. His cookbooks were always spilling out of the kitchen cabinets, the pages stained with the wine and olive oil of thirty years of evenings.

But there is no relief in the stark glare of the dining table, now naked of Henry's clutter. And none either in the neat sheets of the bed, never piled, these days, with Henry's clipped articles or his half-read books, his reading glasses lost somewhere in the blankets.

"Wow," said Nathaniel's daughter the last time she visited. "It looks like no one lives here."

To get at the pipe under the sink, he must lie on his back, his legs spread out on the tile, his shoulder jammed into the wall. It's an antique, this sink, something Henry brought home one summer, more for its beauty than its function. Something about the lines, he'd said. The silhouette. And the mahogany cabinet that stands beneath it.

Inside that cabinet, behind the vitamins and the aspirin, pushed to the far back corner, remains the bottle of secobarbital that Henry got ahold of in the weeks after his diagnosis. Something awful runs in Henry's genes. His father had it, an uncle. He knew what was coming for him. "When I can't remember your name," he told Nathaniel again and again, "give me these."

But the bottle remains unopened in the cabinet. No good reason but this one: every human being has certain things they can do and certain things they cannot.

The pipe is crusted in rust. This is a harder job than he thought.

While he works on the sink, the voices of public radio stream out through the speakers of a refurbished antique RCA that Henry bought online: ten more cases, they are saying now, five more suspected.

It is hard for Nathaniel to say if it is this reference to the sickness that makes him feel suddenly a little tired, or just the time of day—he always gets sleepy in the afternoons.

He makes himself some coffee. He keeps working. When he finally gets the part loose, it's a surprise to feel the cold thread of water landing on his forehead. It takes a moment to understand why it's happening. He forgot to shut off the water—that's the problem. It's a little alarming to forget to do something so simple and so crucial. But the proof that he must have is at his feet: a little puddle is forming on the bathroom tile, and growing.

Now is when the phone begins to ring: it's one of Henry's doctors.

The voice of this doctor, though—it sounds different—as if the voice belongs to someone else, but he knows that the person on the phone is Dr. Chavez, the same doctor Henry has had all along.

"I have some news," says the doctor. Nathaniel sits down on the bed. There is a certain kind of dread that destroys the world with its force. "We really weren't expecting it."

Henry's voice has been gone from his head for months. Henry, the great talker, the reciter of poetry, has gone silent. But now a corresponding sensation suddenly grips Nathaniel: he can no longer assemble in his mind the memory of Henry's face.

"At first," says the doctor, "I thought there'd been a mistake. I thought maybe the nurses had mixed up the patients."

He has sometimes wished, these last few months, that he had done what Henry asked of him. It was supposed to be quick: ten minutes to sleep, four hours for the rest. A quiet release for them both. But now, the more familiar feeling rushes in: a desperate fury to keep Henry alive.

"Is he all right?" he asks.

"I want to warn you," says the doctor. "We think this is related to the sickness, so there's no telling what else is coming, but for now, he has a counterintuitive symptom that we haven't seen in the others."

Nathaniel's mouth has gone dry. He can hardly breathe. He waits.

"About an hour ago," says the doctor, "well, Henry, he started speaking."

So much of the rest of the day will always be blurry in his mind, the drive back to the nursing home, the guard letting him in, a special circumstance, the doctor's explanation, full of hesitations and caveats, how there is no way to know if this period of alertness will last, but the wobble of excitement in the doctor's voice, his use of that word—*extraordinary*. But what Nathaniel will always remember, as vividly as anything else in his life, is that warm look on Henry's face, the old expression he has forgotten about until now, the way his eyes fasten on Nathaniel as they have not done in months. This moment makes rational every ir-rational thought he's dismissed since Henry got sick: that he might return one day, as if from a walk or a trip, that he might, in some way, wake up. Maybe this is what kept Nathaniel from giving him those drugs. This day makes meaning of that be-trayal: It was all for this day, see? It was for this, Henry. For this.

Here is Henry, looking a little younger, somehow, than before he got sick, though a little frailer, too, and he is wearing that old red shirt he used to love. There is a slowness to his words, a slur, but still: "Nathaniel," he says, relief in his eyes. Those are Henry's arms reaching out for him. That's Henry standing up from the chair, the press of his big chest against his. He says something else, but it's hard to understand the words. He tries again: "Na-thaniel," he says. "Where have you been?"

Biology is full of paradoxical reactions. Certain drugs excite the ordinary brain but calm the hyperactive. Tranquilizers can some-times agitate instead of soothe. Certain antidepressants have been known to hasten suicide.

Nathaniel cycles through examples—associations in place of an explanation—as he packs a box for Henry. Books, mostly. That's what he's asked for so far. Books, and chocolate and tea.

They will be studying his case for years, of course, thinks Na-thaniel. Henry: one of a handful of people in Santa Lora in whom the virus produces the exact opposite effect as in the oth-ers, a heightening of consciousness instead of the loss of it.

Four cases have surfaced so far in the nursing home. An unused wing now serves as a makeshift isolation unit. While the other three lie sleeping in their beds, Henry, in a white mask and blue gloves, walks the echoing halls. His long legs, his long arms—he was always the tallest in any room. And now here he is, looking his age again, which is twenty years younger than the other residents. He walks a little slower, maybe, and slightly hunched in the shoulders, but mostly, he is just like before. He hums and he grumbles. He quotes Emily Dickinson to the nurses.

"I feel fine," he keeps telling them, his speech sounding clearer every day. "I feel just the same as I ever did. Tell them, Nathaniel," he says. "Don't I seem fine?"

But there are some famous cases of the catatonic inexplicably coming to, only to slip away again. He needs to be monitored. That's what the doctors say. He cannot go home.

He is allowed this much at least: to walk with Nathaniel in the garden, where one hillside is planted with marigolds, where honeysuckle laces the fence, the lake visible just beyond it. This view—this has always been a consolation.

"I moved your desk back the way you like it," says Nathaniel. This is November, but the day is sunny and warm.

"What was I like?" asks Henry. "What was I like all this time?"

Henry saw his own father this way. And his uncle. He must know what he was like.

"It was like you were gone," says Nathaniel.

There are certain thoughts he does not want to think. Among them: when tides recede, they always rush back in.

"I should be angry with you," says Henry. "You didn't do what you promised."

Nathaniel waits, but he knows what he means. He cannot look into his face, so he watches the lake instead. In the distance, a sailboat drifts, as if nothing remarkable were happening in the town of Santa Lora.

"But I'm not," says Henry. "I'm not angry."

These words—they are the exact right thing. Some kinds of trees require the blast of a forest fire to break open their seeds.

Henry's voice softens to a whisper. "I have an idea," he says. A surfacing of an old rebelliousness, as familiar as the warmth of Henry's hand in his. "Let's leave."

The surprise is how easy it is.

No one stops them. No security guard comes running after them. No police. They just open the gate. They just get in the car, and they go.

They do not listen to the news. They do not follow the protocols for contagious disease. If Henry offers him a sip of whisky from his glass, Nathaniel takes it. They do not sleep in separate beds.

Every day, Henry's walk is more steady, his voice more sure. Here is Henry sitting in his wingback chair with a book. Here Nathaniel, making him tea. Here is Henry, walking at his side in the woods.

These woods: If classes were in session, today is the day Nathaniel would have done his lecture on the pheromones of trees. It's a way of catching the attention of the undergraduates for a minute with the counterintuitive news that trees, so silent and so still, have ways of reaching out to one another, lines of communication, systems of warning. There is something satisfying in it, that the plain reality of the universe reads to us like magic. Henry might go further. He would point out how much our brains are limited by what we believe already—how once, when people expected to see ghosts, ghosts were what they saw.

Henry's presence in the house, and in these woods, triggers a second longing, too, a profound need for his daughter to be here, and not just as she is now—a grown woman in San Francisco, whom he calls on the phone to say, yes, yes, it really is amazing— but also as she was once: a six-year-old girl in blue butterfly barrettes, trailing behind him and Henry, as she did on so many evenings back then, out in these same woods, reciting the names of the trees like a catechism, ponderosa, manzanita, white oak, her pockets bulging with pinecones.

His daughter, as she is now, the grown woman in San Francisco, does not seem to understand what he is trying to tell her on the phone. "He's cured?" she says. "How is that possible?" She has a lot of questions that he does not want to consider.

A rush of anger comes over him, washing everything else away.

"Just leave it," he says to her. "Just leave it alone."

It is on the third or fourth day that Nathaniel's mind begins to feel a little foggy. He and Henry are out on the porch drinking whisky, the way they used to, and Henry is telling a complicated story about a man in Key West in the 1930s. He was in love, this man. He was in love with a dead woman.

"At first, he tended her grave," says Henry, leaning back in his chair. "Then he removed her body and kept her in his house for years." Seven years, he keeps saying. "He kept embalming her body. She was like some kind of doll."

It is hard for Nathaniel to remember the start of the story or why Henry is telling it. There it is, that fogginess again. A confusion. For the first time, Nathaniel worries that he might be getting the sickness, too.

"Are you all right?" asks Henry. His hand is on his back.

How cruel it would be to fall sick just as Henry got well. But there is no law in nature against cruelty. In fact, Henry would argue, with his Victorian rooms and his seminars on Thomas Hardy, it seems, at times, to run in that direction.

Nathaniel's confusion is accompanied by something else, too, a strange noise. "Like water," he says to Henry. "Do you hear that? Like water dripping somewhere."

But Henry does not hear it. The house is dry. The sun is out. But the sound persists, unnerving, inexplicable: like the light sloshing of water against a boat, always there and growing louder.

27.

One hundred twenty cases balloons to 250 in two days. Two-fifty soon cascades to 500.

But with the hospital closed to new patients, these newly sick are spread out in giant tents instead, as if they've been felled on a battlefield in some distant place.

Along with supplies, volunteers are flown in from other places to give the only treatment there is: keeping the hearts beating and the bodies hydrated and fed. It's a lot of work to perform manually every task the waking body does on its own. There are not enough monitors. There are not enough beds. There are not enough workers to turn the bodies back and forth in the sheets.

The story is everywhere now. Television commentators are circling Santa Lora on maps of California: this place is only seventy miles from Los Angeles and only ninety miles from LAX, which might as well be a neighborhood in New York or London or Beijing.

Something needs to be done, that's the feeling. Something big.

On the eighteenth day, three thousand miles away, watchers of
the morning news shows awaken to a series of aerial images of
the town of Santa Lora, California.

From the cockpit of a helicopter, the campus of Santa Lora
College looks serene: sixteen brick buildings, lit with orange
lights, parking lots empty of cars. The lake, or what is left of it,
shines in the moonlight, its former waterline not so obvious in
the dark. Beyond that, the streets fan out in a grid. Swimming
pools, covered over for winter. Station wagons parked in driveways. An ordinary town in the middle of the night—except for
a long line of military trucks clogging the one road in and out.
And also this, visible only faintly through the trees: a line of soldiers standing in the woods.

For now, the people of Santa Lora are sleeping soundly, the
healthy and the sick alike. Hours will pass before most of them
will hear the words that people in Maine and Pennsylvania and
Florida are learning right now: *cordon sanitaire,* the complete
sealing off of an infected region, like a tourniquet, not used in
this country for more than a hundred years.

From the air, all the streets look the same, the houses packed
close like teeth, the artificial lawns indistinguishable from the
real grass gone brown from the drought. But on one of those
streets, under one of those roofs, a baby is crying in the dark.

One floor up, Ben wakes to the noise, knowing that his wife is
with her already, that soon his daughter will go quiet in her arms.

He dozes, a half-sleep. But the crying wakes him again.

He turns in his bed. He begins to wonder if this crying is different from the crying of all the other nights, more urgent, maybe
a kind of screaming. The sickness floats up into his mind—what
if this is how it starts?

Now he's up. He's out of bed. His heart is beating fast. The
way to slow it down is to see her. He wants to see his baby right

away. But her room is empty. They're downstairs, he realizes—that's where the crying is coming from. The kitchen.

"Poor little nut," he says in the dark when he gets there, which is a way of greeting his wife, who he knows is in there, somewhere in that blackness, probably pacing like she does, the baby curled in her arms, or else she's rocking her in that special way they learned from a book. They haven't spoken much since their fight, but he forgets all that now. "How long has she been awake?" he asks.

But there's no answer. The crying gets louder. This is when his foot bumps against something plastic—the warble of a bottle rolling across the floor.

His fingers run along the wall for the light switch, and the click of that switch is proof that a baby's cry is the truest communication there is: something is wrong.

Through his squinting, he sees that his wife is lying on the linoleum. Her eyes are closed. Her limbs are still. His baby is curled awkwardly on Annie's chest, her tiny face bright red from the crying, squinting in the bright light, her blanket coming loose around her feet.

He lifts her, their baby, and presses her to his chest. In his arms, she quiets immediately.

But the relief is brief. There is a bruise spreading across his wife's forehead. Her eyelids are twitching madly, as if she is dreaming a terrible dream.

He calls her name. He squeezes her shoulder. He does not hear the helicopters whirring in the air above the town.

He thinks to press a piece of ice into Annie's hand, like they did in birthing class, as a small simulation of labor pains, a way to practice the breathing—Annie hated it. She could not tolerate it for more than a few seconds. Maybe it will wake her now. But this time, the only detectable reaction is in the ice, which melts swiftly in the warmth of her palm, while Annie goes on dreaming some unstoppable dream.

28.

The crackle of a loudspeaker, the hum of recorded static: the words are sticky and indecipherable, too distant to make out as they drift, like airport announcements, out over the sidewalks and the streets of Santa Lora, and in through the windows of the empty houses, and in through the windows of the big white house, where, once, in a different time, Mei was a babysitter but where, on this morning, she is just waking up, alone in a king-size bed.

"Are you hearing this?" calls Matthew from the hall. She pulls on her jeans and opens the door. It's a surprise to smell the toothpaste on his breath as he rushes past her toward the window—for a moment, it's all she can think of: his nearness.

They can't see it, at first, whatever is making the noise, but the echoing voice is accompanied by a grinding sound, and it's growing—something is moving slowly toward them.

Words begin to emerge from the static. *Health department,* she hears. *Isolation. Mandatory.*

"The whole town?" Mei asks.

"I'm surprised it took them this long," says Matthew.

A Humvee, painted to match a desert, is rumbling past

porches and porch swings and artificial lawns—with a loud-speaker mounted on its hood.

"The military," says Matthew. "Of course."

On the sidewalk, two little boys, their shadows tall in the autumn sunshine, are running alongside the Humvee, as if this were the ice cream truck lumbering down their street, kicking up dried leaves as it goes.

The message repeats. Food and water will be distributed. A website is mentioned.

"It's just the National Guard," says Mei. "Like for hurricanes."

All along the street, doors are swinging open. People are stepping out of their Craftsmans to stand on their porches, hands pressed over their mouths.

There is a feeling that this morning is passing into history, a sudden shifting of scale—far from a story about one floor in one dorm at one college.

If you're sick, says the recording, *or if you see someone who's sick, call 911 right away.*

Four soldiers are riding inside the Humvee, in white masks and sunglasses, shooing the kids from the truck. If they smile at the boys, it is hard to tell through the masks.

"They shouldn't be here waving their guns around," says Matthew. He is on his laptop already, looking for more news, and it's everywhere, this new news, these new words: *cordon sanitaire.*

"They're not waving their guns," says Mei, though she can see them, the guns, long and black and resting in their laps.

Do not gather in large groups, says the message. *Avoid public places. If you think you've been exposed, call the following number.*

"Do you know that the American government once quarantined a Chinese neighborhood for typhoid, and then set the whole place on fire?" says Matthew.

"They're not going to set us on fire," says Mei.

"They did it before," he says. "Hawaii, 1930."

"Maybe someone finally knows what they're doing," says Mei.

"I can't believe how naïve you are," says Matthew. His skin is smooth beneath the little hairs starting to grow on his chin.

All along the street, neighbors are clustered on porches, arms crossed as they talk in their driveways, as if they need to hear the news in more than one person's voice, the way any kind of faith leans partly on what other people think.

"They have no idea what's going on," Matthew says near her. She can feel him resisting the urge to call out to those people, to shout from the window. This boy: a certain kind of logic runs in him like a compulsion. But something stronger than logic is keeping these people bunched together.

To Mei, it's the empty porches that look ominous—in how many of these quiet houses are people sleeping already, their bodies dehydrating as they dream?

Her phone begins to ring.

"I thought you turned that off," says Matthew. "If someone tracked our phones, they could find us."

It's her mother: "Where are you?" she says.

"I'm fine," says Mei.

"We got a call from the police," says her mother.

The Humvee is shrinking in the distance now. The recording is fading away on the wind.

"You need to be somewhere where they can take care of you," says her mother. She can tell by the scratch in her mother's voice that her mother is about to cry.

It is at this moment that Mei sees something almost as surprising as the Humvee: a small group of people in rumpled business suits trudging down the sidewalk with suitcases. Their coats are slung over their arms. They walk slowly, wearily, as if they've been walking these streets for days. The wheels of their suitcases are ticking over the cracks in the sidewalk. Some kind of plastic ID badge swings from each of their necks.

Together, on this residential street, these travelers, steering their luggage past driveways and fire hydrants, look like the incongruous images seen sometimes in dreams.

"What if you get sick?" says her mother, but it is easier to worry about the people outside instead, as they walk slowly, slowly, down the street. One of the women outside is walking barefoot in her business suit. Where are her shoes? Mei wonders, but that's the thing about strangers: you don't get to hear their stories.

29.

Two weeks: that's how long it has been since the girls have left the house, except to water the vegetables in the garden in the middle of the night and, once, with flashlights, on the night their father was taken away, to inspect the giant X painted on the side of the house.

They keep the curtains closed. They keep their voices low. They have an idea that the helicopters might have telescopic sight.

News of the quarantine has not reached their ears. They keep the television going all day and all night, but never on news channels. Infomercials or cooking shows—it doesn't matter. What they like best, these girls, alone in this big house, is to hear from a distance the soothing sounds of voices coming from another room.

Everything they need is in the basement: peanut butter and tuna fish and macaroni and cheese, crackers and cereal and granola bars for a year. They have canned vegetables and canned fruit. They have toilet paper—stacks and stacks of toilet paper—and also the shelves of all those rarer things, each one an act of their father's imagination, just waiting to prove clairvoyance: radiation suits, a Geiger counter, capsules of potassium iodide. Maybe they should be sleeping in the cots down there instead of in their bedroom upstairs, but there are spiders in this basement, and that one bare bulb, the smell of soil coming up from the earth. They never pictured sleeping down there without their father.

They do not know where he was taken or when he'll come home, or if, but the only way to tolerate living alone in this house is to expect him to return at any moment.

On this morning, Sara is washing out the smell of urine from the sheets he last slept in. There is a kindness in not telling. There is love in covering up.

It is only as she is closing the lid of the washing machine that the danger occurs to her: Could she catch it from breathing in that smell? Now she's at the sink. Now she's washing her hands. She washes her hands for five minutes.

Libby is in the kitchen with the cats, handing out scraps of turkey.

"Don't give them our food," says Sara. She dries her hands on her jeans.

"But we're all out of theirs," Libby says.

They've been a good distraction, the cats, the four kittens skating across the wood floors, the two older ones always howling for food. One of the babies keeps throwing up on the rug. Another one pees on the stairs. But it feels good to take care of them—the way it is possible to disappear inside someone else's need.

"We must have more food for them somewhere," says Sara. But then she remembers: her father's survival plans do not include the cats.

One of the kittens steals a piece of turkey right out of the mouth of another; he swallows quickly as if it might be taken back. There's a scuffle on the linoleum, a sudden hiss.

"We have to get them more food," says Libby.

"We can't go out," says Sara.

But she is soon turning the lock on the safe in the basement and pulling two twenty-dollar bills from the envelope her father keeps interred there.

"We're bringing these," she says as she stuffs the two gas masks into her backpack. "And the gloves."

They leave through the back fence, through the woods, and then emerge on a path along the lake, so that their neighbors will not see them leaving the house. This is how they keep the secret of their living alone in the house.

How odd it is to be outside again, their shoes grinding the dirt, the glittering of the lake in the sun. Only two weeks earlier, they were walking this same stretch of sand with their father and his metal detector. As the lake shrinks into the distance, coins lost in these waters decades ago are now hidden by only a thin layer of dusty soil.

They walk slowly, deliberately, like they do on the high dive at the Y. There's the feeling that they might have forgotten the way.

Two helicopters are hovering over another part of town. And some sort of military vehicle crosses an intersection up ahead. It makes some kind of announcement, but they cannot understand what it says.

They can tell from across the street that something is happening at the grocery store. Never before have they seen so many cars circling for spots. Never have they seen so many shopping carts heaped so full—a woman near the entrance is leaning hard to get hers rolling, as if pushing a stalled car down a hill. Some people are pulling two carts at once.

"Maybe we shouldn't go in," says Sara.

"We have to," says her sister, her white cowboy boots clicking quickly into the crosswalk.

They should put on their masks—that's what Sara is thinking.

But it's too embarrassing, now that they are here, now that she has spotted two girls from her class, to walk into a crowded grocery store wearing gas masks.

"Let's at least put on the gloves," says Sara. "And only the cat food. Don't touch anything else."

Inside, the aisles are choked with people. The checkout lines snake to the back of the store. And it is so much louder than usual. The workers are shouting to manage the crowd.

Some people, just a few, are wearing paper masks.

But still the usual music tinkles from the ceiling, not the work of real strings or real keys, their father likes to point out, but some digital imitation, as artificial as the apples that shine in the produce section, genetically modified for color instead of taste.

But on this day, all those apples are gone. And the bananas, too. On the back wall of the produce section, the automatic sprinklers are showering mist over a row of empty bins where the lettuce usually sits.

The canned food section has been similarly stripped. A tightening is spreading through Sara's stomach. This is just as their father predicted.

Only a few bags of cat food are left slouched on the shelf. The girls grab what they can carry, one big bag each, and keep moving.

The clearest way out is through the candy aisle, where the racks still bulge with abundance, the only aisle empty of people. If they stand here among the chocolate bars and the Blow Pops, and if they cover their ears, they can pretend that the store is the same as it always is, the calm cool of packaged food, the aisles wide and clear. Simple.

Libby pauses to pull a big bag of gummy worms down from the rack.

"We don't need that," says Sara.

Candy is not allowed in their house.

But the gummy worms remain wedged under Libby's skinny arm.

Suddenly, a soft voice nearby is saying Sara's name, a boy: "Hey."

She turns and finds Akil at the end of the aisle, with a small black bulldog beside him on a leash. A ping of happiness comes to her, but also the urge to hide her gloved hands, to smooth her unwashed hair.

"Hi," she says.

She has never met Akil's parents, but those must be them, a man in a gray suit, a woman in dark pants, a green paisley scarf at her neck, now digging through the groceries in their cart.

"Where have you been?" says Akil. This rush of gladness—to be missed—is too strong to admit.

The lie comes out almost without her notice: "I've been sick," she says.

"They canceled the play," says Akil.

The loudspeaker crackles with an announcement: they have sold out of diapers, says the voice, all sizes.

Behind him, Akil's father seems agitated. He raises his voice: "This is outrageous," he says.

"I didn't know they could close off a whole town," says Akil, in that crisp way he has of speaking. "Not in the States, anyway."

"Is that what they're doing?" she says. A new tenseness comes into her. This is another of her father's darkest imaginings.

But now Akil's mother is cutting in between them, her accent thick and glamorous, a flash of concern on her face: "Are you girls here alone?"

Sara has the idea that Akil's mother is accustomed to crisis. They had to leave Egypt, he once told the class, after his father was arrested for something he wrote, and when he got out of jail, they left everything behind and moved to Florida, and then here, so he could teach at the college. Maybe what is happening in Santa Lora is nothing for this woman, compared to everything that came before. There is a calmness in the way she is dressed, her dark hair, perfectly parted, those gold earrings, shaped like seashells. But every mother is a little exotic to these motherless girls.

"Our dad knows we're here," says Sara, and the words release a surge of longing—for this wish to be true.

There is a pause that sounds like skepticism. And it is only then that Sara notices how much cat hair has collected on Libby's black sweatshirt. She can hear a gummy worm already shifting around in her sister's mouth, unpaid for.

"Please be careful, girls," says Akil's mother, the curve of her accent giving the words a special weight.

Akil's father agrees: "You should go straight home."

"We will," says Sara.

Akil looks like he might say something more, but he doesn't. He just smiles a small smile, and then walks away with his little dog and his beautiful mother, his father trailing behind them.

One aisle over, a man is leaning down on one knee, reaching for something on a low shelf.

"Hey, you girls," he says as they rush past him. "Can one of you reach that box?"

The turning of his head reveals two facts at once: this man is their neighbor, the professor, and he has the baby with him, pressed against his chest in a wrap, a pacifier pulsing in her tiny bird mouth.

If he recognizes the girls, he does not show it. He looks different. The beginnings of a beard are coming in patchy on his chin. And he is moving awkwardly, delicately—he can't reach the box because of the baby burrowed in the wrap.

"I'll get it," says Sara.

It's formula, the last box. She holds it out to him through the cuffs of her sweatshirt, no contact with her skin.

There's something terrible about the depth of this man's gratitude as he thanks her for an act so simply done.

Suddenly the baby begins to wail. The pacifier has dropped from her mouth, and it is as if, all this time, the noise of her crying has been plugged up like water in a tub.

"Shit," says the professor. He rubs the back of her little bald head and leans slowly toward the floor—like a pregnant woman. She can tell he's not used to carrying her like this. Libby tries to help by scooping up the pacifier and stretching it out toward the baby's mouth.

But the professor lunges forward. "No," he says, grabbing hold of Libby's sleeve. "Don't touch her."

The baby seems as stunned as Libby. She goes quiet for a moment, and then the crying rushes back, even louder.

"I'm sorry," says the professor. He is rubbing his eyes. "I'm so sorry."

He looks like he might cry, and there's no need for the girls to discuss what to do next. They want the same thing at the same moment: to get away from this man as fast as they can.

In the checkout line, Sara begins to feel a strange weariness in her limbs. It's her legs especially, but also her back, as if every muscle in her body is calling out to her for rest.

"Are you okay?" says Libby.

It's just the waiting, she thinks—the line is long and slow, and the cat food is heavy in her arms.

"I'm fine," she says.

What happens next begins with a sound she does not recognize: the cracking of eggshells on linoleum. "Oh my God," someone is shouting from the dairy section. "Oh my God." A single scream leaves a momentary vacuum. Every head turns toward the sound. And what they see when they do is a woman crumpled on the floor, egg yolks pooling around her head.

Sara grabs her sister's hand just as everyone lurches forward, a tidal surge toward the front doors. The girls run like the others, the cat food pressed against their chests.

There's a bottlenecking at the front—the automatic doors keep trying to close, but there are too many people trying to get out at once, that ringing again and again. Here is where Sara sees the professor a second time, just a quick flash of his face, which is desperate and red. He is pressed against a wall of windows, his arms curled around the head of his tiny girl. "Stop pushing!" he's shouting. "I have a baby! Stop pushing!"

The girls burst outside, and they don't stop running for two blocks.

At first, Sara feels better outside, the cool air on her skin, the sun. A gummy worm is releasing its sweetness in her cheek. She's okay, she says to herself as they walk. She's fine.

But when they're a few blocks from home, a sudden pain twists her stomach. It soon spreads to her back. The feeling comes with an intense urge to lie down. And this wish seems to produce right in front of her a patch of dry grass.

"Hold on a second," she says to Libby. She sits down right where she is.

"Do you have your inhaler?" says her sister.

"It's not that," says Sara. She pulls her knees tight to her chest. It feels right to close her eyes.

"Oh my God," says her sister. "Oh my God."

But it is hard for Sara to feel afraid, because, suddenly, the world has been reduced to only this one fact: this massive ache flooding her body. Somewhere very far away is the sound of her sister dropping the cat food on the sidewalk.

"Please don't be sick," says Libby. "Please. Please."

It only lasts a minute, the worst of it, anyway, and then everything eclipsed rushes back to her at once: the smell of the grass, the dry dirt against her legs, the terror in her sister's voice.

The pain comes and goes all the way home. They have to stop again in the woods.

"You can't go to sleep," says Libby, once they've snuck back into the house. "You can't."

But she needs to lie down. She is clenching her teeth on the stairs.

If she curls herself up in a certain way, she feels a little better.

Soon, she can no longer hear the yowling of the cats downstairs, or the rattle, loud as hail, of Libby filling their bowls with food.

She lies curled in her four-poster bed, that old green quilt pulled up to her chin, one socked foot sticking out from the sheets. Her ponytail fans out on the pillow, and the hood of her sweatshirt is crumpled around her neck. Her eyes are closed. Her mouth is open. Saliva is gathering on her lips. Her breathing is light and steady.

Lost, for now, is the buzz of the panic in the grocery store. Gone is the price of gummy worms. Fading away is the face of the woman who was standing two people behind them in line and the man pushing a cart near the entrance.

If, in the months before the sickness appeared, you had asked a specialist why it is that a human being spends part of every day unconscious, you might have heard an answer that's been around since at least the ancient Greeks: we sleep, the theory goes, in order to forget.

Sleep, the experts would tell you, is when our brains sift through the day's memories, sweeping away the unimportant things. What remains for Sara is the soft look on Akil's face when he asked where she had been, the music of his mother's voice, the sweaty warmth of her sister's hand as they sprinted toward home.

Unlike so many of the others, Sara eventually opens her eyes.

She wakes to the sound of shouting. It's Libby. Libby is screaming at the foot of the bed.

"You wouldn't wake up," her sister shouts.

Sara is still a little in her dream—something about her mother, the idea of her, anyway. She was wearing the green cardigan from the picture of her that Sara has in her drawer. And the kitchen. They were sitting together in the kitchen. But matching the words to the dream only dissolves what is left of it, the way certain stars vanish from the sky if you look directly at them.

It takes a second to remember her waking life. Here she is in their bedroom, the sunlight flickering through the boarded-up windows. Here is her sister, her face red from crying.

"You have to go to the hospital," says Libby. She is pulling at the sheets. There are streaks of brown blood here and there. "You're bleeding."

Now the dream is gone from Sara's head—only a tracing is left, like skates on ice, a sadness.

"Wait," says Sara, sitting up in wet jeans. "Let me think for a second."

There's a small swell of relief as the situation becomes clear in her head. "I'm not sick," she says.

Sara is not a girl who has been waiting for this day to arrive. Ever since they showed the video at school, she's been nursing the idea that maybe, hopefully, it would never happen to her at all. It was easy to believe. How could something so bizarre really be so ordinary?

"I didn't think it would be so much blood," she says to her sister through the bathroom door.

A tide of adrenaline pushes her through the first steps: the changing of her jeans, the layers of toilet paper, to be replaced eventually with a washcloth folded in quarters, the swallowing of two Tylenol at the sink. There is the slightest traitorous gladness that her father is not here to witness any of it.

It is hard not to wish for her mother. Akil's mother flashes into her mind—maybe she would know how to help.

She can hear her sister in the hall, through the door. A strange snorting sound.

"Are you okay?" Sara calls to her sister. No answer.

On the other side of the door, she finds Libby sprawled on the floor: laughing. She is laughing so hard she can't talk.

"It's not funny," says Sara.

Libby is giggling so much that she is holding her stomach as if it might otherwise come undone.

"Stop laughing," says Sara.

But she keeps at it.

"Stop it."

"I can't believe I thought you were dying," says Libby. The noise has attracted the kittens, who are nuzzling their faces against her shoulder. "And look at your jeans."

But all Sara can feel at this moment is a vague sense of an animal indifference in the universe, how everything in nature is just as relentless as a virus, replicating itself again and again without end.

30.

The parents: one mile outside of town, at a rest stop where the highway twists into the woods, a group of parents begins to gather. This is the closest the soldiers will allow them to get to Santa Lora.

This is outrageous, the parents say to one another. This is a violation of their sons' and daughters' civil liberties. They call their lawyers. They call their representatives and their senators. They call the media. They watch military vehicles trundle in and out of town. One father tries to climb aboard an army truck but is soon shooed off by the soldiers.

Some sleep in their cars. Some set up tents. They take turns driving back down the mountain for food.

They talk in small groups, exchanging news and blankets. Most of their children are still awake in Santa Lora—why not let them come home and wait out their quarantine in their own houses?

Protest signs begin to appear. Cameras.

Among the parents here is Mei's mother, who, unbeknownst to Mei, has been sleeping in her station wagon. It feels better to

be at least this near. Her daughter has not answered her phone
in two days. And there is no way to know if this silence means
that she has caught the sickness, or if it is only proof of the
natural order of things: how parents are always so much more
focused on their children than the other way around.

31.

The day after the start of the quarantine, Mei and Matthew join the crowd that forms at the barricades of Recuerdo Road in Santa Lora. They stand side by side in sweatshirts and jeans, white masks on their faces, blue gloves on their hands. Mei is looking around. She is nervous. Matthew stares straight ahead.

This is Mei's idea, this turning themselves in. Something unfamiliar is blooming in her, something big, like duty.

But Matthew has agreed. He has thought it over. "This is the greatest good for the greatest number," he says.

For Mei, it is less a thought than a feeling, almost physical, as if it is the muscles in her stomach that know most clearly the right thing to do.

Two rows of barricades stand at the point in the road where the state forest land ends and Santa Lora begins—with a scattering of cabins in the woods. The old sign hangs nearby: WELCOME TO SANTA LORA.

Only two months earlier, Mei came in on this same road, her mother's Volvo packed with new sheets and new clothes and a mini-fridge still in its box. In her head, so much hope and longing, her new life so close at hand.

The crowd here is loud with need, for supplies and for food, but most of all for information. A man here is asking about his daughter. A woman is looking for her husband. "They took him away in an ambulance," she says. "No one will tell me where he is."

Every one of these questions is met with the same response from the two soldiers posted behind the fence: the slow shaking of their heads.

They wear fatigues and big boots, sunglasses. They would help if they could, they say, through their crisp white masks, and they do look sorry, like boys, is what they look like, but with big black guns at their sides.

"You should all go home," one of them calls out through his mask. "That's the safest place to be."

"But we don't live here," shouts a woman in a wrinkled business suit. She is with a group of nine or ten people who were here for a conference, she says. "We're stranded," says the woman. This is the moment when Mei notices that she is barefoot, the same woman she saw the day before. "Where are we supposed to go?"

Two news helicopters are swirling overhead. All the channels have dropped the story of the escaped college kids in favor of the bigger headline: for the first time in American history, a tourniquet has been applied to an entire town.

Matthew calls out to one of the soldiers. "Excuse me," he says. "Excuse me."

"Hey," shouts a man from somewhere nearby. "There's a line."

An hour of waiting produces nothing. A line of wispy clouds drifts in the sky. A dog walks alone in the road, his leash dragging behind him. Whose dog is this? people call out to the crowd. Whose dog is this? They keep asking until that dog wanders out of sight, his tags jingling unread, his leash still flapping behind him. It is hard not to wonder what happened to the person whose hand let go of that leash.

When it is their turn to talk to the soldiers, Mei and Matthew fare no better than the others.

"Who told you to come here?" says one of them, as if they have asked him for some kind of favor. "We can't help you here."

"But we've been exposed," says Matthew. "We're trying to do the ethical thing."

The one soldier meets eyes with the other, like Matthew might be some kind of nut.

The soldier hands them a yellow flyer and taps with one gloved finger the same number that Mei called earlier.

"They said to come here," says Mei.

"Call again," he says. "I guess."

Suddenly someone is shouting nearby. There is the clanging of metal on pavement.

"Hey," shout the soldiers. "Stop."

A man is trying to climb over the barricades.

A woman in the crowd is calling after him: "Sayyid," she shouts. "Come back."

"Stop where you are," shouts the soldier closest to Mei. He does not point his rifle. But if anyone were really looking closely, which no one is at this moment, he or she might notice the way his hand tenses against the barrel.

"You can't trap us here," says the man. He has an accent, Mei can't tell from where. "What about all your talk of human rights?"

He is wearing a gray suit, this man, and dress shoes. He already has one leg over the fence.

The woman keeps calling after him from somewhere in the crowd.

"Sayyid," she says. "What are you trying to do?"

And now another voice joins hers, a boy's: "Daddy, stop." He says. "Please. Come back."

The woman switches her pleading to a different language: Arabic, maybe, but Mei can't say for sure.

The activity attracts the helicopters. They circle tight and low.

The man is wandering now between the two sets of barricades, as if lost in an empty moat. He looks dizzy. He is beginning to cry.

On the other side of the barricades, the woods loom, and the mountains—twenty square miles of state forest stretch out on both sides of this road.

He keeps going, this man. He begins to climb the second set of barricades.

"Stop where you are," say the soldiers, but he does not stop.

The reflective yellow lines of the road are sparkling in the sun beneath the man's shoes. He climbs up over the second set of barricades.

The soldiers half catch him and they half don't, and Mei can see, as the man lands hard on the asphalt, that these soldiers are afraid to touch him.

They are pointing their guns at him.

"Don't hurt him!" shouts the woman. She is wearing a green silk scarf at her neck, beige pants, gold earrings. A boy, maybe eleven or twelve, stands by her side. "Please," she calls to the soldiers. "He's not acting like himself. He's a professor."

The man keeps coming toward the soldiers.

"I need to leave here!" he shouts. "You have to let us go."

"Sir," they say, "please." And then more gently: "Go home."

"I am five thousand miles from home," he screams. "I have fled my home. And now you treat us no better than where we came from."

The woman is shouting. She is crying as she pleads with the soldiers.

Certain experts will later suspect that the virus affects the brain in subtle ways even before the onset of sleep. The waking consciousness, in some cases, takes on certain qualities of the dream state. Heightened activity in the amygdala, the emotional center of the brain. Decreased activity in the cerebral cortex, charged with reasoning. Increased impulsiveness. Some will say later that these effects may have contributed to what happened on this day.

The soldiers are backing away from the man, but he keeps going and going, as if the way to make them understand is to shout the words up close to their faces, as if, by grabbing hold of that one's uniform, he will finally make himself clear.

The crack of the shot comes crisp and cold. That sound—it sucks all the other noise from the world. The man goes right down.

Mei's hand darts down for Matthew's hand, but already he is moving forward. He is surging toward the barricades.

"Shit," says the soldier who shot the gun. "Shit, shit, shit. I told him," he keeps saying. "I told him to keep away. Didn't I tell him?"

The other soldier is crouching over the man. He is calling for help on his radio. Cell phone videos will capture three people from the crowd, Matthew among them, jumping the two sets of barricades to help, and also the woman, who will turn out to be the man's wife, and the boy, his son, climbing the barricades to get to the man, the boy ignoring his mother's pleas. She is sobbing, speaking to her son in a language only the two of them, in this crowd, understand.

From where she is standing, Mei cannot see the man's face, but she can see the shine of his blood on the asphalt. Something is happening in Mei's chest. She can't take a deep breath.

Into this moment comes a small rumbling at high altitude. An airplane is cutting across the sky, the events on this road too small to see from those windows, as if the passengers up there and the people down here are operating on two different scales of experience.

What a relief it is—and a horror—when the man begins to scream.

———

He is soon taken away by an ambulance. His wife and his boy go with him. Mei has a feeling that something more needs to be done for them, but they're gone—there's no way to help them now.

Matthew is talking to one of the other men who tried to help, one of the group of stranded business travelers.

"Our hotel was evacuated in the middle of the night," he says. "That was two days ago. We spent last night on the floor of the bus station."

"We have nowhere to go," says the woman without shoes. She is carrying a pair of heels in her hand.

"How many of you are there?" Matthew asks. A stab of fear comes into Mei. She knows what he'll say next.

Ten, they say. No, nine, someone corrects.

"You can stay with us," says Matthew.

"What if they're sick?" Mei whispers.

Matthew's face stays hard and straight, unreadable.

"What if you are?" he says.

She can hear her mother begging her not to take any risks. They think it was in the hotel ventilation system—that's what they've said. They have probably all been exposed.

They are sales reps, these people, whose suitcases now fill the living room while they take turns in the showers, in the master and the guest, and in the little girl's bathroom, too. Mei thinks of it too late—how maybe just rinsing their bodies there will contaminate the girl's bath toys, her tiny boats, those letters made of foam. A wild panic beats in her chest. She must remind herself that little Rose is far away, for now, floating on a cruise ship with her parents.

At first, they sit around watching the footage of the shooting on television.

"You can't say they didn't warn him," says one of the guys, in a red polo shirt, a company logo embroidered on the pocket.

Matthew is shaking his head. He is pacing around.

"I'm just saying," the man says. "They wouldn't have shot him if he listened."

"Did you know," says Matthew, "that in 1930, in Hawaii, the government quarantined a Chinese neighborhood and then set the whole place on fire?"

"Is that true?" says one of the women. She is wearing two sweatshirts, but she is holding her arms like she's cold.

"Let's talk about something else," says the guy in the polo shirt.

The house has plenty of wine, and Matthew keeps opening up bottles. Everyone is eager to drink. Just the taste in Mei's mouth makes her feel better, even before it hits her blood.

Maybe it doesn't matter anymore that this big house belongs to someone else, as if this patch of wooded earth has been cut loose from the rest of the world, and from all its rules of cause and consequence.

They drift out onto the back porch, and Mei can see the woman next door watching them there. She might call the owners, this woman. But Mei surprises herself: she does not care.

After a while, one of the women asks Mei and Matthew how they met. "I always like to hear how couples get together," she says.

A sudden awkwardness surges between them—isn't that the one feeling that, when shared, widens the gap between two people instead of closing it?

"We're not a couple," says Matthew, as if it's a crazy thing to say.

Mei can feel her face turning hot.

"Oh," says the woman.

In the quiet that follows, moths buzz and flutter against the lights. A Humvee rumbles by. Matthew goes in for more wine, and then appears on the porch with the autographed guitar back in his arms again.

One of the sales reps begins to smoke.

Maybe, in a photograph, it would look like a small party on a back porch, the long light, the late fall, a kid playing guitar in one corner.

There is not much food left in the Sub-Zero, and all the stores, they've heard, are closed.

"I know where we can find something," says Matthew. There's a jolt of excitement in his words, the crackle of a boy accepting a dare.

The porch swing sways in his wake as he stands and then hops over the wooden railing. He lands beside a row of trash cans— the lids come right off in his hands.

"Whoa," says the loudest of the sales reps from the porch. "I don't think we're quite at that point yet."

"I do this all the time," says Matthew, his bare feet in the grass, his bare hands already untying a white trash bag. There are holes in his sweatshirt.

That look on the sales reps' faces, the way they all turn their heads slightly away, as if they can smell the garbage from the porch—it's not something she wants to see aimed at Matthew. She watches him instead, the way he leans his head deep into the bag, his hands at work at a delicate task. His nickname from the dorm floor rushes back to her: Weird Matthew.

Half a loaf of bread emerges, still snug inside its package. One thin line of mold is the only imperfection on a plastic-wrapped block of Parmesan cheese.

The sales reps refuse to eat any of it. Mei, though, she takes it. And it tastes fine, that bread. It tastes better than fine.

"You know what this whole thing reminds me of?" says one of the sales reps. "That sleep aid we used to sell," he says. "Remember?" He has the beginnings of a mustache, this guy, more than a stubble, more like sparse grass. "There was one case where a guy slept for twenty-four hours straight."

"Wait," says Matthew. He sits up fast. He seems suddenly angry. "Are you guys, like, Big Pharma?"

"Here we go," says the guy in the red polo.

The others nod in their folding chairs. That's what the meeting was for, they say: pharmaceutical sales.

Whatever Matthew says next is drowned out by the wailing of a helicopter, which briefly lights and then darkens the yard.

"This just does not seem real," one of the women says. She is shaking her head. She is drinking the wine.

Matthew has gone silent. There he is on the porch swing, arms crossed, staring into the woods.

"None of this seems real," the woman says again. "You know?"

"Maybe it isn't," says Matthew from the porch swing, its chains creaking as he sways. "Maybe none of this is real."

Oh, Matthew. If only she could rescue him from the way this woman is meeting eyes with the others. He does not see it, or he does not care. But these are not Mei's kind of women, anyway—how many hours have gone into the shaping of those eyebrows, the pale pink sheen of those fingernails?

"Like a hoax?" says the woman.

"Have you read Descartes?" says Matthew.

"No offense, dude," says the loud guy. "But I don't think any of us are in the mood for that kind of dorm-room bullshit tonight."

Matthew stays quiet, arms crossed. Mei can feel a fury rising off him like heat.

"Please don't ask me how I know this table is really here," says the guy. He knocks his knuckles on the patio table. His teeth are red from the wine. "Please don't ask me how I know that the blue you see is the same blue I see."

Matthew leans back on the porch swing. Already she has come to know that look, a way of smiling that signals unhappiness.

"Let me ask you something else, then," says Matthew. "How does it feel to get rich off the backs of sick people? How does it feel to be part of a system so fucked up that kids are going without their EpiPens and asthma inhalers because your companies have decided to raise the price by a thousand percent—just because you can?"

"I love college students," says the first guy. "Talk to me in ten years, dude."

Matthew says nothing. He just gets up and goes inside.

"Anyway," says Mei, but she can think of nothing much to say, except this: "How long have you all worked together?"

"Us?" one of the women says. "We all just met on Tuesday."

This news astounds her. How lonely it feels to discover once again how quickly other people can bond.

At a certain point, one of the women dozes off in her chair. It is an uneasy sight, and the loud guy is soon tapping her shoulder. What a relief it is to see her open her eyes.

She is slow to come around. She yawns and asks for more wine.

"I was dreaming that everything was moving backwards," says the woman. "Like time itself was moving in reverse. In the dream, the guy popped up after he got shot. Then the soldiers shouted at him. Then he climbed backwards over the barricades and disappeared into the crowd."

Later, the sales reps set up in the living room, having declined the bedrooms, as if this were the sort of danger that calls for safety in numbers, instead of the exact opposite thing. They use their sweatshirts as pillows once the pillows run out. They are quick to turn out the lights but slow to put away their phones, leaving only the odd glow of their faces, lit white by the screens, as they wait on their backs for sleep.

Mei and Matthew linger last on the porch. A breeze is working its way through the woods, setting the wind chimes ringing.

"I don't think we should sleep in the house with them," he whispers.

A soft sound is coming from inside: one of the sales reps is weeping.

"Let's sleep out here," he says, nodding toward the backyard. "I found a tent in the garage."

A tent. An odd sensation keeps flooding back to her—that this day is taking place somewhere outside of normal time. Not even the strangest possibility can be ruled out.

"We can set it up in the yard," he says.

She worries what the sales reps will think, but there's an urge to want what Matthew wants. It feels good to agree. And so here they are in the backyard, Mei pointing a flashlight at the ground while Matthew unrolls the tent.

It seems brand new, this tent, fresh with the smell of the packaging, not like her own family's tents, so dusty and worn out from use.

"Fucking rich people," says Matthew. "They always have a bunch of shit around that they never bother to use."

Where does he come from, she wonders, with his shabby sweatshirt, his worn-out backpack?

"What did you mean, earlier?" Mei whispers, as he spreads the tent flat on the grass. He is reading the directions. "About things not being real?"

"You've probably heard it before," he says, without looking up.

She waits for him to say more.

"When we're dreaming," he says, "we can't tell that we're dreaming. Right?"

"Okay," she says.

"So if we can't tell that we're dreaming when we really are dreaming," he says, "then, theoretically, if we were dreaming right now, we would have no way of knowing that."

These words in his voice—they're like live current, the electricity of big ideas.

"But actually," he says, "some philosophers think that the whole argument is a moot point. They think that consciousness itself is just one big delusion."

Something bold and brave is surging in her: "I like the way you talk about things," she says.

But he does not look up. Maybe it was the wrong thing to say.

He is still staring at the tent poles, studying the directions, squinting in the light of the flashlight. Somewhere a siren screams. The helicopters go on swirling through the air.

"Do you need some help?" she says.

"I guess so," he says. He hands the instructions to her. But she does not need them: she knows what to do, from years of family trips. She is soon feeding the poles into the sleeves while he holds the flashlight.

"I haven't been completely honest with you," he says.

Her whole body goes tense. A prickling on her skin. She is suddenly aware of the chill in the evening air.

"What do you mean?" she says.

She doesn't know what to do except to keep working on the tent. There's the shuffle of nylon against nylon. All at once, the tent is up, like a ship in a bottle.

"Have you heard of Baker & Baker?" he says.

Television commercials come into her head: pharmaceuticals.

"Yeah?" she says.

"That's my family," he says, like it's some kind of confession.

"I grew up in a gated community. I went to boarding school. My whole life has been paid for by dirty money."

It's true she had not pictured it, this boy in a ratty sweatshirt, old shoes. But there's something about him: he is all present, no past. As if nothing he can do can surprise her.

"But I don't want that life," he says. There's a kind of desperation in his voice, as if he expects her to be angry. "I think it's wrong to live that way."

Now she wonders what he would think of how her family lives, of her father the accountant and her mother the teacher, a Volvo parked in the driveway.

She shows him where to put the stakes for the tent. Together, they hammer them into the ground.

He's in the tent now, kneeling, as he rolls out a sleeping bag inside. He drops the flashlight inside, so that the tent lights the lawn blue like a lantern. It is not very big, this tent, and she likes the idea of them crouched inside it together, that nearness.

He sits down on the grass. He looks up at the sky. He seems so sad sitting there, this mysterious boy.

She sits down next to him. Suddenly his face is close to hers.

A sudden kiss. She does not even think of how they shouldn't be doing it. It's quick and fast. It's shy.

And then he is saying something about the stars, how they can't see them anymore because of all the emergency lights, and how his dream is to just live in the woods somewhere and sleep under the stars.

"I want to live on the same amount of money that the poorest people in the world do," he says. "That's my goal. I think that's the most ethical thing."

Everything in his mind is either one thing or the other. Right or wrong. There's a thrill in that clarity.

He motions for her to crawl into the tent.

She sees now how it will happen, how there's no need to discuss it in advance, as if she can feel it already, the warmth of his arm beside hers before they fall asleep.

But then suddenly he is up and out of the tent again and standing in the grass.

"You sleep in the tent," he says. "I'll sleep out here."

In the morning, none of the sales reps wake up.

A mass suicide is what it looks like, their bodies splayed out in the living room, their hair hanging over their faces, their mouths slightly ajar, saliva pooling on the planks of the floor. But if you listen closely, you can hear the sounds of their living: the slow breaths of deep sleep.

One of their phones keeps ringing. There is a lot of information in that sound, the way it rings so often that it is hard to tell when one call ends and the next begins: the ringing of a person gone crazy with worry. But here in this room, no one is stirring.

There is something terrible about the way the sun streams in over their faces, as if the sunlight were a part of it—and isn't it true that the sun has turned ominous lately, parching the land deeper and deeper into drought?

According to the experts, there is no way to distinguish by sight alone between the sickness and sleep, but Mei can tell right away what this is. It's a deep settling in, a blankness of the face, and they look younger, somehow, than they did the night before, this the kind of knowledge that can never be captured in the results of an experiment or in the lens of a camera, the human mind the only instrument subtle enough to register it.

If, somehow, the sales reps could see up through their dreams, here is what they would find, refracted, at the surface: A boy and a girl with white masks on their faces, bent over their nine bodies in the vast living room of strangers. The press of the boy's fingers—in kitchen gloves they've found under the sink—searching their wrists for the beating of their hearts. The sensation of liquid running down their chins as the girl drips water from a child's sippy cup into each drying mouth. They would hear the sound of the boy's voice getting angry in the other room: *But we've been waiting all day for an ambulance.* And finally, the feeling of someone, that same boy, lifting each one up by the armpits, while the girl holds tight to their legs, the swing of their bodies like sandbags. Then the smell of leather seats. Then the makeshift click of seatbelts over their slumped bodies. The crank of a garage door. The turning of an ignition. The bump of the old streets beneath the tires, their heads swinging forward or back with the turns in the road. And maybe: a glimpse of pine trees, the mountains, the wide sunsetting sky, their bodies so long attuned to the rising and setting of that same sun—but suddenly no longer.

32.

From the window of the third floor of the hospital, now sealed for ten days, Catherine watches helicopters come and go—with supplies and with food. Garbage is piling up on the streets below.

There is something monstrous about the suits that she and the other healthcare workers now wear when in the isolation ward, the way the plastic distorts the faces of the doctors and the nurses, the way it muffles their voices. They look larger in those suits. Less human. People get spooked.

At the back doors of the hospital, sleepers have begun to appear slumped alone against the glass, abandoned like newborns or drug addicts, notes pinned to their shirts. Rumors are flourishing: anyone exposed will be detained.

Seventy miles away in Catherine's townhouse in Los Angeles, Catherine's daughter and her daughter's babysitter are quarantined, too. This is a precaution, in case Catherine brought the virus back home—on her clothes, maybe, or on her skin, or in the very air she breathed as she kissed her daughter's cheeks after those first few visits to Santa Lora.

She should have been more careful, she keeps thinking.

Her phone conversations with her daughter always end the same way: *Okay, but Mama, now can I go outside?*

She has begun to misbehave, says the babysitter, in unfamiliar ways. She pulls on the curtains. She throws her food on the floor. She runs in circles through the house.

The babysitter, so patient otherwise, has begun to sound weary on the phone.

On the following Sunday, Catherine spots from the window a small church congregation meeting outdoors, having dragged the pews out into the parking lot to limit the airborne spread.

There is something about it, those families in their pews, those Bibles in their hands, the faint strains of their hymns floating in the open air—tears come into Catherine's eyes. She has never been away from her daughter so long.

One night, Catherine watches a crowd of people swarm a helicopter at the high school nearby, as it tries to land with a shipment of food.

After that, one of the ER doctors pulls her aside:

"We're moving the opioids out of the pharmacy," he says. He is very thin, this doctor, a new beard spreading across his face. He speaks quickly. None of the staff are sleeping much. The lack shows in this man's eyes. "Now that the town is cut off," says the ER doctor, "street drugs aren't going to be able to get in, either. It's only a matter of time before they come looking here."

"Who?" says Catherine. But she knows who he means. He speaks of them like animals. But she wants him to say it.

"Addicts," he says.

Addiction is not her specialty, but she often sees it in her patients. And why not? Those drugs soothe the same parts of the brain that mental illness sets on fire.

"If there's going to be violence in this hospital," says the ER doctor, "that's how it will happen."

She can see it in this doctor's eyes, how clearly he can picture it: the drug-addicted, like zombies, overrunning the hospital. Worry, she often reminds her patients, is a kind of creativity. Fear is an act of the imagination.

"From now on," says the ER doctor, "you and I are the only ones who will know the exact location of these drugs."

More and more doctors fall sick.

Catherine finds herself performing procedures she has not done since medical school. How strange the sewing needle feels in her hand, the coarse thread, as she stiches up a cut on the forehead of a young boy, after he slips near one of the overflowing toilets. And how odd is the heft of a newborn's head at the moment he finally slips out of his mother and into Catherine's gloved hands—while the only obstetrician in the hospital goes on dreaming in the isolation ward.

A few days later, Catherine finds the ER doctor slumped in an office chair in what was previously the waiting room. It is less and less surprising, how suddenly this sleep takes over the body, though his breathing seems even slower than the others'.

Two orderlies in blue suits are moving him to the isolation ward, when a bottle of pills falls from his pocket.

"Wait," says Catherine. "It's not the sickness," she says. It's

OxyContin. An opium sleep. No wonder he knew so clearly what others might do.

For this, at least, there is a cure, a temporary one, anyway: one shot of naloxone in the thigh. He opens his eyes, awake and embarrassed. He avoids her after that.

That night, Catherine gets a call from her daughter's babysitter.

"She has a fever," says the babysitter. Catherine's breath catches. The sickness, they have come to understand, starts that way, too. If something happens to her daughter, it will be Catherine's fault, she is certain.

"I didn't want to worry you," says the babysitter. "But she fell asleep a few hours ago, and I'm having trouble waking her."

Now it is Catherine's turn to imagine the worst in florid detail.

A crazy simplicity cuts through everything else: she must get home to her daughter.

She will leave this hospital, which no one has left for two weeks. She will leave this town, surrounded by soldiers and military vehicles.

She peels off her gloves and rushes downstairs.

She does not even make it past the front door. There are guards, of course. This is not a voluntary quarantine.

Catherine spends the whole night on the phone with the babysitter. On the small screen of her phone, her sleeping daughter looks just like the sick do. Sometime after midnight, she realizes with a burst of panic that she cannot remember the exact color of her little girl's eyes. People comment on it, an unusual shade of hazel, but she cannot picture it. She cannot remember her own daughter's eyes.

Finally, at 3 A.M., relief: her daughter opens her eyes and asks the babysitter for water.

This is not the sickness, then, just an ordinary childhood fever.

The sound of her daughter's little voice on the phone releases in her a tenderness for the whole world, for everyone, awake and asleep, in this hospital. It feels like a drug spreading through her body. It feels like the moment her daughter was born.

33.

At the center of that hospital, in the wing where the first patients are now tended by nurses in Level 4 Tyvek suits, beneath the sheets of one particular bed, beneath the thin cloth of the hospital gown, and beneath the smooth skin of the belly of one young woman: a tiny heart begins to beat. It is a secret, fluttering, hummingbird beat, four weeks in the making.

Rebecca experiences none of the emotions she otherwise would, pregnant by accident at eighteen—the panic, the disbelief, the excruciating need to make a decision.

Ten feet away, dreaming in another hospital bed, Caleb feels none of that, either.

The whole thing, too young yet to call a fetus, has grown to the size of a pea.

A face is beginning to surface from the tissue of the head, the earliest components of eyes. Those eyes: they will show her everything she will ever see. Passages are forming that will one day become the inner ear. Those ears will deliver every voice, every note of music, every drop of rain, she will ever hear in her life. Already, there is an opening that will later become the mouth, the same mouth that, if mother and child survive, might ask, someday, what God is and why we need the wind, or where she was, anyway, before she was inside her mother's belly.

In the room, the monitors hum and whir. The suits swish as nurses and doctors come and go, performing the same diagnostic tests they have been doing from the start: the massaging of the sternum, the tickling of toes. No change.

Nutrients travel through a plastic tube up through one nostril, then down her throat and into her stomach.

Meanwhile, Rebecca sleeps and sleeps, the conscious brain, it turns out, as superfluous to the process unfolding inside her as the sunflowers that are right now wilting on the windowsill beside her.

34.

He sleeps when she sleeps. He wakes when she wakes, which is six times or eight times or ten times a day. And every one of these wakings is also a remembering, a collecting again of the facts: Ben is alone with his six-week-old baby.

Wherever he goes, he is the man with a newborn curled up on his chest. You should stay home, he is told again and again. That's the safest place to be. But he has to go out, for formula and for diapers—they've started handing out supplies at the high school.

No one can tell him where his wife is. Not the operators who answer the phones at the hospital. Not the soldiers outside the emergency room. Not even the paramedics, on that first night, sheathed in blue suits and white masks—as they lifted Annie up from the kitchen floor, her fingers fluttering slightly, the way they always do when she sleeps—could say exactly where it was she would go.

The morning after, when the nurse comes to take the baby's temperature, she wears plastic goggles and a full-body suit. The baby cries and cries. Already the baby can recognize what is ordinary and what is not.

That nurse never comes again.

Every so often, a Humvee drifts down the street. An ambulance roars by. The neighbors come and go from their houses, tense and watchful. But all Ben can see is the face of his baby. All he can hear is her crying. The only way she will sleep is in the bend of his arm, her lips going loose against a bottle. All his clothes smell like urine and sour milk and the sweet stink of her diapers. There is no time to take a shower. There is no time to wash his face. Dirty laundry litters the floor.

One of Annie's colleagues stops by those first few days with formula and wipes. "Doesn't it seem like no one knows what they're doing?" she says, arms crossed, voice shaking a little. "I don't think they know what the hell they're doing."

They are not very close, this woman and Annie, but they have lived in this town for only three months, and you ask whoever you can.

Annie, Annie, Annie: her name sounds suddenly sacred—and strange—rendered somehow extraordinary by not saying it thirty times a day. *Come home,* he whispers, like a prayer.

He calls his mother in Ohio every day. She wants to fly out, but it's no use, he tells her, whispering into the phone, while the baby dozes on his chest. "They would never let you in."

It has been decades since he has felt this way about his mother, the simple need for her presence. "You should have let me come when she was born," she says, but he and Annie had decided in advance that they wanted to be alone with the baby for a while before letting their parents come. He sees now that this was a teenager's notion of what it is like to be an adult. "If I had come when she was born," says his mother, "then I'd be trapped there with you now and could help."

Sometimes, he is so tired that it does not sound so bad: to fall asleep and not wake up.

Scraps of news from public radio drift through the house between feedings. Six hundred cases and counting. Seven hundred.

In Los Angeles, seventy miles away, the stores have run out of masks; people are stockpiling food in case the sickness spreads.

Every ordinary thing turns ominous. A black bulldog wanders leashless in the street. Somewhere nearby, a teakettle whines for many hours. A trickle of water runs all day through the gutter, as if someone somewhere has collapsed while watering the lawn.

On the third day, when Annie's friend does not arrive when she said she would, and when she does not answer her phone, Ben does not need to be told why.

After that, he sets up a system with his mother—he will call her every morning. "If I don't call you by eight," he says, "call the police." But time with a newborn is shifty. The hours roll away. On the third day, Grace wakes up wailing and spitting up, and he forgets to call his mother—something is happening to his memory, some kind of disintegration. Two hours pass before he looks at his phone. Ten missed calls and a message: his mother has called the police.

"Thank God," she says when he finally calls her back, and that rush of relief in her voice, like some kind of high—he understands it right then for the first time in his life: the special suffering of loving a child. "So," she says, her breathing still quick in the phone. "What did you say when the police showed up?"

"They didn't," he says.

Two days later, a police officer arrives with a crew of workers in blue suits.

"We have a report," says the officer, "that there might be a sick man here, and that there might be a newborn baby alone in this house."

"That was two days ago," says Ben.

The police officer sighs through his mask. His eyes look tired and red.

After that, Ben leaves the windows open all the time. His mind is fertile with visions of a terrible future. If the windows are open when he goes under, maybe some good stranger will hear his baby crying before the dehydration takes her away.

In a surge of the kind of unlikely luck that is just as possible in a disaster as it is in daily life, Ben eventually tracks Annie down. Someone on the phone at the hospital can finally confirm that she is a patient, his Annie. But not in a regular room. She has been moved to the campus library, says the woman on the phone, which has been converted into a ward. No one can enter the building, which, like the hospital, is quarantined and guarded, but, says the woman on the phone, the thing about the library, she says, as if passing on a secret that is not hers to share: there are floor-to-ceiling windows.

When he gets there with the baby, he finds a small group of people already crowded near those windows, just normal people in white paper masks, a few children, holding hands with their parents. Soon the soldiers will fence off this whole area, but for now, on this day, it is still possible to press two hands against the tinted glass and peek in.

Here is what he sees inside: maybe fifty beds, lined up in rows, someone sleeping in each one, a few nurses or orderlies in blue suits moving between the beds. The old lamps and the tables have been pushed to one side of that vast room, the books looking down from their shelves.

He does not see her right away, but soon he notices someone in the far corner with curly brown hair. And he knows immediately that it's her. He takes a sharp breath that jolts the baby on his chest. "There she is," he whispers to the baby, his lips making contact with her bald head as he speaks. It is upsetting to see Annie that way, lying flat on her back, the tubes, but it is also a relief. It's her, it's Annie, and she looks like herself, the way she looks on the rare mornings when he wakes before she does. It is a comfort to know where she sleeps.

He pulls the baby out of the carrier and holds her up to the window to see, her little legs curling up under her like a bug. A newborn's eyes cannot see more than four feet into the distance, say the books, but by now, he has stopped trusting those books. Babies know so much more than the experts think—he is sure. There is a difference between what is not true and what cannot be measured.

"Do you see her?" he says. "Do you see?"

But even then, even as he stares at Annie's body, even as he knows for certain that this is her, that this is his wife's hand lying on her lap, that this is his wife's hair falling in her face, even then, with the proof of her right there, the same questions bob back to him anyway: Where are you? Where have you gone?

But also, somehow, there is this: walks with the baby at sunrise when he can spend not one more minute in the house, her little body zipped into his fleece and her eyes squinting shut in the sunshine, the crunch of his footsteps in the woods.

He spends all day telling her the words for things. Those are the mountains, he says as they walk. This is a lake. This here is a hummingbird, hovering over the neighbor's bougainvillea, and that buzzing up there, that's called a helicopter, and it is hovering, too. And the sky, that sky, so clear of clouds and blue. Blue. That's what we call that color: blue. She stares at everything as if in amazement. She begins to babble. That little voice. This is the voice of his daughter. A surprising feeling sometimes surges in his chest, quick and bittersweet, a little guilty, even, given the circumstances, but what other word for it is there but this: *joy*.

He tries to commit it all to memory, every small smile and every new trick—this is how he misses Annie most, as the person who would want to know the baby at this level of detail, the contents of her diaper, the long-awaited burp, that thing she does with her toes, the scale of the love expressed in minutiae. He tries writing it down, but it is all whooshing past him. It would take as long to retell it as it does to live through it. The only way to preserve these days for Annie would be to preserve every hour, every minute. In one way, at least, this time is just like any other: it goes.

35.

In the beds in the hospital and in the cots in the library, and in the giant tents rippling across the college quad, and in the cots set up in the dining halls, and in the cots set up in the classrooms, and in the brand-new tents, a second wave, built from supplies meant for use in Liberia or New Guinea, and in the special tents set up for the soldiers who themselves have now begun to slip under, and in anonymous beds in anonymous houses now scattered throughout Santa Lora—the dreamers go on dreaming.

There is a feeling that the town is emptying out, though no one is going anywhere. The sensation persists among the survivors, though, a feeling of exodus, as if we can all sense without knowing it, like lights in the periphery, the consciousness flashing in other people's heads.

At this point, it becomes hard to keep an accurate count of cases. A thousand, they think. Maybe more.

The hair grows. The fingernails curl. There are not enough workers to keep the toenails clipped or the faces shaved. And besides, these tasks are dangerous to perform with hands wrapped in three pairs of latex gloves.

More of them are dying than before. Malnutrition. Dehydration.

If a bedsore appears and fails to heal, there is not always someone nearby to notice.

The Victorians famously feared being mistaken for dead and then buried alive, but now the opposite begins to happen in Santa Lora—some of the people lying so quietly in those cots are mistaken instead for alive.

36.

Observant watchers might have noticed them by now: a scattering of civilians working alongside the National Guard. There they are, unloading boxes of food at the high school, their jeans stark blue against the green of fatigues. And there they are again, setting up cots in the campus chapel. Among these volunteers are two college kids, faces never quite clear, rushing here and there.

But one of their mothers notices, in the background of a news photo—isn't that her daughter, that girl handing out masks? It is a relief to see her alive. And who is that boy beside her, unpacking those boxes of plastic suits?

Mei: a loose string pulled taut. There is so much confusion in Santa Lora, but some facts are obvious: they are awake, Mei and Matthew. They are alive. And they have two hands for helping and two feet for walking and a desire to do whatever they can. And it *is* like desire, like a craving, somewhere deep: to put themselves to use.

Matthew's dark eyes above his mask, the echo of his voice

through the paper, the way he always knows exactly what is right and what is wrong, as if nuance were a conspiracy made up by the weak—it feels good to be near him. They move in only the one direction: to wherever they are needed. They are always together, always, as if operating as a single unit, the way his arms tense, for example, as he lifts her up by the hips to peek into windows to search for the sleeping and the dead.

She keeps forgetting to charge her phone. She keeps forgetting to call her parents—she has no idea that her mother has joined the group of other parents and relatives camped out in cars a few miles outside of town, waiting and waiting for news. But can it really be true that a week has already passed since she spoke to her mother? Time here is as slippery as it is in a dream.

They are only eighteen years old, but the past has fallen away. The future has shrunk down to this, like a shadow foreshortened suddenly at midday.

They run errands for whoever needs help. They use the last of the gas in the SUV to bring food from the high school to the nursing home. They find the sick in houses and in cars, sometimes slumped on sidewalks or benches.

One day, they wander past the Humane Society, and hear the dogs howling and whimpering through the walls. Mei is the one who spots, through the window, a man passed out at the front desk. The doors are locked.

They do not discuss what to do—Matthew simply picks up a trash can and throws it through the glass.

The cats cry out when they hear the window shatter.

Who knows how long these animals have gone hungry? Matthew throws open the cages. Two dozen cats and dogs spill out the front doors, while Mei empties big bags of food onto the sidewalk.

As they're leaving, two men wander in through the broken glass and then rush out with boxes under their arms.

"Probably drugs," says Matthew. "Horse tranquilizers and shit. But who are they harming?"

On another day, they come across a section of sidewalk oddly darkened by water. The sun is out. The air is dry and clear. They can't tell, right away, where the water is coming from. But when Mei steps into the yard of the nearest house, the grass is swampy beneath her feet. The water, they see, is quietly streaming out of an open window.

Through the screen, they discover this uncanny sight: the ripple of standing water, knee-deep, in a living room. A hidden flood.

That water, they know, may as well be blood—the people inside might have drowned in their sleep. How quickly human spaces, unattended, come to rot.

"Maybe no one's home," says Mei. Books and papers float on the surface, furniture knocking like boats. "Maybe this happened after they left."

"Or maybe they're inside," says Matthew.

There he is: her boy. He is already kicking off his sandals, swinging one leg over the windowsill. The sound of a splash. Mei hangs back, a pang of admiration and fear. It might be contaminated, that water. From inside, he opens the front door and releases a gush of water out onto the porch.

"Come on," he says. And she comes.

Inside is the soft sound of running water. It is coming down the stairs in a thin but steady stream.

Parts of the ceiling have caved in. Through those holes, they look up and see the walls of an upstairs bedroom, water pouring around the edges like a sinkhole.

"I don't think it's safe to be in here," says Mei.

But Matthew is already heading for the stairs.

He is a little excited, a chance to save a life.

"We have to see if anyone is here," he says.

But Mei's fear comes washing back: this is too much. She has the sensation that something terrible might be hidden in this water, creatures unseen. Or bodies. Unconscious, a person can drown in only a few inches of water.

"We should call the police," she says, but she knows as she says it that this is an idea from a different time—who knows when they could make it here?

Soon, like jumping off a cliff, she takes a deep breath and she follows him up those stairs. The carpet is spongy beneath her bare feet. Water is dripping down the wallpaper.

"It's the sink," Matthew calls down to her. She hears the squeak of a fixture turning off. "It was leaking from a pipe under the sink."

Mei kicks into something hard, a laptop submerged.

"Holy shit," says Matthew. "Look."

On an antique four-poster bed, as if floating on a raft, a man with white hair and glasses is lying, fully clothed, on his back. He looks so alone, this man—the shape of his life suggested by the fact that two strangers have found him before anyone else has.

Mei leans down toward him and hears no breathing. She puts a hand on his chest, and there it is, the relief of that rising and falling.

"He's alive," she says.

Matthew turns him over and gently moves his limbs back and forth, an idea they have that this needs to be done to prevent sores.

On the floor all around the bed are journals, the ink mostly leached off the pages, smears of blue and black ink, the letters lifted away.

"Wait," says Mei. "I think this is my biology professor." Those classes are beginning to seem hazy, but she liked him, this professor, his obsession with trees.

By now, they have driven dozens of sick to the medical tents. This professor of biology makes one more.

When they sleep, they sleep in the tent, as if that big house has become a source of two kinds of contaminants, not just the sickness but something else, too, a kind of decadence in a time of suffering.

But they sleep as little as possible—there is so much work to be done. And the nights are for doing, too. Everything is urgent. Everything is new, even the way he reaches for her in the dark, his mouth finding hers so quickly, the press of his body against her. There's no talking. No lights. There is almost no thinking. Here is the same clarity that drives them all day.

After that, they sleep hard, not waking for hours, the sleep of the young and the tired, and of bodies exhausted from purpose. The stutter of helicopters no longer wakes them from their dreams. They have learned to sleep through the sirens, too, and the rumblings of Humvees. They sleep through the worry, also, which floats free in this town like a sound.

Meanwhile, in the woods that loom over the tent, the crickets perform their own ancient rituals while the bark beetles hollow out the trees, slowly, slowly felling them.

In another time, under the watchful eyes of the girls of the dorm floor, Mei might have wondered what it was that was happening between them, whether she and Matthew were a real couple or not. But she is not thinking much about any of that. They are connected like this: two people in peril every day. Here he is beside her. Here is his hand, laced in hers at the end of the day. Here is his hip pressed into hers in the night. What does it matter what they call it? How about this, she thinks, as she floats off to sleep one night, nursing the kind of grand idea she would never speak aloud: a love for the end of the world.

37.

Every tensed muscle must eventually relax. Adrenaline cannot flow unending. At a certain point, a new feeling begins to dominate these long homebound hours: boredom.

This is how it comes to be that Sara and Libby resurrect one of their oldest games, to go exploring in their own house, to open the drawers they are not allowed to open, to comb the closets they are not supposed to enter. Their father is a keeper of secrets, and there is usually some small thing to find.

It does not need to be said out loud what kind of treasure they are really after: traces that their mother once lived in this house. This is how they have learned most of what they know of her days on earth. She wore pastel nail polishes and faintly silver eye shadow; she once bought eight jars of baby food and one bottle of wine at Ralphs; she once bought a book about Italian painters from the used-book store; she once took a watercolor class at the college; she was once prescribed antibiotics for pneumonia and was late to pay the bill. She once got a speeding ticket. She had a library card. A driver's license. She kept a photograph of the girls in her wallet.

"I know you're going to say we shouldn't," says Libby, suddenly cheerful with possibility—or risk. "But let's check the attic."

The attic: the only time that little door has ever creaked open is for the few moments it takes for their father to set the mousetraps in the corners. Those mice—or else the possibility of some creature much worse lurking up there—have always kept them clear of the attic.

But on this day, Sara surprises her sister. "Okay," she says. "Let's go."

The door is locked but Libby knows where their father keeps the key. The door sticks a little in its frame, but one hard push and it flies open.

It is smaller than Sara thought, this attic, and a little brighter, too. Sunlight is streaming in through a dusty oval-shaped window, the light catching on the fluttering wings of moths.

Mouse droppings litter the floorboards. There is a stink in the air.

But this, too: a stack of cardboard boxes, sealed shut. Libby goes straight for them, as if she knows just what she is looking for.

Maybe Sara has seen these boxes, too, years earlier—because when Libby slides one of them toward her, it does not surprise her to see what is written on the side, in their father's handwriting, all caps: the letters of their mother's name. MARIE.

"Did you know these were here?" says Sara.

"I've been up here before," says Libby.

It is a shock that her sister has kept this small secret, that she has maintained any private life in this house.

"But I've never opened them," she says. And Sara has the feeling that this might be true or it might not be.

The cats have followed them in through the open door and are sniffing around. Daisy soon finds a mouse, a dead one stuck in a trap.

"Let's open these downstairs," says Sara.

They hide their trail into these boxes, like thieves. They are careful with the tape. Their fingers get dusty with the work of it.

As Sara pulls back the last bit of tape on the first box, an intense anticipation rises in her body, as if these boxes might finally answer some unanswered question, as if they might finally tell the girls who she was.

The first box is full of clothes.

These were her clothes, Sara thinks to herself as she lays them out on the couch, like sacred relics.

"I think I remember this one," says Libby. She holds a green one up to the light—moths have eaten holes in the sleeves.

"Really?" says Sara. She wants to remember them, too, these sweaters and these jeans. But this is the truth: those sweaters seem as alien as the ones that hang at the Salvation Army downtown.

Libby lays everything out on the living room floor. The summer dresses, the sandals, a set of black ceramic birds that say MADE IN PORTUGAL on the bottom, but bought in this country or that one—who knows? What they do know, or can assume, is that her hands once touched them, and so they want to touch them, too.

There is a tiny magic in a box of jewelry. This turquoise necklace hung on her neck, these silver hoops from her ears. But it is less than Sara wants to feel. There is a disappointment in objects.

But Libby is far away, deep in concentration, as if these things have succeeded in taking her somewhere else.

Something outside soon catches Sara's attention: the wanderings of a small black bulldog, who, at that moment, is lapping up what little water there is in the gutter. There is something familiar about the shape of his head, that red collar.

"Hey," says Sara. "Isn't that Akil's dog?" Akil: a private shimmer always accompanies his name. But this time, it comes with a new dread—why is his dog outside all alone?

"He must be lost," says Libby, face pressed up to the window. It is a relief to have her back. "Poor little guy," she says. "We should take him home."

Sara feels the weight of what her father would say. "We can't risk going outside again," she says.

She rushes to the bathroom. She is still busy with her bleeding, soaking the last of it up in her own made-up way: washcloths and toilet paper and not much walking around. Of all the supplies their father requisitioned, he never thought of this.

By the time she is out of the bathroom again, she hears the banging of the screen door hitting its frame, and then the unmistakable clink of a water bowl landing on the patio. Libby has corralled Akil's dog into the backyard.

He is friendly and grateful, this dog—what else could that wet look in those dark eyes mean? His tongue lolls wildly as he drinks, as if it has been a while since he has done it, the water splashing out of the bowl and onto Libby's bare feet. He does that thing dogs do with their teeth, an almost smile.

The cats are lined up at the kitchen window, scratching at the glass as Libby rubs that dog's back like he's hers. Libby's little brown curls fall over his ears as she lets him lick her mouth. They have this in common: they are both so quick to love.

His tags confirm who he is. Akil's last name and address are engraved on the piece of metal dangling from his thick neck. That tag, shaped like a bone, looks suddenly alien to Sara, like an artifact from a lost time, like touching a parallel world. The dog's name is Charlie.

"I should call Akil," says Sara. There is a certain excitement in the idea. But once the phone is in her hand, her heart begins to pound so hard she can't speak.

"I'll do it," says Libby.

But no one answers Akil's phone.

"Let's just walk him home," says Libby.

It is only a few blocks, but the neighborhood is full of soldiers in fatigues and big boots, rifles perched on their shoulders, and those trucks in camouflage, rumbling around like tanks.

"What if someone sees us?" says Sara. The soldiers might take them away: two girls living alone in a contaminated house.

But Libby is already sliding her bare feet into her white cowboy boots, no socks. She is tying a piece of old rope to Charlie's collar, a makeshift leash. She is going, she says, whether Sara comes or not. And anyway, there is a certain thrill in the idea: to do something nice for this boy.

They take the back way, through the dead and drying woods. They will never remember the way these woods looked before the drought. To these girls, it is the nature of this place that every tenth tree will be a dead one, a skeleton standing amid the ones still trying to survive.

There is a feeling, as they walk, of being watched. Every rustling of pine tree might be a soldier shifting his weight, every fluttering of wings a whisper. They walk fast.

But they see no one, not in the woods and not on the streets they glimpse through the trees. Sometimes, the air is so quiet that it feels like they are the last ones left awake.

Through the trees, Akil's house looks the way it always does: those big clean windows, the red curtains, the potted plants on the porch. The garage door is open, leaving exposed the bicycles bunched in the corner and Akil's science fair project, a model for some kind of robot. Beside it are three suitcases stacked against the wall—is that the luggage they brought with them from Egypt, she wonders, when they left in the middle of the night?

A shiver of shyness moves through her body.

Only later will Sara think about the lights, how the porch light is on in the middle of the day, how the chandelier in the dining room is blazing like it's night.

And then Charlie is suddenly sprinting across the street, up onto the porch and right into the house. This is when they realize: the front door is standing open.

"Hello?" says Libby.

Akil's green backpack is slumped by the door. Books are scattered everywhere.

They are inside for only a minute, just long enough to discover a dinner spread out on the table, flies drifting from the soup to the bread.

Charlie is barking and barking.

"We shouldn't be here," says Sara, and at the same time, she notices what they should have seen before: a drippy black X spray-painted on the front door.

Oh, Akil: to survive one terrible thing, and then be caught by something else. Tears rush into Sara's eyes.

Someone is suddenly shouting at them.

"Hey, girls," a man's voice is calling. A neighbor is leaning out from an upper window of the house next door. He has a full mask on his face. "Get away from that house."

They run all the way home through the woods, pinecones cracking beneath their feet. Charlie runs with them, suddenly silent, his black fur going dusty.

Once they are home, sitting, panting in the yard, a new worry comes to Sara:

"What if he has it on his fur?"

So they pull out the hose. They put their gloves on first and long sleeves, but they forget to wear the masks. Sara sprays him from far away, as far away as possible. What they do not think of is how much he will shake once he's wet. He shakes that water all over the vegetables. He shakes water all over them. Then it's their turn to take showers.

"Try to hold your breath," says Sara as the steam fills the bathroom, but it is too many minutes. They breathe it right in.

They feed the cats. They change the litter. They arrange and re-arrange their mother's things.

That same afternoon, when a terrier comes wandering down the street, his leash snaking behind him, tangling with the fences, Libby runs out and scoops him up, too.

Now they have two dogs to feed. Two dogs and five cats.

From the widow's walk, the neighborhood seems drained of neighbors. Whenever the helicopters float briefly out of earshot, a strange quiet rushes in: no lawnmowers whirring, no children yelling, no basketballs bouncing in driveways. No buzzing of ga-rage doors opening and closing on tracks. No slamming of car doors. No one is out for a run. In the house across the street, a television has been flickering, unattended, for days. And some-where out there, their father sleeps.

But the birds go on singing. The squirrels rummage through the garbage, which has not been collected for days. A group of stray cats has started living in the wreckage of the nurse's house across the street.

At these times, and these times only, Sara feels suddenly grateful for the rumbling of a Humvee—proof that she and Libby are not the last ones left.

That night, Sara falls asleep in one of their mother's sweaters.

38.

In other parts of the country, certain skeptics remain. A new hashtag begins to trend: #SantaLoraHoax.

The government, they are sure, knows more than it is saying. That's the real reason they've cut off the town: to hide whatever it is they have done.

The only thing that's real are the soldiers. That's what this is really about: an excuse to let the government take control. Think about it. Santa Lora is probably only the beginning, a test case.

Or if it is real, it's our own damn fault. It might be Russia that's behind this, or North Korea. Some kind of nerve agent, maybe, released by a drone. Haven't we been asking for something like this for years? Going around the world and dropping our bombs? Or more likely, the government just wants us to *think* we're under attack.

Just open your eyes, people. If you really believe this Santa Lora story, then you probably think that the fluoride in the water really is for our teeth and that a passenger airplane really did crash into the Pentagon on 9/11.

And have you heard the latest numbers? Fifteen hundred cases in six weeks? Come on, nothing spreads that fast.

39.

It is around this time that Ben's dreams begin. They come quickly when they do. No matter how brief his sleep, the dreams rush in immediately, as if his consciousness can hardly keep them away. And always—always—at the center of these dreams, like a song that lives for days in his head, is Annie. In the dreams, she comes back to him in the smallest possible ways, in the form of things he did not know he knew: the click of her ChapStick rolling across the counter, the crisp scent of her practical soap, the way she lets her nails grow until they break, so that they're always a little ragged and each one a different length. Sometimes, he dreams of what she sounds like moving through the rooms of the house, the flush of the toilet through the wall, the small splash of her spit landing in the sink, or her humming interrupted by the stubbing of her toe, once again, on the same loose floorboard she always trips on, that small familiar chirp: "Shit."

These dreams always end the same way: with the wailing of the baby for milk.

———

Walking soothes the baby. And it soothes Ben, too, and what else is there to do? So they walk: two, three, four times a day.

This is a pine tree, he says as they drift once again down their street, and here is a pinecone. This is our shadow, yours and mine, long on the sidewalk because the sun is low in the sky at this time of year. And what we call it, this season, is fall.

Those people on that porch, he says, his eyes going watery, that woman looking weary and saying, "No, no, we have to stay inside again today"—we call her a mother. And that boy in the doorway, we call him her son.

Here is a sidewalk, he says. Here is a street. Here a spider web. A birdhouse. A car.

But not everything is so easy to name.

What are the right words for this: someone in a blue plastic suit who is crawling around in the middle of the street.

Ben and the baby are half a block away when he notices. The person's hands are pulling at the rubber of his hood, yanking at the mask, the movements urgent but inefficient. Panic is a feeling you can recognize from a hundred feet away. Finally, those hands succeed in lifting that hood up and off the head. A face is revealed: a young man with sweaty black hair.

He is saying something, this man, sounds without meaning, an urgent mumbling. Something is wrong with his eyes— a blankness.

Ben steps back. His arms encircle the baby on his chest, as if the muscles of his wrists are separate from him, as if they know what to do before his mind can decide.

"Are you okay?" Ben calls out to the man.

But the man does not answer, this man in the blue plastic suit, and he does not turn his head. Instead, he begins to climb onto the hood of a parked station wagon. His feet keep slipping because of the booties he is wearing over his shoes.

A few neighbors now appear at their windows.

"Are you okay?" Ben calls out again.

But it is obvious what this is: the man is asleep, a walking dream. What is not clear is where he came from or who he is—a paramedic, maybe, left behind by his crew?

For a moment, his mumbling turns clearer, swiftly rising to a shout: "I can't swim," he says to no one. "Help me. Please. I can't swim."

A few people have collected on their porches now, watching, but they stay where they are: the unkindness of fear.

Ben is sure he would do something to help if he didn't have the baby, her warm head resting against his chest. The baby makes everything simple. All he can do is get her away from this man. All he can do is get her home.

He calls 911 on the way. An ambulance will come, he is told. But it takes a long time. Ben can hear the man shouting for more than an hour, his voice drifting farther away, as Ben fastens and unfastens one diaper and then another and as he opens another package of formula.

All this time, while the man is shouting on another street, Ben's baby girl stares at Ben's face, as if she understands every-thing better than he does, and her whole growing up will be a slow coming-to. "Someone will help him," he says to her, as if she has asked or accused. "Someone will help."

If Ben were to turn on his television at that moment, he would discover that one of the news helicopters has begun to trail the man in the blue suit, so that millions of people are watching live as he zigzags down the street, disappearing at one point into the woods and then reemerging, barefoot, a few minutes later.

Ben is not one of the millions who see what happens next: how the man walks right into the path of a speeding Humvee.

But six blocks away, Ben hears the sound—a screeching of brakes, a breaking of glass—not knowing, or at least having no proof, that the man in the blue suit, this volunteer from Tennessee, as the world will soon learn, has been crushed beneath those oversized wheels.

The dreams: the more often they come, the stranger they are. Maybe it's the sleep deprivation. Maybe it's the isolation. Maybe something is happening to his mind. Whatever it is, these are not normal dreams. They contain, somehow, the heft of lived life. It's hard to explain, but there's a sensation that these experiences are real, as real as anything in his waking life.

At first, he dreams of the past: he and Annie in their old neighborhood in New York, he and Annie at a concert, cold beers in their hands, the feel of her waist in the dark as they sway to the music, real days unspooling in her dorm room, real afternoons in the park.

But he does not dream of that trip they took to Italy. He does not dream of their wedding. He never dreams of their favorite places: Venice, Mexico, the hammock in Maine. He dreams of her body—of course, of course. But he never dreams of her in that green dress he likes, or with glossed lips, or with her hair blown shiny and straight. Instead, he dreams of her in sweatpants. He dreams of her in smudged glasses. He dreams of her drinking a beer in her pajamas on their old vinyl couch in Brooklyn, the shape of her breasts just visible through that old T-shirt as she laughs. He dreams of her watching a documentary on his laptop. He dreams of those ice cream sandwiches she once made for a road trip—who makes ice cream sandwiches for the car?— the way they dripped and crumbled everywhere, the steering wheel sticky for weeks.

Sometimes he dreams of old arguments or small annoyances, how she never does the dishes and never takes out the trash, how she is never the one to think to buy the toilet paper, and how she was afraid to let them use the wobbly ceiling fan on the hottest night of the year. But there is a certain pleasure even in these dreams, the pleasure of problems that can be solved in the morning—with only a screwdriver and a stepladder, a quick trip to the drugstore.

And he never dreams, anymore, that Annie has left him for her advisor. In these new dreams, she is always at his side, sturdy and constant and calm.

He cannot always tell which are the real memories and which are not. Like those ice cream sandwiches, now that he thinks of it. "Did we really do that?" he asks the baby as he bathes her one morning in the kitchen sink, her eyes big and blank like a fish's. He can no longer remember where they were going with those ice cream sandwiches or whose car it was or how old they were then. Or that wedding in the middle of the woods—was that real? "Whose wedding was that?" Maybe that wedding was only a dream.

But this is when a certain strange sensation begins to come over him—the feeling that these dreams are somehow glimpses of days yet to come.

He dismisses it, of course. Of course. It's a crazy idea, like some kind of hallucination, he figures. An idea from the old stories he assigns to his students, where angels carry messages and witches speak in riddles, where kings and princes are visited by ghosts in their dreams.

Something is happening to his memory. For example, if his mind were working properly, would he have forgotten to clear the silverware from the kitchen sink before using the sink as a bathtub for the baby?

The serrated edge of a knife comes suddenly bobbing up in the soapy water near the baby's thigh. His horror comes in the shape of Annie's voice in his head: Ben, he hears her say, what the hell?

And this, too, didn't this, or something like it, happen once before, in a dream?

A symptom of delusion, he recalls, is the inability to distinguish between reality and dream.

One afternoon, Ben discovers what everyone else in town already knows: the two gas stations have run out of gas. More is coming, the soldiers keep saying, but they won't let the gas trucks through.

"Think about it," says the guy in front of Ben in line at the gas station, as Grace begins to cry in her seat. "Why would they want us to have gas in our cars? This way, we stay put, like sheep in a pen."

That night, he dreams of a beautiful sunny morning. They sleep late, he and Annie, luxuriously late. She goes out for chocolate croissants and strawberries. They spend the morning in bed, reading the paper and drinking coffee, the strap of her camisole sliding down her shoulder. What should we do today? she asks, stretching slowly, and the question comes with a feeling that they could do anything, anything at all. Time: that's what the dream is really about. There is so much time in this dream, endless hours to spend however they like. An intense feeling of leisure.

How painful it is when the dream slips away, the bed empty beside him, but in the wake of its leaving comes that odd feeling again, that this exact morning lies somewhere up ahead.

It takes a moment to remember what is missing from that dream: the baby.

Now he wants to check on her. He is suddenly desperate to see the baby.

When he gets to the crib, he sees right away that something is wrong. Her blanket—it has come undone. Her face is completely covered. What relief it is when he sees that she's fine under there, a little hot, maybe, but fine, and still asleep. But could she have suffocated? What if he hadn't woken up?

An outlandish idea is beginning to bubble in his mind. Or is it only a wish? That these dreams really are a sort of travel, a kind of vision of a time yet to come.

It isn't like him to think this way. He would never say it out loud, but he is different than he used to be, different from who he was before the baby. He believes in more—or is it less? It is so much harder to say, these days, what is true and what is not true. After all, the most unbelievable thing has already occurred— what could be more uncanny than an infant? Hadn't it required a certain magical thinking to believe that what was swelling beneath Annie's skin all those months really was a human being? And wasn't she a little otherworldly when she came? A *criatura*. That's the word that came to him, the Spanish word for a newborn, according to their book. A creature. She was born with a silky layer of hair all over her body. Fur, said Annie in delight. Lanugo, the doctor called it. Our baby has fur, she liked to say, as if Grace really had traveled from some supernatural realm. She knew exactly how to breathe without ever having done it. She knew exactly how to grasp a human finger. And isn't it true that even now, whenever Ben wakes in the night, worried about the baby in her crib, she answers right away—as if by some midnight telepathy—with a small and reassuring cry? The point is this: after all that, who is he to say what is possible and what is not?

Morning: there's a sudden dripping sound, and he cannot at first make sense of what he sees—coffee streaming across the kitchen counter and down the linoleum. He has turned on the coffeemaker while the carafe is still in the sink.

As he warms another bottle for the baby, his most recent dream still clinging to him, he begins to believe that maybe—he would never say it out loud, but maybe, maybe, like collective unconscious, like ESP, maybe—he really is seeing the future in his dreams.

40.

It is easy to mistake a wish for a fact, a hope for a lie, a better world for the one that is. For example, our children: we don't expect we'll ever lose them.

And so, when Ben finds his baby girl in her crib, sleeping late into the morning, it is hard for him to believe that anything might be wrong. She looks so much like she always does in sleep, those peach cheeks, those fat lips. Her eyelids are fluttering like they always do. Her little legs are pumping slightly as she snores. Nothing seems amiss, except for this: no matter what Ben does, she will not open her eyes.

"Come on," he says. She is so warm in his arms, and, if he puts his thumb in her palm, her fingers still close around it. "Come on, little nut."

But no tickling of her feet, no brushing of her cheek, no splashing of water on her face—none of it will rouse his daughter.

No matter that he has imagined this exact scenario constantly for weeks—all those visions turn out to be useless now, his worst fears proved flimsy by the real experience. This, this is ghastly: a sudden draining of meaning from the world.

Later, he will think of all the ways he might have saved her from this: maybe they should have stayed inside all this time, or left town earlier, broken the barricades—anything.

But for now, he just kneels down on the floor as if to pray or to beg.

"Please," he says, his hands on her chest like he might still find some magic there. "Please, wake up."

There is a reason that time seems to slow down in moments like these, a neurological process, discovered through experiment: in times of shock, the brain works faster—it takes more in. And so, some might say that this—the increased rate at which his neurons are firing—makes these first few seconds even more excruciating than they might otherwise be.

But forget all that. The only way to tell some stories is with the oldest, most familiar words: this here, this is the breaking of a heart.

41.

That night, something wakes Sara up.

Maybe it's the creak of the hinge in the front gate. Maybe it's the crunch of footsteps on the gravel of the driveway. Or the quick clearing of a man's throat on the front porch.

But these are possibilities that predate her awareness. The only thing she knows is that she is suddenly awake in the dark.

All she can hear, for now, is the drip-drip of a faucet, and the small stirrings of the kittens in their sleep, and one more slow metronome: the steady rhythm of her sister's breathing in the bed beside hers.

The room is warm from their bodies, and she can see her sister's face in the moonlight. But a strange sensation keeps creeping into her body, the feeling that she is alone in the room, that her sister is not there at all.

It's her sister's breathing—that's what it is: too slow. The possibility hits her with the heft of a fact: her sleep is too deep.

Maybe ten seconds pass between the moment this thought surfaces and the one when she's poking Libby's shoulder.

Libby wakes up right away.

"What are you doing?" says Libby. Her voice is scratchy and grouchy, and the most wonderful noise Sara has ever heard. It is hard to remember in the dark that every worry is more worrisome in the middle of the night.

Libby turns over in her sheets, already bobbing back to sleep. The clock glows midnight, and Sara aims for sleep, too. She is close to a doze, dipping in, when the kittens suddenly pop up from their box. Sara sees them in silhouette, eight ears twitching in the same direction, as if they have caught some ominous sound, too low for the girls to hear.

But then comes another noise, much louder: the tinkle of breaking glass.

Now she is up and out of bed. The cats are running everywhere. She is shaking Libby's shoulder.

"Get up," Sara whispers. "There's someone in the house."

This house is a hundred years old. The floor shudders whenever anyone takes a step. Huddled in a closet, the girls listen through the vent. Someone is moving around downstairs.

Her sister is so close she can feel her warm breath against her shoulder. She is so close she can feel her shaking.

Now the creak of the wood is replaced by the sticky smack of linoleum. Someone has passed into the kitchen.

The refrigerator swooshes open. It suctions closed. Open again. More steps. And then a crashing sound, as if someone has overturned the table. From the backyard, Charlie begins to bark.

"Maybe it's Daddy?" whispers Libby, a sudden blast of optimism.

"I don't think so," says Sara.

Now they hear the squeaking of hinges as the kitchen cabinets swing open and slam shut. There is a scraping sound. There is the clatter of dishes.

A few seconds of silence precede a terrible new noise: the creak of the stairs. Whoever it is—he is coming up. And he is coming quick.

Now the bedroom door clicks open. They hear the cats scurry away, their claws sliding on the wood.

In the closet, Libby is squeezing Sara's hand so hard it hurts. Her little nails are digging into her palm.

On the other side of the closet door, drawers are opening and closing. Things are crashing onto the floor. There's another sound, too, an intermittent static, like a radio or a walkie-talkie.

Every dark scene her father has ever painted comes flashing into Sara's mind: someone has come to hurt them. Maybe it's the government, like in that movie their father likes. Maybe they're killing everyone in town to stop the epidemic.

She begins to cry. Her sister reaches over to cover her mouth.

And then it happens: the closet door swings open.

By the low light of Libby's night-light, they can see the outline of a man.

"Are you in here?" he says. There is panic in his voice. "Are you here?"

The girls keep quiet.

They do not imagine what he might see at this moment, the faces of two little girls in nightgowns, squeezed together among their sweaters and their coats, one crying, the other burying her head into the other's shoulder. But that is the thing: he does not seem to see them at all.

They can see his feet now—no shoes. And his chest—no shirt.

He parts the coats in the closet like curtains.

"Please," he keeps saying. "Please tell me where you are."

That's when Sara recognizes him. It's their neighbor. This guy is their neighbor, that professor with the baby.

It is a relief to know that this man is a father, as if one parent will always look out for the children of others.

Now she sees that he is bleeding. His hands are running with blood. Bits of glass sparkle on his bare feet.

"Where is my baby?" he says. "I can't find my baby."

There is something about his eyes, seeing but not seeing, as if, it comes to her suddenly, as if he is dreaming.

There's that sound again, the windy swish of some kind of electronic device. He holds it up to his ear. A baby monitor. The noise comes in like an old recording, or a radio station losing its signal. A surge of noise, but no baby sounds.

And then he rushes out of the house as suddenly as he came.

He does not flinch or shout out, when his bare feet step on broken glass. He never makes it home. From the widow's walk, the girls spot him passed out on his porch.

Libby runs out to put a blanket over him. Sara calls the police. Only late the next day does an ambulance come to take him away. Those suited-up workers spend a long time in the house and then mark it with an X. If they find the baby in there, the girls do not see her.

In the morning, they discover that among the things he shattered in his sleep are their mother's black ceramic birds from Portugal. There they are, in pieces on the floor. Libby spends all day trying to glue them back together. But time moves in only the one direction. Not everything that breaks can be repaired.

That night, Sara wakes again, gripped by another ominous feeling. This time, her sister's bed is empty. Sara rushes for the lights. And this is how she discovers Libby, lying perfectly still on the wood floor. But worse than that: her brown eyes are wide open.

For five seconds, Sara knows she is alone in the world—only the dead lie like that.

But then an odd mumbling begins to come from Libby's mouth, singsong, as if she is speaking in her sleep, eyes still open.

Not so uncommon, she will later learn, in the youngest victims of the virus.

Sara puts a hand on her back, gentle at first. "Wake up," she says.

But she knows already that the thing she has been dreading for weeks has finally come to pass: the sleep has come for Libby.

42.

They carry her sister in their arms, these strangers, college kids in college sweatshirts. A boy and a girl who seem to know what to do. They wear white masks and green gloves.

"I kept calling 911," says Sara. Her voice is shaking with a desperate gratitude—it feels like some kind of love. "I kept calling, but they never came."

"They don't have enough ambulances," says the boy.

He is lifting her sister up from the wood floor, where she has been lying all day. Libby—green pajamas, bare feet, her cheek creased from the knots in the wood. Her lips, Sara worries, are beginning to chap.

"Are you guys staying here alone?" asks the college girl through her mask.

An urge keeps rising up in Sara: to apologize for the trouble.

The boy is holding Libby as if he has never held a child, careful and stiff and way out in front of him, as if her body were an heirloom, a thing that might break.

But he walks quickly once he has her, in running shoes, skinny legs, long strides down the staircase, quick steps across the living room and out the front door.

"The hospital is full," he says, squinting on the sidewalk. "But they can help her on campus."

His mask has fallen down over his chin, and the girl works to fix it—she is tender as she pulls the elastic back over his ears. But the boy wants to rush.

"That's good enough," he says, and he turns away from the girl.

"You should put some shoes on," the girl says to Sara.

"No," says the boy. "She should stay here. She'll just slow us down."

Their eyes conduct a brief argument. The girl wins.

She hands Sara a fresh pair of green latex gloves.

"Put these on," she says. They are too big on her fingers, but she wears them anyway—she will do whatever these people say.

And then the three of them start walking, Libby in the boy's arms.

The sky is loud with helicopters. But down here, the streets are empty. Here and there, a distant voice comes through, or sometimes a face in a window. But mostly it is only the sun and the woods, the birds on their branches, the soundless shuffling of the pine needles in the wind.

It is warm for December, but a breeze reminds Sara that she has left the house in only a flannel nightgown and sandals.

Libby's eyelids keep shuddering, as if she is dreaming, even then, even as her head bobs in the crook of this boy's elbow; even now, she is dreaming some secret dream. There is something unsettling about it, to see so clearly this fact: how unreachable the inside of even her sister's mind.

The front door of the Garabaldi house stands wide open—no Garabaldis. Sara spots a bird flapping around inside.

Her father was right about everything.

When an ambulance swings around the corner, the college girl waves it down. But the paramedics, in their goggles and full-body suits, shake their heads through the windshield.

"We can't take anyone else," they call through their masks. All you can see are their eyes. "We're full."

This is the moment—as that ambulance fades like a dream in the distance—when something begins to happen inside Sara's chest. A sudden tightening, a resistance to the task of breathing.

She stops where she is on the sidewalk. She bends over, feels faint. Someone's hand is rubbing her back.

"Have you eaten anything today?" asks the college girl.

Food—the whole idea is surprising. And water, too. The information comes to her suddenly: how dry her mouth is.

"We don't have time for this," says the boy. "Her sister is the one who needs help."

"Have this," says the girl. She pulls a few things from the pocket of her sweatshirt.

A few gulps of water and a granola bar put Sara back on her feet. Or maybe it's something else: to be cared for like this.

A Hummer whooshes by without stopping. A policeman rushes past them on foot.

The boy shifts Libby's weight in his arms, so that her head rests on his shoulder, her hair on his neck, the way a father might carry a toddler. The boy's mask has fallen down again—and again, the girl tries to fix it, but he shakes his head.

"Just leave it," he says.

You can see she wants to say something but doesn't. Instead she drips a little water into Libby's mouth, and Libby coughs a tiny cough as the water runs down her chin.

"She needs an IV," says the boy.

That's when the college girl takes Sara's hand in hers, which feels weird at first—Sara is not that young, and it's strange through the gloves. But the longer they walk, the more it feels like a good idea.

When they get where they're going, outside the campus gates, when she sees the crowd that has gathered there, Sara remembers something awful: they are not the only ones who need help.

From far away, they look lifeless, all those people spread out in other people's arms. The heads hang back, the necks exposed. Their arms, like Libby's, dangle loose like something wilted. Worse are the ones on the ground, lying on their backs on the sidewalk or facedown in the grass. Who knows how they got there or who they are? Workers move through the crowd in blue suits, but Sara can see from half a block away how much the need outweighs the aid.

Slowly, very slowly, the sick are being carried onto campus on stretchers and into the white tents that loom on the college lawns. And always the helicopters, arcing across the sky, as useless as flies.

Someone in a blue suit is going around handing out gloves. Another is walking through the crowd, spraying something clear on the ground and on people's shoes. Bleach, maybe.

A stab of longing for her father comes into Sara—she has no way of knowing where he sleeps.

An enormous man lies snoring on the sidewalk, his belly showing under his shirt. No one can lift him. He looks so alone, lying there—she can't bear it: Maybe his family has only gone on an errand and will be back to sit with him soon. Maybe his wife has only gone to find a bathroom. Four blue suits struggle to get him onto a stretcher. The smell of urine wafts in the air.

A rumor is traveling through the crowd. An evacuation is coming. Buses.

But the boy is skeptical.

"Why would they evacuate anyone now?" he says. "That's the exact opposite of what they're trying to do."

To Sara, it feels as if there is no one left out in the world, anyway, as if this is the last town on earth. The feeling stays with her, like a thing you know is both true and not true at the same time.

Some people are angry. A man keeps shouting at the soldiers. "Shame on you," he says. "Shame on you."

In the grass between the road and the sidewalk, a woman and a little boy lie unconscious together. Names and phone numbers are written on the boy's overalls. Who wrote them? Sara wonders, but there's no one to ask. A bee lands on the woman's face. The college girl shoos it away.

On the fence around the campus, boots and suits hang from the posts, a creepy batch of laundry, drying in the sun. In the distance, the smell of burning.

"They burn the masks and gloves," he says.

The boy and the girl leave Sara with Libby and help whoever else they can. She watches them handing out water.

Libby is lying on the grass, her head in Sara's lap. She is holding Libby's hand.

Libby begins to mumble in her sleep, but it's nothing Sara can decipher. Maybe they are the lucky ones, the ones dreaming more fortunate than the ones awake. Sara drips a little more water into her sister's mouth.

The boy is gone for a long time, and then returns with a couple of workers—for the woman and the little boy. What about her sister? she thinks. But she is too afraid to ask. It is hard to tell whether there is no order here, or if she just does not understand the order that there is. The woman and the boy are eventually scooped up by the workers—they want to take the little boy first, alone.

"Can't you keep them together?" the girl asks. "He's so young."

One worker sprays the grass where they were lying.

The boy brings to Sara a piece of thick paper, like a notecard, but with a string attached.

"Write her name down on this card," he says to Sara.

To see the letters of her sister's name in her handwriting brings a fresh sadness. He ties the card around Libby's little wrist and then disappears again.

After a while, Sara spots someone she knows in the crowd, her drama teacher, Mrs. Campbell. The surprise of seeing a teacher outside the classroom, and the further surprise: to see the look of suffering on her face. She is holding someone in her arms, someone sick, a man in short sleeves, a blanket draped around his narrow shoulders. She knows that man, too, she realizes. The sleeping man is Sara's math teacher, Mr. Guitierrez. But for no reason she knows, Sara pretends not to see them.

The college girl soon comes back to check on her. She squeezes Sara's hand. On another day, this college girl would have made her shy, this Mei, with her thick hair and her closeness to this boy, how she knows how to be in the world. But Sara thinks of none of this. There is only the rising and falling of her sister's chest and the warmth of this older girl's hand in hers.

"Come on," says the boy to the girl. "You're wasting time."

"This is important, too," says the girl. She stays where she is, on the sidewalk with Sara.

The feeling of that girl's hand in hers is how she makes it through that day—to the moment, hours later, when the girl and the boy give up on the workers and carry her sister through the gates themselves, and then the way that girl walks her home to the house, where Sara will fall asleep alone—curled in her sister's bed.

She promises, this girl, to come back later to check on Sara, but hours pass. The whole night passes. The college girl does not return.

43.

The second floor of the college library is where the youngest sick now sleep.

Here, in the makeshift pediatric ward, they sleep in cat shirts and ballet skirts. They sleep with feeding tubes taped to pink cheeks. They sleep with IVs peeking out from the sleeves of fire truck pajamas. Some sleep with stuffed animals in the crooks of their arms, put there by who knows who, a worn elephant, a floppy rabbit, a plastic baby nestled in the arms of a toddler. Some sleep with notes pinned to their clothing: their names and their phone numbers and PLEASE HELP. Some sleep, like Libby, with eyes half open to the ceiling, their little bellies rising as they dream.

Maybe their parents sleep in other rooms—in the hospital or on other floors of this library, or in the tents on the lawns outside. Or, maybe, their parents have ceased to sleep. Wherever they are, those parents are not here.

The bookshelves, pushed to the sides of the room, loom over the children's cots while doctors and nurses in blue plastic suits check vitals, one by one.

A kind of sacredness suffuses this library. It is quiet here, except for the small sounds of their snores, the occasional cough, the steady beep and whir of the monitors, which track the workings of their little beating hearts.

But there is a certain amount of chaos here. Always, there are one or two workers wearing less protection than they should, by accident or ignorance or a shortage of the proper gear. Volunteers sometimes carry sick children right into this room with only gloves on their hands and thin paper masks, the rest of their skin exposed to contaminated air.

This is how Mei and Matthew end up in here, carrying the girl through the big double doors and up the stairs, after many hours of waiting for someone else to do it. They are suddenly breaking their last remaining rule: to stay outside the wards.

"Let's go," says Mei, as soon as they have left the girl in the care of a nurse.

But Matthew hesitates, mesmerized by what he sees: there must be a hundred children sleeping in here, and only a few nurses and doctors to care for them. He is suddenly alive with the work there is to do here.

"Matthew," Mei says. "We need to leave."

But instead, he heads toward a nearby bed. A young boy is sleeping there; his IV has come unhooked. It's a quick fix, but no one has yet noticed.

"Come on," says Mei. She is hot with fear.

But Matthew will not leave, even when the nurses try to shoo him out.

"I'm leaving," says Mei.

"So then go," he says.

And she does. Out in the sunshine, the open air, a mix of relief and guilt comes to her. He can be so infuriating, this boy, so brave and so rash—what good will it do if they get themselves sick?

It is late that night before Matthew comes back to their tent in the yard. She wakes to the sound of the zipper coming open.

"Please don't do that again," says Mei.

But Matthew is vibrating, electric with a day of doing the most vital work.

"Think of how many years of life are ahead of those kids," he says. "Their lives are worth so much more than the adults'."

"We don't have the right masks or suits to be working in there," says Mei. "We're not trained."

He sighs hard and lies down beside her. A sticky silence comes into the tent.

"I've been thinking," he says. "I think you're too attached to me."

A lump rises instantly in her throat. It is a surprise how close these feelings are to the surface.

"Aren't you attached to me, too?" she says. She reaches for his hand. He pulls it away.

"Let me ask you something," he says. She can tell by the way he says it that he is heading toward something abstract, some example from philosophy he read in a book. It can be tiring, late at night, this constant talk of logic, this daily parsing of ethics.

"If I was drowning," he says. "And two strangers were also drowning nearby. And if you had to choose to save either me or the two strangers, who would you choose?" he says. "Me? Or the strangers?"

"What do you think?" says Mei.

She knows what he wants her to say. But it's not true. Him—she would save him. Of course she would. She has not dared, these weeks, to say the word *love* out loud, but it feels like the right one.

"But that's the wrong choice," says Matthew.

A set of sirens zooms by outside, the faint flashing of red lights on his face.

"Two lives are always worth more than one," he says. "It shouldn't matter that you know me."

"I don't just *know* you," she says. He can be so cold sometimes. "I guess you're saying you wouldn't save me?"

"See?" he says. "This is why I think love is unethical. I don't believe in it."

It is a shock to remember that she has only known him for a few weeks. There is a feeling of the ground falling away.

He gives more examples, but she has stopped listening. At least it is dark in this small tent—he can't see her tears. But they are coming fast and hard. She can't hide it for long. Maybe she doesn't know him at all, this boy, who does not, at this moment, reach over to comfort her, even now, as she begins to sob.

"This is what I mean," he says. "You're too attached."

A sudden longing for her parents blows through her, an old memory from a lonely childhood: how at least her parents would always care what happens to her.

"Why are you being so mean?" she says finally.

He answers by unzipping the tent.

"You're missing the point," he says as he climbs out onto the grass like he is trying to shake her off of him, get free.

Next she hears the sound of his feet crunching quickly on dried leaves as he rushes off somewhere, leaving only the noise of the crickets in the woods, the distant thrum of helicopter blades, and in her, the longing to be somewhere else.

After that, she cries so hard her head hurts. She thinks to call her parents, but she can't bring herself to try. She is all alone in a strange place. A kind of numbness follows.

She finally drifts into sleep, or something close to it.

That's when it happens, an unfamiliar feeling: some kind of presence is with her in the tent.

"Matthew," she says or tries to say.

But Matthew is not here. Some kind of dark figure is here with her. This figure, like something human and not human— now it's climbing up onto her chest. Something is pressing down hard on her whole body. Something is pinning her arms.

She tries to scream, but nothing comes. Her throat is closing up.

Her entire body, she understands now, has slipped out of her control, like some kind of paralysis.

It is hard to think past the immense pressure on her chest, but there is the tiniest sense of the larger possibility, that maybe this is it: the sickness. Maybe this is how it starts.

44.

First is the feeling of hands—Matthew's—as he lifts her up from the bed. Now the echo of his voice calling her name. *Mei, Mei, wake up, Mei, wake up.* She is aware of a shift in the light. A breeze on her skin. He has carried her out into the yard.

It is not at all how she imagined it would be, this sleep: a twilight more than a night. The waking world is somehow seeping through.

He will take her to the campus, she knows, like they have taken all the others. But this time, those arms hanging from their sockets—those are hers. And that head lolling back, that hair streaming over the face—it's hers.

Her eyes are closed, and yet, somehow, she can see—or she sees without seeing, without needing to see. She knows the way the cracked sidewalk glints in the sun. She can picture the ragged line of the mountains against the sky. And the clean waft of eucalyptus in the air gives rise in her mind to the spidery image of that exact tree.

One other fact glows clear in her head: the pleasure of Matthew's attention and concern.

At some point, they arrive at the college, her body still draped in his arms. Now the cool of old buildings, the murmur of many voices, the scent of bleach in the air.

"How long has she been like this?" someone says, voice muffled, as through a mask. Someone official.

A sudden urgency swells in her. I can hear you, she wants to say, but she can't, or she doesn't. I'm here, she thinks, but she cannot seem to make use of her voice. I'm here.

"I don't know when it started," says Matthew. He is out of breath. He is talking fast. She has not heard him like this before: afraid. "I think she's been asleep for twelve hours," he says. "Maybe longer."

His bare hand, unprotected, brushes the hair from her face. His goodness comes into her like electricity through his palm.

Next comes the cold penny of a stethoscope on her chest, and then her spine sinking slowly into a cot.

She will try speaking again in a little while, she decides, just a little later, when she is not quite so tired as she is now.

She has a confusing sensation that she is surrounded by books, old ones. Maybe she smells it in the air—that mustiness, the decay of thin pages. Or maybe she hears someone say it through her sleep: that they have brought her to the library, one floor down from the children's ward.

She is aware of certain gaps. She has lost hold of the passage of time. Each moment floats alone, disconnected from any other.

At one point, an old story floats up, murky, into her head, from a book she read once or a movie, or just an article she saw somewhere, years earlier, about a man paralyzed in an accident. Everyone thought he was brain-dead, but he wasn't. No one knew he was in there, still thinking and noticing and longing to connect—for years. Locked in, they called it.

A sudden terror washes through her. Can Matthew sense it, somehow, this fear? Maybe this explains why he always seems to return to her bed at these moments, his warm hand squeezing hers.

Other times are inexplicably peaceful, a gliding, everything white and distant, as if somehow leached of meaning and consequence.

There might be a feeding tube in her throat—there must be. But if there is, it is painless. And because her hands no longer move in accordance with her will, it is easy to avoid running her fingers around the plastic tube that must be taped to her cheek.

She is sometimes aware of her legs moving slightly, but she is not in control—they move like reeds drifting in a mild current.

She is sometimes a child again, walking on the beach with her parents or helping her grandmother with the cooking, while her grandmother tells stories she only half understands in Chinese. But sometimes, instead, Mei is the grandmother, retelling those stories to her own grandchild.

She can hear the other sleepers, the snores and the breathing, a moan or a shout—the noise of their nightmares and their dreams. And otherwise: the crinkle of plastic suits, the squeak and the drone of carts rolling across the hardwood floors, the helicopters chopping in the distance.

And always, there is the musty smell of the old books rising up from the stacks around her, like soil, like roots, like the trees they once were. Maybe she is not in the library but on the shady floor of a forest. Maybe she is asleep in some unrecoverable woods.

At some point, her mother arrives. What a surprise it is to hear her voice—and a relief. How did you get in? she wants to ask her but cannot.

"What's wrong with her eyes?" her mother asks, and keeps asking. "What happened to her eyes?" Mei worries that her eyes have been disfigured in her sleep, as if gouged out or removed.

When she tries to open them, she understands suddenly and with a terrible certainty what has happened: the skin of her eyelids has grown down over her eyes.

And her mother, she realizes, is not here in this room. Of course she's not. She is on the phone. Someone must be holding a phone up to her ear. Or else her mother is on speakerphone—maybe that's why her voice is warbling like that. Or she might be on the radio, even. Her mother's voice might be coming from the television on the other side of the room. Or through some deeper channel, as if through her brain, her blood.

"Why is she moaning like that?" her mother asks. "Is she trying to talk?"

One night—or it seems to her like it's night—Matthew whispers something in her ear: *I'm sorry.*

It may as well be *I love you.* And she has the idea that she can say it, too, not with words but with thoughts instead, or with the sound of her breathing in and out, like a code that only he will hear.

That same night, or maybe another one, or maybe the middle of the day, Matthew climbs into her cot, and after that, he sleeps there with her for a long time until it becomes the main thing she knows, her surest truest fact: his body curled against hers.

45.

There is no one part of the brain in charge of keeping track of time. In the conscious brain, the system of timekeeping is loose and diffuse and subject to distortions of various kinds: love, for example, and grief, and youth. In the mind, time dilates, and time contracts. Different days travel at different rates.

But certain other parts of the body keep time with more precision. At the beginning, we all grow at a certain, fixed rate.

Thus, as Rebecca begins her seventh week of sleep, ten fingers begin to flower, and ten toes. A pair of tiny nostrils opens in a nose. The eyelids are starting to form. The skull, at this moment, is translucent like a jellyfish. And inside it are blooming the earliest passageways of a brain.

Soon, the reproductive organs will coalesce. The ovaries will begin to fill with eggs, and those eggs will travel with this tiny girl—if she survives—for the whole rest of her life.

The air in Rebecca's room is still. Her only movements are the occasional shifting of her head in sleep, and the cyclical fluttering of her eyelids, her eyes darting beneath them in a way suggestive of dreams.

But soon, hidden inside her, those feathery limbs will begin to move. The arms will bend. The knees. The hands will meet and come apart. A thumb might make its way into the mouth. A million neurons will emerge every minute.

A blood test has finally revealed her secret to the doctors, who take it as a worrying surprise. There is no way of knowing how the virus might affect the fetus, or if they can keep Rebecca's body well enough for the baby to grow to full term. From then on, the nurses treat her with extra care.

While Rebecca sleeps, and while the nurses change in and out of their suits, and while, outside, the soldiers go on and off shift, and while the world watches the continuing coverage of the Santa Lora sickness, the small developments of one minute human being go on unfolding at a perfectly predictable rate, like the intricate ticking of the most delicate clock on earth.

46.

The news travels quickly. It is a rumor, really, at the start. A development more shocking, in a way, than all the facts that have come before it. Seven weeks in, news like this is difficult to believe. But it is true: one of the sleepers has woken up, only the second to open his eyes since the outbreak began.

At first, says the nurse, she assumes she is mistaken. It can be hard to see through the rippling plastic of the masks. But a second look, at that man in the corner, four rows in, shows that she is right: his eyes are open. And it's not only his eyes. It's the way he is suddenly shifting around in his sheets, his movements so different from all the other sleepers, more purposeful, more direct. He whips his head back and forth. He is looking around.

His cot is one of two hundred cots set up in the college dining hall. There is a sleeper in every bed. There is an IV in every arm. The sight of one of them sitting up like this—it is as startling as it would be to see a corpse rise up from the dead.

Not described in any of the early reports is how the nurse

feels in that first moment: a pang of fear she cannot quite explain.

The man begins to speak.

Often, they mumble and they moan, but this is different. This is speech. How alien it is to hear this man's voice, hoarse at first, but his first word so crisp and so clear: "Hello?" he says. "Hello?"

He raises his head. He turns it quickly. He pulls the wires off his body. He waves his arms in front of him, as if he is blind, which, it turns out, he is, in a way—his glasses have been lost during his long weeks of sleep.

All the nurses soon gather around him, a clutch of yellow suits, the sound of Gore-Tex boots.

A contagious disease, they say. You have contracted a contagious disease. It is hard to tell if he can hear them, their voices echoey through the plastic. It is hard to tell if he understands what they are saying.

He has pale green eyes that shine blankly at them.

Later, these nurses will confide to one another about the strange sensation they experienced as they spoke to him, as if they were attempting to communicate with a traveler from some faraway land.

The man speaks quickly. His words tumble too fast to be discerned. And also there is this: he is shouting. He is shouting something about a fire.

"Did they put it out?" he shouts. "Is it out?"

You were dreaming for a long time, they tell him.

"There was a fire," he shouts again. "At the library. The whole place was on fire."

His voice grows louder and louder, but the sleep of those around him continues undisturbed.

He calls for water.

"Please," he says. He keeps pulling at his beard. "I'm thirsty. I'm so thirsty."

He drinks and drinks. He drinks so much water that the water comes right back up, splashing the rubber boots of the nurses, as if, after a while, a body grows to prefer even the worst of circumstances to any sudden change.

"A fire," he shouts again. "It was a huge fire."

The nurses nod together in their yellow suits. They are volunteers, these people, flown in from other states after most of the local nurses slipped under. They want to be comforting, but the man will not be comforted. One of the nurses touches his shoulder with her gloved hand.

"And my girls," he shouts. "Where are my girls? Where are they?"

There is no mention of relatives in his chart. It seems possible that these girls, like the fire, are part of some deep and indecipherable dream.

He asks for pen and paper. This is how he spends the next few hours: writing in a notebook with the speed and urgency of a person facing his death.

What a shock it is to receive the message after so many weeks in quarantine in the hospital: she is needed on the campus, Catherine, one of the few psychiatrists left awake in Santa Lora, and the only one who witnessed the waking of the first boy. His body on the pavement—it still glows bright in her mind.

She is escorted the three blocks from the hospital to the dining hall by two soldiers, her first time outside in more than a month. The weather has changed in that time. December. Dead leaves drift across the empty sidewalks as they walk, the seasons more apparent up here in the mountains than they are in Los Angeles, where her daughter, thank God, has been released from quarantine into the care of Catherine's mother.

In the time they have been apart, her daughter has learned to count to twenty, and to put her own shirts on. Her bangs, she knows from their nightly video calls, have grown into her eyes.

The patient, when Catherine gets there, is writing in a journal—they have moved him to a separate room in the dining hall.

She wants to be more careful this time, after what happened with the first boy. She approaches this man quietly.

"Do you know," she asks him, "how long you've been asleep?"

The man does not answer right away. He looks into the distance, the way one might if looking out over a vast remembered space. The other boy did that, too, Catherine remembers, as if the world inside his head were more arresting than the one outside of it.

A sudden burst of suspicion comes into the man's face.

"You can't keep me here," he says. "You can't keep me."

"It's normal to feel disoriented," says Catherine through her mask.

Often, the comatose have the feeling afterward that they have been unconscious for only a short time, a few hours, maybe, or a single night. It can be traumatic to learn how much time has passed.

Catherine notes several unusual symptoms in the man, not present in the other boy: a tendency for palilalic speech, the repetition of certain words and phrases. And also the shouting, megaphonia, as the textbooks would call it. The patient seems unaware of both symptoms, as if his perception of the world is out of scale with ours.

"I'm not answering any more questions," says the man. He does not speak for the rest of the day, but he goes on with his writing late into the night.

Only later that evening does Catherine discover one more eccentric symptom, familiar only from case studies she read in medical school: the pages of the man's notebook are filled with miniature writing, the letters so small that they are legible only with a magnifying glass.

From what she can read when the man briefly dozes off, his writings are marked by delusion and confusion, and in particular, a conviction that he has been asleep for much longer than five weeks.

47.

Six A.M.: a barking of dogs in the yard, the clink of the chain on the back door.

Three floors up, alone in the house, Sara goes stiff in her bed, as if whoever is out there might sense the small movements of a twelve-year-old girl through the walls. She is sleeping again in one of her mother's sweaters.

Now the crunch of footsteps in the dirt. Now a rattling of the side door.

The dogs go on barking and barking—she does not even know most of their names, each one rescued by Libby, hungry, from the street, but thank God for their loyalty, thank God for their noise.

Now the scrape of metal on wood. Something is being dragged across the loose boards of the back porch.

She wishes for her sister like a prayer. And in the darkness of the bedroom, still shadowed with the dolls they once imagined had the power to talk, she almost believes it: that some similar magic might call Libby back from wherever she sleeps.

She tiptoes to the window. Her hands shake as she pulls back the corner of the curtain.

The kittens are agitated, too, the littlest one pacing and pacing the floor, the others waiting deep under Sara's bed.

When she peeks out through the boards on the bedroom window, what she sees in the early morning dark is a man standing on a trash can. It's not the neighbor, this time. It's someone else, this man who is right now reaching up toward the second-floor window.

He calls out to the dogs to be quiet—and this is when she recognizes him, his voice.

He arrives like a stranger and a thief, but here he is: her father.

At first, it's a relief. Of course it is. Of course. Here is her father, sitting at the kitchen table. Here he is: alive and awake.

He keeps saying her name. "Thank God," he says. "Thank God." She does not remember a look like that showing up on his face before, a relief that seems somehow explosive.

"I didn't mean to scare you," he says. He is a little out of breath.

His head has been shaved clean. His beard is missing.

He does not say much at first, as if there is not much to say, as if, after five weeks, he simply woke up and walked home.

"I don't know what happened to my key," he says. "Do you know what happened to my key?"

His skin is very pale, and he is squinting through a pair of borrowed glasses. He looks even skinnier than usual in a loose green T-shirt she has never seen before. But it's him. It's him. Those are his arms resting on the kitchen table, and those are his tattoos, the intricate wolf with the yellow eyes and the blocky black spider on his elbow, and her mother's name fading gray on his forearm beside the birth dates of both of his girls. This cataloguing of his body feels necessary because there is something about him—there is something about him that is different.

"Do you know what happened to my key?" he says again.

His fingernails have grown long like a woman's but ragged, the thumbnail so long that it is starting to curl.

"What happened to your hair?" Sara asks. "What happened to your beard?"

"I don't know," he says.

His skin is so pale, and that bare chin—she tries at once to look and not look, as if a section of his face has been removed. A phantom impulse rises in her: to point it out to her sister.

"You're okay," he says. "Right?"

"Are *you*?" she says.

By now, the sun is coming up. There is a quiet comfort in that milky light, the way it streams through the cracks in the boards so like the way it would on a more ordinary morning.

"Where's your sister?" he asks. He glances toward the stairs.

She cannot look at his face while she tells him, so she looks out the window instead, toward the dogs. Every word of the story must be pushed, one by one, over the hard knot in her throat.

Her father seems confused by what he hears.

"You already told me that," he says. "Didn't you? You already told me she got sick."

"What do you mean?" she says, her eyes going blurry.

"We talked about her, earlier," he says.

She is afraid to say no, but he can see the truth on her face. It is hard to know what to say.

"Never mind," he says, rubbing the bald ridges of his head. He has a mole up there she has never seen. "Never mind."

She has the urge to replace the confusion that follows with a nice, clear idea: "If you got better," she says, "then she'll probably be okay, too, right?"

Her father stays silent. He looks like a man struggling to make mathematical calculations in his head.

She brings him a soda, the cool reassuring pop of the tab beneath her fingers. She brings him the nail clippers, too, leaves them on the table beside him. There is a certain confusion in the room about who is the caretaker and who the one in need of care.

Now that her father is home, she is suddenly aware of how the house has gotten away from her—that's the way it feels—like weeds taking over a garden. The kitty litter is pebbling out of the bathroom, and there is the clamor of dishes in the sink, the scatter of soda cans, and all those forgotten cereal bowls, licked clean by the cats.

But her father does not seem to notice any of it.

He does not ask whose dogs these are, wagging and whining and lapping water all over the linoleum.

"Can you get these dogs out of the kitchen?" he says, and that's all he says about them. "I have a lot to figure out."

Thank God he does not think to go down to the basement, where, if he did, he would discover what those dogs have done to the neat stocks of toilet paper and the cereal boxes, the many jars of preserved carrots they've cracked on the cement.

Her father spends that first day right there at the kitchen table, bent over an unfamiliar spiral notebook.

"What are you writing?" she asks after a while.

"I don't know exactly," he says. "I'm just trying to sort some things out."

He hardly moves all day, as if his body has grown used to it: the motionlessness of sleep. And when he does move, he moves slowly, as if pushing through a thicker kind of air. His pen inches across the page, leaving a trail of tiny words.

This is only the first day, thinks Sara, an uneasiness creeping through her. Maybe he's still waking up.

Chloe skids across the linoleum when she sees him for the first time, a hiss.

"That's Daddy," says Sara as Chloe's tail puffs up like a duster. "He's your favorite, remember?"

Maybe it's the baldness of his head that bothers her, or that bare chin. Or maybe it's the unhealthy color of his skin. Whatever it is, Chloe stays away, her path to her water bowl arcing unnaturally wide.

On television, the same headline is running on all the news channels: "Man Awakens from Santa Lora Sickness."

"I think they're talking about you," she calls to her father from the living room.

But he stays at the table and goes on with his writing. From a distance, he looks as if he is performing the careful work of a clockmaker.

The news channels do not seem to have much information about him, no picture, no name, no sense of his condition.

"Can you find me another pen?" her father calls from the kitchen, shaking his pen in the air, his mind having drained it of ink.

Among the many things her father fails to notice that day is the way her mother's belongings are spread out around the house, those attic boxes now gutted in the living room, the treasures spilling out: the wedding pictures and the cassette tapes, her collection of turquoise jewelry, all the objects they've been lovingly studying, like clues to an old mystery, and her tarnished silver charm bracelet, which is right now revolving around Sara's small wrist, clinking lightly against the table.

Sara uses the last of the bread from the freezer to make tuna fish sandwiches for dinner, but her father leaves most of his on his plate.

All day, the nail clippers sit on the table beside him, untouched. All day, the scrape of his nails on the soda can.

"You should go to bed," he says finally, the kind of thing no one has said to her in weeks. And it is appealing, in a way, to be told that and to do it, these the normal words of a father to a daughter.

Much later, in the middle of the night, she can still hear him down there, not sleeping, moving around in the kitchen.

In the morning, two policemen come to the door.

Sara watches them from the widow's walk, afraid to find out why they have come—in their white masks and their green gloves, tucked tight beneath the cuffs of their uniforms.

The knocking on the door sets off the dogs.

"Daddy," Sara calls to her father. He is sitting at their bulky old computer, waiting and waiting for a page to load. "The police are here," she says.

"Just ignore them," he says, as if they are salesmen who will go away on their own.

They keep shifting their weight on the porch, these police. They keep looking around, as if eager to get away. Behind them, on the other side of the street, the frame of the nurse's house leans forward like a shipwreck. After so many weeks, the caution tape has frayed in the wind, and the birds have built a nest in the stove, which stands, rusting, in the open air.

The police knock again.

Sara can hear the dogs whining and scratching at the door from the inside. Maybe the police can hear it, too, that whining and that scratching.

At some point, the knocking stops. She watches, flush with relief, as the policemen step down off the porch, and then stand for a moment in the weeds that have overtaken the front yard. One of them says something into his radio.

Instead of walking back to their car, they disappear around the side of the house. Then comes the creak of the side gate, the terrible crunch of their shoes in the gravel that leads to the back-yard.

The knocking starts again, this time at the back door.

"Hello?" they call. "Hello?"

Sara listens from the kitchen, hidden by the boarded-up windows. But she can hear the swish of the static on their radios outside.

She is not prepared for what comes next: the creak of the back door, the cry of its hinges, the way the thin crack of sunlight beneath the door explodes to the shape of the whole doorway. Her father must have left it unlocked in the night, which is not like him, to make a mistake like that, not like him at all.

"Oh," say the police when they see Sara, the way she is squinting in the kitchen in pajamas. It's too late for her to hide.

"Oh," one of them says again. He is a dark figure in the doorway. Sunlight blazing around him. "We didn't know if anyone was home."

The dogs begin to jump up on their tan police pants, friendly tongues lolling out of their mouths, but the policemen are backing away, as if the dogs, too, might be contaminated.

One of them is holding the door open. He is using only two gloved fingers to do it, and he is leaning way back as if for access to fresh air.

"Is Thomas Peterson here?" the other one asks. It sounds like a stranger, the way they say his name. No one calls him Thomas.

"If you know where he is," says the one holding the door, his voice softened by the mask, "it's very important that you tell us."

She is not sure what the right answer is, or if this is a time when a lie is right. She settles on silence, and for a moment, the only sounds are the panting of the dogs and the squeak of their black police shoes as they dodge the leaps of the dogs.

One of the men finally crouches down to talk to her, as if she is a much younger child.

"Listen," he says through his mask. He is looking past her, searching the living room over her shoulder. "He wasn't supposed to go home yet. He might still be sick."

She wonders if they know about the slowness of his walk, the strange writing. She wonders if they know how little he has been sleeping.

"It was too soon," he says to her.

But she will not watch her father leave again.

"He's not here," she says finally, her voice scratching from so long without speaking.

The two men look at each other. She can see only their eyes over the tops of the masks, but their eyes are where the skepticism floats.

"Have you been staying here alone?" one of them asks, which seems to raise a new threat.

An answer comes in the form of her father's footsteps on the stairs behind her. He walks differently—that's another thing that has changed. He takes smaller steps than before, a wobbly stride, almost like a limp.

"You don't have a right to be on my property," he says to the police. He is wearing the same clothes as yesterday.

They just want to monitor him for a while, they say, the doctors.

"That's why they sent us here," one of them says.

"I'm not going to the hospital," he says.

"It's a matter of public safety, sir," says the one holding the door.

"It's not safe for you or your daughter," says the taller one.

"I'm not going to be some guinea pig," says her father.

And this is how the conversation ends: he closes the door and locks it. Then he goes back upstairs to the computer.

It is a surprise when the police really do leave, that after all that, words are enough to chase them away. Before they get into their car, she watches them pull their green gloves off, one glove at a time, dropping them into a trash bag.

There is a feeling that they will be back, or that someone else will. It's a feeling of a leak plugged only temporarily.

That night, a sound familiar but hard to place drifts up from the kitchen after midnight. A soft sandpaper scrape. And then again: scrape, scrape, scrape. She knows, from the occasional cough, that it's her father down there. She is not sure he should be left alone.

The smell confirms it at the same moment as the sight: her father at the kitchen table, a lit match burning between his fingers.

"What are you doing?" she asks.

On the table beside him is a scattering of burnt-out matches, a whole pack from the basement, used up in a night—it isn't like him to waste.

"This thing did something to my brain," he says.

He watches the flame for a while and then gently shakes it out. He drops it in the pile with the others.

"What are you doing?" she asks again.

He takes a sip of beer. He pulls a fresh match from the box and begins again, the slow striking of the match to the box, too slow, at first, to make the match light. But he keeps at it, a determined, careful scrape.

The helicopters are still thumping outside in the dark, but she knows from the news that the reporters are wrong about which house is his—they think that the man who woke from the Santa Lora sickness lives in an old white house a few blocks away, a place abandoned for years, since before Sara was born, wildflowers growing up through the planks of the porch. Maybe it's the boarded-up windows that make them confuse that house for theirs, that lead the helicopters to hover over that other roof and not theirs. But after she has watched the footage all day, that other house, a stranger's house, a dead man's house maybe, begins to take on a feeling of familiarity for her, the way, in a dream, a place you have never been can somehow stand in for home.

Finally, the match blooms in his hand. He lets it burn for a few seconds. Then he shakes it out again.

"I had these dreams," he says. "While I was sick. Dreams that were like no dreams I've ever had before."

He takes another drink of beer. It is not his first, she can see. Two other cans are sitting on the counter.

"What were they about?" she says.

"What do you mean?" he says, as if she is the one who brought it up. This is the way he has been since he got home, his mind always running on some second, unknown track.

"The dreams," she says. "What did you dream about?"

He rubs his bald head. His fingers move slowly, as if tracing an alien terrain.

"I need to ask you something," he says. He looks right at her. A layer of stubble has grown where his beard used to be. "Was there a fire while I was gone?" he says. "Was there a fire at the college library?"

"There was one in the woods," she says, and it seems amazing that he could know about that somehow, though he slept through the whole thing. "On the night you got sick."

But he shakes his head in frustration as if he has been trying to get this point across to her for hours.

"No, no," he says. "I'm not talking about a brush fire. I mean in the building. Was there a fire in the library? On the second floor," he says. He is closing his eyes as if remembering. "Or maybe the third?"

"I don't think so," she says.

"I had this dream," he says. "That there was a fire at the library, and somehow, the fire—it woke up all the sick." He takes a sip of his beer. He swallows hard. "The fire," he says, "it worked like some kind of cure."

After that, he goes quiet again. He goes back to his matches, lighting them one by one. Every once in a while, a look comes into his face that she has not seen before—spooked but satisfied, as if to say, Aha, there it is, that's it.

"I've been having this strange feeling," he says. "Ever since I woke up, I've been having this feeling that things are happening out of order."

He scrapes another match. It doesn't light. He tries again.

"Like just now," he says. "When you came into the kitchen, I had the sensation that you were standing beside me, but that was before you walked in."

It's like everything's out of order, he says, like there's something wrong with the sequence, as if the future were coming before the past.

She understands already how powerful his imagination is. After trauma, she's heard, people sometimes have hallucinations.

He picks up another match.

"Sometimes," he says, "I see the flame before I strike the match."

48.

The library: on the hundreds of metal bookshelves, now shoved flush against the wood paneling and the floor-to-ceiling windows, the ten thousand volumes now gathering dust in low light contain all the usual products of human thought.

In the Classics section, a visitor could read about the oracles of ancient Greece and Rome, how the people of those eras believed that dreams could sometimes reveal the future.

One floor down, in the Psychology section, one might eventually discover that Carl Jung, at a certain point in his life, became convinced that he had dreamed of his wife many years before he met her.

On another part of that same floor, in Philosophy, one could entertain the theory that if you could truly understand the complexity of reality, you could also accurately predict the future, since every moment of the future is set in motion by the events of the past—the whole system simply too complex for the human mind to model.

Upstairs, in Physics, one could find journal articles theorizing that the concepts of past, present, and future are artificial constructs, that in fact all three may exist at once, simultaneously, in different dimensions.

In Linguistics, one would find a similar intuition reflected in the grammar of certain languages. In Mandarin, for example, verbs operate entirely in the present tense. There is no special tense for the past or the future.

Time, said Saint Augustine, exists only in the mind.

But no one is reading any of the books in this library. At least one slim hardcover is right now being used to stabilize a wobbly army cot, where a small boy lies sleeping alongside a hundred other sick in the cavernous main reading room.

And even if one were to read every book in these stacks, certain mysteries would persist.

Think of William James, one floor down, back in Philosophy, who once compared any attempt to study human consciousness to turning on a lamp in order to better examine the dark.

49.

Certain real events are familiar only from the horrors of our dreams. And so, when smoke begins to pour into the main reading room of the library, drifting out over the bodies of a hundred sleeping sick, the same word rushes into the minds of more than one of the nurses: *nightmare.*

There will be much discussion later about the silence of the smoke alarms, offline for reasons no one can explain—whether tampered with, or simply unplugged to accommodate the heart monitors and the EEG machines.

Some will blame the masks, designed to filter out the smallest microbes on earth—but also the fine dust that swirls inside of smoke. If they had not been wearing masks, maybe the nurses and the doctors would have smelled the fire before it spread.

In the long minutes before the fire crews arrive, there is no time to argue over whom to rescue and whom to leave behind. Instead, people make their own choices. And who can blame the health workers if some of them carry out their own sick friends and family before attending to any of the others?

———

Ten blocks away, Sara is feeding the cats when the fire engines begin to wail. The sound sends the cats leaping from her lap and Sara rushing up to the widow's walk to check for signs of forest fire. But through the wavy glass of the windowpane comes instead an uncanny image—it is just as her father described it: a thick cloud of smoke is surging not from the woods in the distance but from the windows of the college library.

"Daddy," she calls out, a tightness coming into her chest. "Daddy," she calls again, but he does not answer. Her heart begins to pound. "It's just like your dream."

A snowy quiet. A cool, calm bliss—this is how the sleep has come to be for Mei.

But now, an interruption. Something is pulling her away. Loud noises. Shouting.

She has the sensation that she is waking up in her childhood bedroom, but the idea falls away immediately—this room is enormous.

Also: some kind of urgency is thumping in this place. People are moving quickly.

It is painful to listen after so long in silence.

It is hard to open her eyes. All she can do is squint. A crust has formed on her eyelashes. It is impossible to say whether the haze of her vision is a cloudiness of her corneas or of the room.

Her thinking is cloudy, too, slow and prone to stalling, but an important word does drift across her mind, tentative and abstract: *fire?*

People are coughing around her. Glass is breaking. Her throat begins to ache.

And then: Matthew appears across the room.

She has the feeling that she has not seen him in a long time. But here he is, running, as usual, those long legs, that frenetic way he has of moving. He is good in a crisis. One thing is different: his face is full of worry. When he gets close to her, he shouts something she cannot quite understand and keeps running. Then he sprints away, farther into the building, without touching her.

After that, she loses track of him, but he will take care of her. He will do whatever needs to be done. This is what she's thinking as she sinks back into the quiet relief of sleep.

There exists in the annals of medicine a rare phenomenon performed by the otherwise catatonic. In cases of emergency, someone previously immobilized may suddenly awaken—and regain miraculous abilities: to stand or to scream or to run. A hand, long dormant, may suddenly accomplish some necessary task: grab hold of a bedrail, perhaps, in the last seconds before a fall from a bed.

On this day in Santa Lora, some similar effect is observed in a small number of the sleepers.

Ben: first, he is at a party with Annie. It's at some kind of hotel, this party. Or not a hotel, a loft. In Brooklyn, maybe, or maybe not. But the loft is filled with furniture that reminds him of his grandmother's house in Wisconsin. That silky cream-colored couch from the sixties. They are drinking punch, he and Annie, out of tiny crystal glasses. How weird, she is saying, that they have the same couch! It's a Halloween party—that's why Annie is wearing that vest and that tie, that floppy black hat, khaki pants. Everyone loves her costume. She is Annie from *Annie Hall,* which is perfect for her—that's what their friends are saying. Perfect. It is very crowded, this party. And it is very loud. The punch tastes like gin and rosemary and a little like smoke, and people are having a very good time—this is the main thing Ben knows as he stands beside Annie, his hand on her hip, as if the goodness is built into the room itself, as if it's suffusing the air and the drinks, these minutes, her costume, that couch.

But then, a sudden sound quiets the party. It's like something breaking, like the snapping of wood. The feeling of an old ship cracking in a storm. Are they on a ship? Yes, a ship. It has been a ship all along.

Holy shit, someone is saying, it's the floor. There's some kind of problem with the floor.

Annie squeezes his hand hard, so hard that it hurts. That's when the whole middle of the floor just falls away like a sink-hole, and Annie—

His eyes flutter open.

For a moment, all he can hear is the sound of his own gasping, his own heart thudding in his ears. A surge of relief washes over him—it was only a dream.

But above him now looms an unfamiliar ceiling, dark wood and very high, a vast room, dimly lit. And also, there is this: people are shouting.

Someone leans over him. A firefighter.

In that moment, as if the visual parts of his brain are suddenly doing the work of smell, the yellow of that firefighter's coat triggers an associative burst—he is suddenly aware of the smell of smoke in the air.

He tries to sit up, but something is holding him down, as if he is tied to this bed. He remembers then about the sickness. He must have caught it like Annie.

Where is his baby? he asks. But no one is listening.

"Where is she?" he says. "Where is my baby?"

A thick smoke is filling the room. His throat is beginning to burn. All his confusion is distilled down to this: to get away from this smoke. It is a complicated procedure, this unhooking of tubes from his body. The firefighter helps free him from the cords and then disappears into the gloom.

The lights flicker and then flash off. A little sunlight is stream-ing in from somewhere, dim through the gathering smoke. He begins to cough. The idea comes to Ben that this is a library, a library crowded with beds.

He can't stop coughing now. And soon he is crawling along the floor with the others. His body is stiff and sore, but he keeps moving, oddly aware of its separate parts, as if the parts are operating just slightly out of synch, how the one hand moves before the other, his knees on hard wood. It is hard to find the exit through the smoke, but people are calling into the room from outside, strangers, strangers are calling to him, and the truth of it, that strangers would help other strangers, makes his eyes fill with tears, right there in the dark and the smoke: *Here, here,* they are shouting through the dusk, *the door is over here.*

Later, Ben will forget almost all of these details, how he finally got out—onto the lawn and into the sun with the other survivors. He will forget the way people looked at him, the shock to see him awake, he and the few others, skinny in hospital gowns, IVs still hanging from some of their arms. Perhaps the mind can only catalogue from any given day a fixed amount of experience. It is what happens next that he will always remember—in almost photographic detail—from the events of this day.

There is a woman out there—she is standing barefoot in the grass. And this woman—she looks a little like Annie. But he knows that it happens, how longing can do that, conjure the shapes of loved ones in the faces of strangers. This reminder of Annie—it is a part of the waking up, he knows, the familiar groove of missing her.

But the way this woman is standing, a little hunched, and the way she is chewing on her hair—he keeps looking.

She turns a little. Her profile comes into view. And there, on that woman's face, is a little notch in her nose, just like the one Annie has, from when she broke it as a teenager. Annie. She is standing in the sunshine in a hospital gown, a fire blanket wrapped around her shoulders, looking skinny and a little unwell, unsteady on her feet, her face smudged gray from the smoke. But it's her. It really is Annie. There she is, squinting up at the sky, as if in disbelief. There she is, awake.

50.

As the newspapers will later report, arson is suspected. Matches are found in the basement, the torn pages of books used for kindling. The setter of the fire is never found.

But many of the sleepers survive. Most are carried out in their sleep.

The big news, though, is this: fourteen of them wake up and walk out.

It's amazing, everyone agrees, miraculous, even. There is a great appetite for the miraculous. Among these survivors is a husband and wife, the Romeo and Juliet of Santa Lora, as several news outlets soon take to calling them in place of their real names: Ben and Annie.

Another survivor is an eleven-year-old girl, who, as the media widely reports, was carried out by her own father, himself only recently recovered, who rushed to the building when he saw the smoke, calling her name until he found her: Libby.

The media pays less attention to the sleepers who do not survive. There are nine of them. The cause of death is smoke inhalation, the gradual dissipation of oxygen from the blood, which, once, was thought to cause unusually vivid dreams.

Among these dead are two nurses, a CDC specialist in infectious disease, and the dean of the College of the Arts and Sciences.

Also on the list is a Santa Lora College freshman from San Diego: Mei Liu, age eighteen.

Her body is found too late by firefighters in a far corner of the smoky reading room of the library, still prone in her cot, curled beneath a blanket, saline still draining into the main vein of her swiftly whitening arm. She slept right through it, her parents are assured. She passed away peacefully, they say, in her sleep.

In the days after the fire, one story is circulated more than any other—people love when a crisis brings out the goodness in others: as smoke filled the library, one student, a college freshman and heir to the Baker & Baker pharmaceutical family, Matthew Baker, rushed inside and saved a baby from the fire. The story is shared again and again, how he grabbed the very youngest of the sick, the one who had the most life left: an infant, nine weeks old, wrapped in blankets, who went on sleeping all the while.

This story stands above the rest, this hero of Santa Lora, as proof of what human beings are capable of—who among us does not love a simple song?

51.

They report only minor residual symptoms, Ben and Annie. A mild dizziness, in her case. A slight impairment of his peripheral vision. They notice nothing else at first.

A year earlier, or two years, or any number of years before this one, their reunion would have felt different, like a wild piece of luck, miraculous, some might say, like a rising from the dead.

But in this particular year of their lives, they do not feel lucky. They feel almost no gratitude, as they hold tight to one another's hands or lean into the warmth of one another's arms. Each of them is entirely preoccupied with someone else. He is a father. She is a mother. Their child is sick.

The college dining hall is where the youngest surviving sick are moved after the fire. Here is where—after much waiting and calling and calling again, and much signing of paperwork—Ben and Annie find their baby.

They see her lying in a clear plastic bassinet. She is swaddled in unfamiliar blankets, her little mind locked in that deep, un- reachable sleep.

A feeding tube is taped into her tiny nostril.

"She's so much bigger than the last time I saw her," says Annie, her eyes continuously welling with tears.

Already, she is holding her up in her arms, the tubes dangling behind her. Even in sleep, the baby resettles her head on her shoulder, as if the memory of her mother resides entirely in the muscles of her neck.

Masks are suggested, and gloves. But it would be impossible, with gloves on, to wipe the crust from their daughter's eyes, or to rub Vaseline on her dried and cracking lips. There is a tremendous need to touch her skin.

She is two weeks older than the last time Ben saw her. Just the continued fact of her body, just her existence, is proof of the work of other people, those nurses, now swishing through the room in protective suits, how they have cared for her every day since he last saw her, and the college student they will never meet who rescued her from the fire.

She could have died—this is the knowledge that lights every moment with her now. The things that could have happened but did not are just as crucial to a life as all the things that do.

A few other mothers and fathers lean over some of the other children, or they sit, like Ben and Annie, in plastic chairs beside their cots. But most of the children lie here alone save for the nurses—and not enough of them—who turn them and wash them and fill the feeding tubes and change the diapers.

One of the last dreams Ben dreams before waking from the sickness goes like this: He and Annie are in a boat, a canoe. The sun is shining on her back, which is bare except for the strings of her green bikini. They are floating in some kind of bay. He does not know where. They paddle out to a small island on which grows a single pine tree. They leave the canoe and the paddles on the small beach and walk up to the tree, where they drink the beers they have packed in a cooler and watch the other boats drift by in the sun. There is an intense feeling of happiness, as the light glitters on the water, and something else, too: possibility. A lightness.

But suddenly someone is shouting at them from a passing boat.

"Hey," they say, "is this your canoe?"

And there it is, their canoe, floating empty in the middle of the water. The tide must have come in, they realize as they swim out to catch the boat and collect the drifting paddles. Like all the other dreams, there is something about this one that does not feel like a dream at all. It feels—how else can he put it—real. Here is that feeling again: that what he is seeing is the future.

In those first few days after waking, the dream hangs over Ben, a kind of background noise to his days in this converted dining hall.

He wants to tell Annie about it.

But it seems suddenly too intimate to mention, and too ridiculous, too. He keeps quiet. The act of matching words to the experience saps his belief.

Instead, he can only say this: "Did you have any weird dreams?" he asks her.

She does not look up from the baby.

"No," she says. "I didn't dream at all."

She feels so far away these days, like a stranger sitting across from him on a train.

On the second day, an older baby nearby begins to whimper in his sleep. His face is wincing. His diaper, Annie soon discovers, has leaked. Ben calls for a nurse. After a few minutes of waiting, the boy moaning, Annie changes it herself. There are certain circumstances under which the changing of a diaper is a sacred act.

———

One day a small boy in a bed nearby opens his eyes. The movement of those eyelids, the white around his eyes, sends hope surging through the whole place.

"I want my mama," he says. He is calm for a moment, as if the request will be granted. "I want my mama."

But when she does not appear right away, he begins to cry.

Ben tries to comfort him, but he will not be comforted.

Finally, the mother is located and brought to his bed.

"He asked for me?" she says when he jumps into her arms. "With words?"

Not quite two years old, this boy, says the mother, had not yet begun speaking in sentences.

But now listen to him:

"Mama," he says, "I had a bad dream."

But Ben and Annie's baby sleeps on. They cut her nails. They bathe her body. They sleep on the linoleum beside her bassinet.

Ben thinks more and more about his dreams. So strong is his feeling that those dreams were premonitions that they begin to frighten him. One thing was missing from those dreams: his baby. If those dreams were of the future, where was she?

52.

In a famous experiment, a geologist once subjected himself to eight weeks alone in a lightless underground cave. Among other things, he wanted to test the accuracy of his own internal clock. He woke and slept as he pleased. He marked his days in a notebook. Without the ticking of clocks or the rising and setting of the sun, his body's rhythms soon fell out of synch with the earth's. At the end of the experiment, he was sure he had spent only thirty-five days underground, but sixty days had passed at the surface.

Libby: she sleeps for three weeks but she dreams of a single afternoon.

She wakes with a smile on her face, a calmness. She yawns and stretches in her sheets.

With the opening of those eyes comes an elation that Sara has never known before. Nothing is more potent than relief.

"How do you feel?" Sara asks her sister.

Libby has awakened in her own bedroom, where their father brought her after the fire—during the first minutes of chaos when no one was guarding the patients. He and Sara have been tending to her for a day without the help of doctors or nurses.

"I had the most amazing dream last night," says Libby.

Her voice is hoarse. Her curls are tangled. She does not seem to understand how much time has passed.

"What kind of dream?" says her father, an odd intensity to his voice.

Libby meets eyes with Sara, their old habit.

"What happened to your beard?" asks Libby.

"Those dreams," says their father. "Those were not normal dreams, okay? What did you see?"

The hair on his head is starting to grow back, but it's coming in white instead of brown. And he is just as skinny as he was on the day he woke up.

"It was about our mom," says Libby. There's an unfamiliar quiet in her voice, a reverence. "We were by the lake."

But her father is shaking his head.

"No," he says, his hand up, like a stop sign. "That's not the kind of dream I'm talking about. What else?"

"Just that," she says.

He keeps asking if she's sure, and she is, and then he disappears downstairs.

"How long did I sleep?" Libby asks once he's gone.

"Three weeks," says Sara.

Libby's reaction is almost physical, as if the wind has been knocked out of her chest.

"It felt like just a few hours," she says. "Like a nap."

The cats have collected around Libby, cuddling in the sheets of her bed.

"You were there, too," says Libby. "In the dream. We were down at the lake with her."

If Libby closes her eyes, she can remember everything about those minutes: the lavender cables of their mother's sweater, her fingernails, chipped with pale peach polish.

"And these earrings," says Libby, picking up a pair of silver hoops from a scattering of jewelry on the nightstand. "She was wearing these earrings."

There was a newspaper spread out on a picnic table by the lake. Finger paints set out.

"We were making handprints with the paint," says Libby. "And she was painting a little picture of the lake with her fingers."

The air smelled like barbecue. Someone was grilling down on the beach. Their mother had a certain way of wiping her hair from her face with the back of her hand.

"You were wearing a sunflower-shaped barrette," says Libby. "And a white sundress."

Their mother handed them milk in plastic cups, a ziplock bag of Goldfish.

"I started to throw the paint, and she said: 'Girls, I've told you three times.'"

The blue paint drying in the creases of her palms, the sound of the birds, the voices of other children splashing in the water.

"Do you remember a day like that?" says Libby.

"No," says Sara.

"I think it was real," says Libby, a distant afternoon recovered, intact, from the deep.

Libby was so young when their mother died—she has never before remembered anything about her.

"It can't be," says Sara, suddenly filled with envy. "You were too young to remember."

But she makes Libby tell her the whole thing again, in even more detail, until the time it takes for the telling far exceeds any minutes they spent, once, years ago, by the lake.

Libby lowers her voice. "What did Daddy dream of?"

"He dreamed there would be a fire at the library," says Sara.

"Don't talk about that," her father calls from the other room.

Sara whispers: "And then there really was a fire there."

An uneasiness comes into Libby's face.

"What happened was just like your dream," says Sara. "Right, Daddy?"

He shakes his head. He is adamant. "In my dream," he says, "no one died."

While the Humvees continue rumbling down the streets of Santa Lora, their father checks and rechecks the supplies in the basement, obsessed with new worries.

He had other dreams, too.

"The oceans moved a hundred miles inland," he says. "Los Angeles was swallowed. The ocean came all the way to the base of these mountains."

He takes a sip of beer. He swallows hard.

"And then today," he says, "this news comes out: the biggest ice shelf in Antarctica is about to collapse. Do you see what that means?"

They wait for him to explain.

"It's happening," he says. "The dreams I had. They were all real."

Sara at once believes it and does not believe it. She has not yet heard the rumors circulating that some of the other survivors claim to have seen glimpses of the future, too. But isn't the future always an imaginary thing before it comes?

53.

A tiny heart goes on beating in the dark. A spinal cord coalesces. Electricity begins to flow through the synapses of a brain. Bones form, the beginnings of teeth. Eyelids. The first flapping of hairline arms, the minute flowering of fingernails. The knees and the wrists—they begin to bend.

Rebecca, ten weeks in, goes on sleeping all the while. Her cheeks, flushed with extra blood, now take on a certain fullness as her chest rises and falls beneath the hospital sheets. A surge of hormones is responsible for the extra oil in her skin, and the nurses—sheathed in their masks and their suits—like to point out the one nice thing in this dark place: she really does have that pregnancy glow.

That same week, inside one of the vast medical tents on campus, the professor of biology opens his eyes in the quiet middle of the night. Above Nathaniel looms a bright white ceiling, fluorescent lit. He is not at home—this is Nathaniel's first thought. The air smells like soil.

He is lucky, says the first doctor—his was a mild case. Only three weeks. That's their best guess, anyway. "Some kids brought you in," he says through his mask. "A boy and a girl carried you here."

He is too weak to sit up, at first, but he asks about Henry, if Henry is here somewhere, too. It takes hours for the answer to come back to him: no, there's no patient here by that name. He borrows a phone. He calls home. No answer.

Here marks the beginning of a period of confusion, not uncommon among the survivors, he is told by the doctors. Now marks the start of a slowly bubbling dread.

At home, he finds a black X spray-painted on the front door. Inside, he discovers a house transformed, as if by the flow of time as well as by water. The wallpaper is peeling like eucalyptus bark. Mold is already growing in the corners. The rugs weep like sponges beneath his feet. The coffee table is crooked, the dining chairs overturned, as if every object in the house has been lifted by water and then set down again when the water receded. A vague recollection comes into his mind—at some point, he was trying to repair the bathroom sink. The offending pipe is still dripping, taped up by someone else's inexpert hands.

He calls Henry's name. "Hello?" he says. "Henry?" But the house is quiet. He half expects to find Henry drowned on the rug. "Hello?"

Instead, he eventually locates Henry back in the nursing home, hunched in an armchair, trapped once again in his stupor. It is hard to make sense of it—seeing him that way again.

"We've been trying to reach you," says one of the doctors there.

"How did he get back here?" Nathaniel asks.

"What do you mean?" says the doctor. There is no mention of Henry's extraordinary awakening.

That slack face. Those blank eyes. If you ask him his name, he makes no attempt to reply.

The facts as others will see them are clear to Nathaniel immediately: that he only dreamed Henry back to life, that his great awakening was only a wish Nathaniel wished in his sleep. And yet, something in him resists the idea, as if this is only one interpretation of the events.

The memory of Henry's return feels nothing at all like a dream. Those few days are as clear as any other memory. Clearer, even.

"Did you have any weird dreams?" his daughter asks over the phone—she has flown down from San Francisco, but the nearest she can get is the next town over. "They keep saying that dreams are a part of it."

"I didn't have any dreams," says Nathaniel. The truth is too embarrassing to admit.

He sets up giant fans to dry out the house. He makes a call to the insurance company. He goes back to his work in the woods.

But a heaviness lingers in his limbs, a weariness—and no diagnostic test can register whether it's a symptom of the sickness or of grief. The darkest moods sometimes descend after periods of unexpected light.

He begins to research the work of one of his old colleagues, a proponent of an outlandish thread of physics: how maybe everything that could have ever happened *has* happened—each permutation unfolding in its own parallel universe.

He goes to sleep alone each night, and each night, he dreams of nothing.

In the thirteenth week, the hair starts to grow. The eyebrows. Marrow begins to fill the bones.

And in the other beds of the same wing of the hospital where Rebecca goes on sleeping, some of the first to get sick—the other girls of the dorm floor—begin to open their eyes. One has dreamed of a long and glittering future. One has dreamed of a series of tragedies. One complains of nightmares so extreme that the ordinary waking world is an extravagant relief.

At the end of that week, officials in Santa Lora report a new milestone: no new cases in seven days. Here is the moment they have been waiting for. A virus can only burn for so long—only a certain percentage of any population is susceptible to any given germ.

That same week, in the children's ward, Ben returns to the bassinet one day to find that in the minutes he was gone, everything has changed: their baby has opened her eyes.

Annie is holding her in her arms—that look on her face, that simple, silent joy. The baby is staring up at her like she did on the day she was born, her eyes a slightly darker blue. Her return is even more precious than her arrival—he understands this time what it means to have his daughter with him in the world.

Later that week, back home in their bed, while Annie gives the baby a bottle, Ben finally tries to tell her about the dreams.

"They were like premonitions," he says. Worry comes over Annie's face. "I know it sounds weird," he says.

But he goes on. He begins with the dream about the canoe and the paddles, the way they floated out into the water while he and Annie were drinking beer under a tree.

"Are you all right?" she says. She shifts the baby in her arms.

"I know," he says. "But listen." He half closes his eyes to remember, shutting out the low light of the bedside lamp. "In the dream, we are somewhere where there's water. And trees. Pine trees that grow right up near the water."

Annie begins to laugh a little, a low and nervous laugh. It was a mistake, he suddenly knows, to tell her any of this.

"That's not the future," she says. "That's the past."

It is as difficult to believe what she is saying as it would be to grasp the idea that time moves backward as easily as forward.

"That was Maine," she says. "The summer after college. You don't remember that? We tell that story all the time."

He tells her about another dream, the party where the floor begins to buckle.

"That was Halloween at Rob's old place in Brooklyn," she says.

He understands what she is saying. But it does not seem possible. Maybe the sleep has confused her mind even more than his.

They go through the dreams one by one while, outside, a light snow begins to fall, catching in the low glow of the streetlight.

"You just dreamed we were young again," says Annie.

The baby is watching his face now. He feels a sudden longing to be alone with his daughter, to tell her and not Annie about the meaning of his dreams.

"Your daddy loves looking back," Annie says to the baby, who stares, blinking. "He's always so sure that things were better before than they are now."

Ben doesn't tell her any more about it. That night, he lies awake for a long time, unable to fall asleep.

Maybe there will always be evenings like this one when he lies down beside his wife and misses the wife from his dreams.

By the seventeenth week, the bones of the inner ear have hardened. And into these ears begin to flow the sounds of Rebecca's beating heart, the swish of shared blood traveling through the umbilical cord, the slight sloshing of amniotic fluid as she turns in her sleep, and, maybe, the muffled voices of the nurses and the periodic beep of the fetal heart monitor.

With the remaining sick dwindling, and no new cases in four

weeks, the CDC announces the end of the outbreak of what will forever be known, should it appear again, or even if it doesn't, as the Santa Lora Virus.

The last case ever reported is in an eighty-nine-year-old man in the nursing home—and then, like the passing of a storm, the virus disappears.

But where does it go? Perhaps it recedes back to wherever it came from—the woods, maybe, some animal carrying it through the underbrush. The researchers return to their labs in different states to keep studying the virus, in case it someday returns, which, they all agree, it will. In a year or in ten years, or a hundred. It might mutate by then, turn milder perhaps, or it might go the other way, a pestilence moving across the country—how much quieter that ending would be, a whole world drowned in sleep, than all the other ways we have to fall.

A federal judge orders the lifting of the cordon sanitaire. The barricades come down. Relatives and reporters flood into Santa Lora. Survivors pour out, the superstitious ones never to return again.

After four months in the quarantined hospital, Catherine is finally allowed to go home to Los Angeles.

But when she walks into her house, her daughter hides behind her grandmother's leg. How excruciating it is, not to see her little face. But Catherine feels it, too, this upsetting nervousness, the feeling of meeting someone new.

She kneels down as if her daughter is one of her patients. "Can I give you a hug?" she asks.

Her daughter shakes her head. She is wearing a green dinosaur T-shirt that Catherine has never seen.

"You look different," her daughter says, peeking out for a moment. And it's true: Catherine has grown thin during the time away.

At least there is this, a comfort and a sadness: her daughter will not remember any of this. Whole years of her life will pass before anything more than flashes will register in her long-term conscious memory.

But Catherine will always worry that this time will stay with her child somehow, this period of separation from her only parent, the way the root of a tree grows around a rock in its path, or a broken bone without a splint heals crookedly beneath the skin.

At twenty weeks, the part of the hypothalamus responsible for the circadian rhythm begins to regulate the rate of the heartbeat and the tides of certain hormones in a pattern that matches almost exactly the length of a day on earth.

Caleb wakes four doors down from Rebecca. He does not pass her room. He does not touch her hand. He does not know what lives inside her, growing, as he leaves Santa Lora with his parents, who have camped out all these weeks right outside the barricades, waiting for news of their son.

Rebecca sleeps on with eighty-five others, the last of the sleepers consolidated now into one wing of the hospital.

At twenty-eight weeks, the brain becomes complex enough to be startled by sudden noises and to turn the head in the direction of voices. At this age, the brain begins to dream. But of what? The sensation of floating, perhaps, the subtle shifts of light and dark? Or perhaps brains so young dream dreams unimaginable to us, beyond the reach of science and language, unrecorded and unrecoverable.

Soon the mouth begins to open and close. The lungs are growing fast, in preparation for the task of converting the air of this planet into something the body can use.

The schools reopen.

Sara goes back to eating lunch alone each day on the quad. What a relief it is to one day spot Akil, finally back at school.

"Hey," she says.

"Hi," he says. There is a heaviness in the way he speaks. He does not need to tell her that he had the sickness. She can see it, somehow, in his face.

"Is your family okay?" she asks.

"Yeah," he says. "We're okay. And yours?"

She nods.

Often, they eat lunch side by side, while the other kids careen around the quad. There is a comfort in sharing a silence. The spring flowers have returned, pink roses near the science lab, marigolds along the gym. Dandelions are everywhere in the grass.

One bright blue day at the end of lunch, the woods looming in the distance beyond the playground, Akil tells her about what happened to his father.

"He could have died," he says.

Instead, he walks with a slight limp and a long scar on his hip.

"I can't get rid of this weird feeling," says Akil. "That it's all still in the future." There is always the sense, he says, that one day soon, his dad will be taken to jail in Egypt, that they will have to leave everything behind, and that on another day soon, he will be shot by American soldiers right here in this American town.

The bell rings. The other kids begin to stream toward the classrooms. But Sara stays right where she is beside him, listening.

"I know that it all already happened," says Akil. "I know that. But that's not how it feels. It feels like it's all coming up ahead, and always will be, around and around again."

Rebecca sleeps through the early contractions. She sleeps through the insertion of a needle between two rungs in her spine. She sleeps as the anesthesia spreads through the tissues in her body.

She sleeps while, in another room, the obstetrician and the nurses don Tyvek suits and Tyvek hoods. She sleeps while, thus protected, they rub her belly with iodine, in preparation for the cesarean.

Even the scalpel does not disturb her sleep.

She does not wake when the obstetrician, with double-gloved hands, having sliced through the layers of her skin, spreads apart the muscles of her abdomen. She sleeps while this same doctor cuts through the wall of her uterus, and while the nurses sponge the resulting blood. She sleeps through the prying of the baby from her body—like pulling a tooth from its bed. She sleeps through the baby's first moments outside.

It is the quietest birth anyone remembers.

Everyone is hoping for a cry, but no cry comes. Rebecca sleeps through the good news: that the baby is breathing, at least. And she sleeps through the bad news, too: that her baby, like her, is sound asleep. The Santa Lora Virus, it turns out, can travel across the placenta.

After the cord is cut and clamped, and the baby weighed and wrapped and the nasal passages cleared, one of the nurses thinks to move Rebecca's hand to the baby's forehead, a pantomime of a mother meeting her child.

Rebecca sleeps while they sew up the incision. She sleeps while they cauterize the wound.

She sleeps when they settle the baby on her chest. And, when they move the baby to her breast, and when the baby begins, somehow, to nurse in its sleep—Rebecca sleeps through that moment, too.

54.

The dead: they are doctors and nurses, teachers and artists, professors of philosophy and French, the mayor of Santa Lora. They are young, they are old, they are in the middle of their lives. One whole family, three hearts, goes quiet within a few hours, like lightbulbs winking on a string. For the undiscovered dead, the cause is dehydration. But under medical care, it is most often the heart that gives out, a slowing so extreme that, at a certain point, the pumping can no longer support the body, like certain Buddhist monks who, in deep meditation, have been known to attain a state of such relaxation that their hearts no longer beat.

The dead are mourned with flowers left at the roadblocks outside of town, or funerals, sparsely attended, the pews moved out onto the lawns of the churches for the continuing fear of contagion.

More dreamers quit breathing each day. One in ten never do wake up. At least, some say, they die good deaths, peaceful. They are spared the experience of their own endings.

The names of the dead will one day appear on a plaque beside what is left of the lake, shaded by pine trees, browning where they stand.

55.

Rebecca, five years older, is holding her little boy's hand as they walk one day in the woods. His fingers pull dandelions in a field. He blows the seeds through the air. She sees wisdom in the sight of him, his growing body announcing it every day: life goes on.

Soon he is a boy at six years old, standing on a diving board in aqua blue swim trunks, calling: "Mama, Mama, watch this." She is sitting on the weedy grass beside the pool. They are at her parents' house on a Sunday afternoon. She is holding her boy's flip-flops in her lap. His church clothes lie in a heap beside her. From inside the house comes the soft clinking of plates, the sounds of her mother making lunch in the kitchen.

Her boy jumps into the pool. A cannonball. That look on his face as he leaps: his eyes pressed shut, as if by the force of his smile.

Rebecca calls to him from the grass as he bobs afterward in the water. "Amazing," she says.

He looks like her brother did at that age. Goggles, a gap between his teeth, lanky legs and long feet. The smell of the neighbors' orange trees is wafting over the fence. The sounds of her mother in the kitchen, the low heels of her church shoes clicking on the linoleum.

Now the boy is up and out of the pool. Water is streaming down his legs, dripping on the same pavement where her own small feet once dripped, and she is speaking the exact words that her mother used to say to her: "Don't run," she says. "Don't run. You'll slip."

But this is only one afternoon in a certain year. One day in a whole life.

The boy keeps moving forward. He gets older. He grows up. He starts college. He drops out. There are arguments, misunderstandings, forgiveness. He moves away the year Rebecca loses her mother. He moves back the same year her father dies. He quits his job. He becomes an artist. He goes back to school. He gets married. He has a baby of his own and then another.

One evening, Rebecca and her son go out for a walk in his neighborhood at dusk. Rebecca is an old woman now and her boy is a man in middle age.

They've had a minor fight, but it is passing now, as they walk.

"You have to let me make my own decisions," he says.

An odd feeling comes to her—it's the way he says that, the way he turns toward her when he speaks, his words, almost exactly like something she once said to her own parents a long time ago.

56.

Rebecca wakes in an unfamiliar room. White walls. Fluorescent lights. An IV twisting out from one arm.

In her confusion, she recognizes only one thing through the window: the mission-style bell tower of Santa Lora College. She is back, somehow, in Santa Lora.

A soft beeping is coming from a nearby monitor. She has the sensation that she is not alone in this room. She becomes aware of a soreness in her abdomen. Her fingers find a bandage there.

A door opens—someone walks into the room. A nurse, maybe. She is wearing a yellow plastic suit, this nurse. The suit covers her whole body, even her shoes, like in a movie, thinks Rebecca. The nurse behaves as if Rebecca is not in the room. Instead, she leans over something in the far corner. A crib, Rebecca sees now, a clear plastic crib on casters. Inside the crib, swaddled in a cream-colored blanket with pink trim, a newborn baby lies sleeping in a little pink cap. Rebecca's first thought is this: Who is that baby?

But now the nurse comes to Rebecca. Now she is saying something through her mask. She is shouting to someone else, someone outside the room.

"She's awake," the nurse is saying. She is calling to someone else down the hall. She is pointing at Rebecca. "The mother is awake."

It is hard to understand what it means. But a panic is rising in her chest.

More people rush in—all wearing those yellow suits.

Already a deep sense of absence is welling in her, a loss: Where is her son? she asks.

But they do not seem to understand what she is saying. "My son," she says again. "Please ask him to come right away."

It is hard to talk. It is hard to make herself clear.

But no one is answering her, and a dark thought comes into her mind. "Is he okay?" she whispers, her eyes already filling with tears.

"You had the sickness," says one of the nurses. "You've been unconscious for almost a year."

Rebecca hears the words but cannot understand them.

"It's normal to feel confused," says the nurse.

At some point, Rebecca's mother walks through the door, just like that, her mother, back from the dead, as if she's been waiting in that hallway all these years. And not just alive but younger, her mother as she was thirty years ago, in middle age, when Rebecca left for college. Her red hair, her white teeth. She rushes to Rebecca's bed. "My God," her mother keeps saying. She takes hold of her hand. "My God."

And it is good to see her face—that joy, that relief. It feels good to see her mother after so many years moving through the world without her. But it's frightening, too, a visitation from the dead.

"Where's my son?" Rebecca asks her.

But her mother does not seem to understand the question. "I don't know what you mean," says her mother. "You've had a baby girl," she says. "Look."

"Did something happen to my son?" Rebecca says again, a sob growing in her throat.

There is fear now on her mother's face. Her eyes flash back at the nurses.

"The doctor," says her mother. "She says that you might have had some strange dreams."

57.

For years after Rebecca wakes, acquaintances will comment that she has a sense of wisdom beyond what is common in someone so young. Left unsaid, perhaps, a certain tiredness, too.

It takes her months to believe that she is a girl of nineteen and not a woman many decades into life. How uncanny, it seems to her, that the baby girl on her lap is hers.

And her son: his absence informs every moment of her life. No one can understand it—how she could cling so tightly to a dream. But for her, her son is a truth as certain as anything else: she knew him for forty years. Sometimes, for a moment, she is sure that she sees him on the street. The sound of his voice, the shape of his face—these are as crisp and as dear to her as her daughter's small fingers, her round cheeks.

There is no grief like the grief for one's child.

Rebecca's doctors find the intricacy of her delusion uncanny; whole decades persist in her mind, a whole life. Her symptoms align with several known psychiatric disorders: the delusion that her baby is not her baby, that her body is not her body, a difficulty distinguishing between reality and dream.

A generalized murkiness also remains. A certain slowness of thought, a confusion in her memories.

"Isn't that to be expected," says her mother, "after so long unconscious?"

Although her mother caught it, too, and her father, her brothers, none slept as long as Rebecca or recall such realistic dreams. The specialists still cannot explain much about the nature of the sickness, or about what it might have done to her brain.

The main thing, say her parents, is to be grateful. Think of the others. Think of the dead. "Give thanks in all circumstances," that's what her father says. "For this is God's will for you in Christ Jesus."

She does not keep in touch with anyone from those days, not even Caleb. How expert we are at looking away from what we would rather not see.

Unmarried with a child—she never would have predicted that it would happen this way or that there would be so little judgment from her parents. If they had any objection, she does not recall it. A gift from God, they say. This girl, your girl, is a gift. No matter how she got here. They leave it at that. They do not ask. And the exact circumstances of her making—so scandalous in her mind that she would have thought it would break the family apart—have drifted away from her thoughts.

But a sensation persists: that pieces are missing. The brain is a mystery, say her doctors, and it takes time to heal. It will get easier—that's what her mother says. We've come through something terrible, she says, but we've come through.

Certain thoughts Rebecca keeps to herself, like how can anyone say for sure that the other life was the dream, and not this one? By what instrument can she ascertain that these moments right here—with her girl on her lap, looking up so sweetly, those cheeks, her first tooth—are not part of a strange and pleasant dream she is dreaming in old age?

But some things are simple: She holds her baby girl just like she once, long ago, held her son. She sings her the same songs she sang to him. She loves her with that same madness. Or with more, maybe, her love suffused, this time, with the loss of the other one.

A year after the lifting of the cordon sanitaire, Nathaniel leaves his house for the last time.

He is brief in the final email he sends to his daughter—they are going to seek some kind of treatment for Henry, experimental, he says, but promising. The unproven, he says, should not be confused with the impossible.

He checks Henry out of the nursing home. They drive to the airport. They fly from Los Angeles to Mexico City, and then on to a smaller town farther south, where an anesthesiologist has promised that he can induce with drugs the same dream sleep that the Santa Lora Virus did.

A needle is inserted into Henry's veins. And then a second one is inserted into Nathaniel's. He holds Henry's hand as it happens. It takes less than a minute for the sleep to overcome them both.

And this is where they lie even now, side by side in a clinic in the mountains of Mexico, tended by nurses, hearts beating, lungs breathing, eyes closed to this world.

And who are we to say that they are not, these two, together somewhere even now, in the woods behind their house, those trees as healthy as they were thirty years ago, or in the old chairs on their back porch, drinking Henry's favorite Irish whisky, now discontinued. Who are we to say that they are not right now dreaming a better world?

The college reopens. Classes resume. Kegs can once again be seen rolling up the ramps of fraternity houses.

But it will be years before enrollment returns to previous levels. A petition circulates to have the town of Santa Lora renamed.

The virus persists not only in the freezers of Level 4 labs of this country, but also in the form of empty houses in Santa Lora, and lost pets, untended gardens, the station wagons abandoned in the parking lots of the supermarket and the church, eventually towed one by one, also the dead patches of grass, shaded for too many weeks by the medical tents on the lawns. It lingers also in the weariness in some people's faces, a slowness of gait, and someday, perhaps, a sunken fishing boat will emerge in the middle of the lake, whenever that water finally dries up completely.

Some dreamed of their youth. Some dreamed of old age. Some dreamed of days that might have been—all the lives they did not live. Or the lives that, in some other world, they did. Many dreamed of lovers, former and continuing. Some dreamed of the dead.

One man reported dreaming again and again of being trapped inside an elevator—he had the feeling that this tedium continued for years. This sort of thing turns out to be common in the dreams, these distortions of time, as if each dream contained its own unique physics.

Past, present, future—a physicist might say that these distinctions are illusions anyway. The human brain is subject to all kinds of misperceptions, and the waking mind not always more attuned to reality than the dreaming one.

Some of the children dreamed exquisitely beautiful worlds, the shadows of which will appear in their drawings for years. And what the infants dreamed we will never know, but perhaps those visions will live secretly in their habits and in their desires, their sense of what is familiar and what should be feared.

Researchers will be studying the virus for years—why some

survived it and why some didn't, and why it receded when it did. But the content of the dreams will be of little interest to science, just as a neurologist has no use for the soul.

Left almost entirely unstudied are the most famous claims—that some dreamers saw visions of the future. Anecdotal evidence suggests that certain dreamed-of events have indeed come to pass: the end of the drought and the deaths of several relatives. A rumor circulates around the elementary school that one of the fathers saw the library fire in his dreams.

These stories bring certain kinds of travelers to the streets of this town, in search of the mystical power of the Santa Lora sleep. Searchers and seekers, they camp out in the woods or in vans by the lake.

And as they wander the streets of Santa Lora, these hopeful travelers might notice, on many nights, a man on a porch swing with a baby resting on his lap, his wife sometimes beside him and sometimes not.

Ben: he will never escape the sensation that what he saw in his dreams—all those good days with Annie—was the future and not the past. Even later, when he understands that it must be true that those days have already come and gone, it does not feel true, the way those who argue that there's no such thing as free will continue to deliberate carefully over big decisions.

The more time that passes, what begins to seem uncanny to Ben is the fact that all the days ahead are such a darkness, that all of us move through our hours as if blindfolded, never knowing what will happen next. How can he send his daughter out into a world like that?

But even an infant's brain can predict the rough path of a falling object in flight.

And so, maybe, in a way, Ben *can* see what's coming:

His girl will love and be loved. She will suffer, and she will cause suffering. She will be known and unknown. She will be content and discontented. She will sometimes be lonely and sometimes less so. She will dream and be dreamed of. She will grieve and be grieved for. She will struggle and triumph and fail. There will be days of spectacular beauty, sublime and unearned. There will be moments of rapture. She will sometimes feel afraid.

The sun will warm her face. The earth will ground her body.

And her heart—now thrumming strong and steady, against her father's chest, as he rocks her to sleep on a porch swing one evening in early summer, at the very start of a life—that heart: it will beat, and it will someday cease to beat.

And so much of this life will remain always beyond her understanding, as obscure as the landscapes of someone else's dreams.

Acknowledgments

I'm very glad to have this chance once again to say thank you to the people who helped make it possible for me to write this book.

For years of friendship and insight—on writing as well as life—thank you: Alena Graedon, Nellie Hermann, Nathan Ihara, Tania James, Susannah Kohn, Dina Nayeri, and Maggie Pouncey. For particularly generous support of this book, I especially want to thank Karen Russell.

For various kinds of support and good times, thank you to Sara Irwin, Heather Sauceda Hannon, Shiloh Beckerly, Kelly Haas, Liz Guando and Dan Guando, Rachel Burgess, and Jack Hostetter and Carrie Loewenthal Massey.

For an endearingly weird non-book-club book club, thank you, Brittany Banta, Jenny Blackman, Hannah Davey, Meena Hart Duerson, Paul Lucas, Devin McKnight, Finn Smith, Pitchaya Sudbanthad (and Nathan Ihara and Casey Walker).

For their wisdom and generosity, thank you, Jim Shepard, Karen Shepard, Dani Shapiro, and Michael Maren.

Thank you again to my teachers, whose insights continue to guide my work as a writer and as a teacher: Aimee Bender,

Nathan Englander, Mary Gordon, Sam Lipsyte, Mona Simpson, and Mark Slouka.

Thank you to my wonderful and talented colleagues at the University of Oregon: Daniel Anderson, Lowell Bowditch, Jason Brooks Brown, Marjorie Celona, Geri Doran, Garrett Hongo, and Brian Trapp. Thank you also to all of my students, whose work continually challenges and inspires me. Thank you to Julia Schewanick for smoothing the way.

Thank you to Amelia Duke, who made it possible to leave the side of a newborn baby for a few hours at a time to finish revising this book—and to do so without the slightest bit of worry.

I feel extremely fortunate to have such a kind and brilliant editor, Kate Medina. Thank you, Kate, for putting so much thought and so much care into these pages.

Thank you to the rest of the Random House team, especially Anna Pitoniak, Erica Gonzalez, London King, Gina Centrello, Susan Kamil, and Evan Camfield. Thank you also to copyeditor Deb Dwyer for a particularly thorough and thoughtful read.

Thank you to Suzanne Baboneau at Simon & Schuster UK for your continued enthusiasm.

Thank you to Eric Simonoff at WME for your encouragement, savvy, and freindship. Thank you also to the rest of the amazing WME team, especially Laura Bonner, Tracy Fischer, Jazmine Goguen, Alicia Gordon, and Lauren Szurgot.

I am also grateful to have come across the following books in my research, all of which were crucial: *Awakenings* by Oliver Sacks, *Strangers Drowning* by Larissa MacFarquhar, *Spillover* by David Quammen, *A Paradise Built in Hell* by Rebecca Solnit, *The Hidden Life of Trees* by Peter Wohlleben, *Dreamland* by David K. Randall, and, from the Oxford Very Short Introduction series: *Sleep* by Steven W. Lockley and Russell G. Foster, *Dreaming* by J. Allan Hobson, *Freud* by Anthony Storr, *Jung* by Anthony Stevens, and *Consciousness* by Susan Blackmore.

And now to my family:

For treating me like a sister, thank you, Liz Chu and Kiel Walker. For love and enthusiasm—and many hours of crucial babysitting—thank you, Cheryl Walker and Steve Walker.

Thank you to my parents, Jim Thompson and Martha Thompson, for all your love, help, interest (and babysitting!)—and for being my biggest fans.

Thank you, sweet Hazel, for your amazing brain, your enormous personality, and for generally enlarging my life—as well as this book. (I added a newborn to this story when you were eleven days old.) Thank you also to tiny, mysterious Penny for big smiles and inspiration and for sleeping so soundly on my chest while I finished this book.

Lastly, thank you, Casey, to whom I owe so much it's hard to settle on the right words, so I'll just say this: for everything.

THE DREAMERS

Karen Thompson Walker

A Reader's Guide

A Conversation Between Karen Russell
and Karen Thompson Walker

Karen Russell: The epigraph of *The Dreamers* comes from José Saramago's *Blindness*, in which a mass epidemic of blindness sweeps through an unnamed city, resulting in a quarantine. How is *The Dreamers* inspired by and in conversation with Saramago's work?

Karen Thompson Walker: *Blindness* is a touchstone book for me, the book that first inspired me to consider writing fiction with a fantastical element. It's a huge influence on both of my books. I'm obsessed with the way Saramago described his own work as being about the "possibility of the impossible." What he said was: "I ask the reader to accept a pact; even if the idea is absurd, the important thing is to imagine its development. The idea is the point of departure, but the development is always rational and logical."

I like to use unreal elements to explore the real territory of human life. The intensely contagious sleeping sickness in *The Dreamers* is an invented virus, but it allows me to play with certain fundamental mysteries of human experience: dreams, the subconscious, fear, the bonds between people and what happens to those bonds in a crisis. And I know that the thrilling experience of reading Saramago's imaginary contagion of blindness lived in my own imagination, and made me want to find a way to write my own contagion story and to treat it with the same kind of "realism" that Saramago treats his.

KR: The way *The Dreamers* is able to toggle between intimate moments and a panoramic capture of the crisis in progress really floored me. We eavesdrop on characters' innermost thoughts and feelings; we also see and know things these characters do not, as when the narrator informs us, "If anyone were really looking closely, *which no one is at this moment,* he or she might notice the way his hand tenses against the barrel. . . ."

How did you decide on this elastic, omniscient point-of-view? What guided you as you chose when to alternate between individual storylines and the collective experience of the virus? Did certain moments feel better suited to an aerial omniscience, with its darkly glinting authority? How did this uniquely mobile point of view help you to build suspense?

KTW: My first book, *The Age of Miracles,* was a kind of keyhole perspective on a global disaster. It appealed to me to try something different this time. There's also something irreducibly social about a contagious illness: you don't catch a contagious disease if you live alone with no human contact. So it felt natural to show the way this strange illness ripples through the lives of various people in the town, rather than focusing on only one person or one family.

I was interested in seeing how a variety of people would respond to the situation, but the individual characters came to me slowly. There's not always a rhyme and reason to how they ended up in here. It was just a matter of who I could make feel real. I added some of them late in the process: Nathaniel and Henry, and Catherine, the psychiatrist. At least one early character got cut because he never seemed to fully emerge on the page.

Finding a perspective for this novel that could make the best use of all of these competing voices was a constant struggle right up until the end. My first book had a first-person voice, and when you write in first person, the limits and possibilities feel more obvious and intuitive—they are the same limits we all live with as people in the world. A third-person narrator who can inhabit various people's thoughts is a creature that only exists in fiction—which is part of the appeal of writing it. For a while, though, the limitlessness was overwhelming. *Does this voice know everything?* I wondered. *What are its rules and boundaries?* I find that limits—in time, in place, and in point of view—are often good for fiction. It can be hard to find the tension and the suspense in a voice that seems to know everything—why not just reveal the whole story at the start? The solution for me was to use the omniscience sparingly, so that the voice travels internally the way a camera can externally, zooming in and out, as needed. And I eventually came to feel that the combination of intimate moments against the backdrop of a larger scope would be the signature of the book. I'm obviously nowhere near the first to try this, of course—I fell in love with Virginia Woolf in college and how she skips from mind to mind so effortlessly. I also looked back at books like *Blindness* and Ann Patchett's *Bel Canto*, which use a similar perspective, and all of that helped me find the way.

KR: A cordon sanitaire ropes off Santa Lora from the rest of America; fences are patrolled by the military. And yet even as these walls feel terrifyingly real, inside Santa Lora, the membrane between dream and reality continues to thin. At one point Ben muses, "A symptom of delusion . . . is the inability to distinguish between reality and dream." He begins to question the very foundation of his "everyday reality."

Part of what makes your novel so frighteningly powerful is its ability to expose the cracks in the rigging of consciousness. The plot shines a light into the profoundly unstable nature of what we call "reality." As I read on, the walls of my living room began to shimmer suspiciously; like Ben, like Mei, I began to wonder how I could really be so sure that I wasn't sleeping myself, in some parallel dimension.

How did writing this book change the way you think about time, space, and this shared dream we call "reality"?

KTW: I find I have certain preoccupations that surface again and again in my writing: disaster, fear, time, varieties of love, the way the extraordinary is often hidden in the ordinary (and now a new obsession has joined that list: the experience of having children, which refracts all of those interests in a new way).

But another recurring interest of mine is how much we as human beings still don't know about our reality. At the moment, I'm reading a book called *Reality Is Not What It Seems* by the physicist Carlo Rovelli, all about the weirdness of quantum gravity. "The more we discover," he writes, "the more we understand that what we don't yet know is greater than what we know." I think we all need to recognize that unknowingness more often, be a little less stubborn in our certainties, and welcome the unknown and the inexplicable. I love to spend time in that realm in my fiction. Why do we sleep? Why do we dream? Why are we conscious at all? A premise like the one in *The Dreamers* is just the way I have of calling attention to all that beautiful unknown.

KR: I know at one point you were considering setting the novel in Iowa, where you and I got to be neighbors in 2014, two insomniacs on the tornado flats. What inspired you to move the setting to the small college town of Santa Lora, California? Did the novel undergo any other major changes in the drafting process?

KTW: I sometimes forget that the book was originally set in Iowa! I only lived there for two years (while my husband completed his MFA) and I found so many aspects of that landscape fascinating (and terrifying—I'd never heard a tornado siren, let alone cowered in a basement while one was going off!). What I realized eventually is that I just wasn't sufficiently in touch with the minutiae of the Iowa landscape to write about it—the weather, the plants, the style of the houses. I felt pulled to move the book to California, where I grew up and where I set *The Age of Miracles*. I don't know if I can ever know a place as deeply as the place where I grew up. There's something about childhood that really puts one in touch with the landscape, the dirt, the plants, the way the air smells in all weather, in all seasons. Even though Santa Lora is a fictitious town, and it's in the mountains instead of on the coast where I grew up, it still feels like a landscape from my childhood—the eternal threat of drought and wildfire, the mild winters, the dried-out pine trees. The one thing I had to sacrifice when I switched the location was a scene that involved a tornado, which I eventually replaced with a California-appropriate wildfire.

The other major change I made middraft was to switch the book from past tense to present tense. I made that change when I was about a hundred pages in, and I loved how the present tense heightened the sense of urgency, which seemed perfect for the story of an unfolding crisis. I once heard Charles Baxter say about the present tense that it's especially useful for characters who have no usable past, who are stuck, for whatever reason, in a kind of perpetual present. A crisis has a way of imposing that condition on people—a giant, blinking YOU ARE HERE sign.

KR: Novels are such a commitment—unlike the nine-month gestation of a child, they can be with us for years and years! What was the seed of this book, the catalyzing spark? Did you have any kind of outline or blueprint for *The Dreamers*? And if so, did this novel mutate away from your original vision? What surprised you the most, as you wrote it?

KTW: I never expected to be writing about college students or dreams, which is part of the pleasure of writing fiction, I guess: the way my own imagination can surprise me.

Living in a college town like Iowa City, where I started the book, brought back a flood of memories from college. A dorm floor—which is where the novel begins—might as well be a kind of quarantine: the small spaces, the hours and hours of time you spend with roommates and floormates, whether you want to or not. It suddenly occurred to me that writing about a mysterious contagion spreading through a dorm floor might be an interesting way to explore the complex ecosystem of that quarantined college world. That was the wispy way *The Dreamers* began—a world of memories I'd mostly forgotten that came back when I was suddenly surrounded by twenty thousand eighteen-year-olds again.

I had been working on it for maybe a month before I decided that the sickness would have something to do with sleep. And this idea—as convenient as it sounds—came from a dream. One morning, I dreamed that I couldn't wake up. And when I actually did wake up, I knew right away what the book's mysterious illness should be: a sleeping sickness that traps its victims in sleep. Sleep felt like a necessary ingredient in the premise, a way to make the story more than just an epidemic story. Sleep made room in the book for something more imaginative, the kind of thing we can only do in fiction: explore the unknowable. The idea that unusual dreams would be a part of the story came much later, and I was a little hesitant to include them. Dreams can be tricky in fiction—because they're like a fiction inside of a fiction, so there's a risk that they will feel diluted on the page. Also, the lack of a discernible logic in dreams is dangerous for fiction writers. Dreams have a kind of randomness that can be unsatisfying in fiction. So I had to find clear role for the dreams, a kind of specificity and a way that these dreams would be different from ordinary dreams.

KR: *The Dreamers* is a love story and also a horror story: a sort of literary Möbius strip, both dream and nightmare. One of my favorite lines gets at this duality: "This is how the sickness travels best: through all the same channels as do fondness and friendship and love."

Love makes us profoundly vulnerable; and yet as I read, I understood why certain characters would choose to risk exposure to the virus over the pain of isolation from their loved ones. Did you set out to examine what love becomes and does under this sort of extreme pressure?

At one point, Ben, a new father clutching his infant daughter, thinks, "The baby makes everything simple." Ben is desperate, understandably, to keep his family safe. It's impossible not to root for these individuals to escape the quarantine. At the same time, you never let us forget the larger stakes: If this child escapes, it puts a world of other children at risk.

How does love refreight the moral calculus for these characters? And their perception of risk and reward? When does a love story turn into a horror story, and vice versa?

KTW: One of the pleasures of spending years on a novel is the way it gradually leads you in unexpected directions, how one's interests evolve over the course of a project. One of the more unexpected subjects I began reading about was altruism in its most extreme forms. Larissa MacFarquhar's wonderful nonfiction book *Strangers Drowning* is full of provocative stories of people living in very radical ways as they attempt to live truly ethically. The idea that the life of your child means more to you than the life of a stranger, or even five strangers, has a kind of gut-level truth for most us. But, if you believe that people are all created equal, that every life should be equally valuable, then you get into difficult territory pretty quickly once you start running certain thought experiments. Take this famous example: if you had to make a choice, would you save your own child or two strangers from drowning? What about ten strangers? Or a hundred? The radical altruists in MacFarquhar's book would say that you should always go by the numbers, and save the greatest number of people. They would argue that it would be wrong in that situation to save your own child over the others. There's something cold and counterintuitive about that idea, and yet it's hard to argue with the ethics of it. Our sense of love can lead to all kinds of ugly consequences if you follow it out: my family before your family, my tribe before your tribe, my nation before yours. Matthew was my vehicle for exploring these thorny conflicts through a particular experience and psyche—he has an extremely austere and rigid sense of ethics that leads him to make choices that run counter to what almost everyone around him would do.

KR: For all the research into sleep, there is still no consensus on why we dream, or what, if anything, the purpose of our dreaming might be. What kind of research into sleep and dreams did you do while writing your novel? Do you think our dreams carry special meaning?

KTW: Can I just quote back to you the genius thing you wrote to me when you first read the book? "In some way, dreams seem to me to be the most honest communication a body can have with itself: the mind becomes its own captive audience, doing a stupendously weird shadow puppetry on the cave walls." I think that's a stunning way to sum up the primal fascination that most of us have with dreaming.

Sleep—and what happens in our minds while we do it—is exactly the kind of weird element of human life that fascinates me most. It's great territory for fiction: a kind of vast, mysterious unknown embedded right in our daily lives. And I love the idea that even in sleep we are storytelling beings.

As part of my research for the book, I went to a conference on the science of sleep, where I watched videos of people sleep-walking and having night terrors and listened to discussions about the connections between sleep and memory. But they didn't talk much about dreams, and it gave me a certain imaginative confidence, I think, to hear that the smartest people studying sleep and dreams still haven't reached definitive answers on these subjects.

KR: "How could something so bizarre really be so ordinary?" Sara muses to her sister. She has just gotten her period for the first time. They may be living through a horrifying, unprecedented sleep epidemic, but this hasn't stopped the animal clock inside her body from moving forward. Ordinary life, illuminated by these extraordinary conditions, seems newly miraculous. A first kiss. Hands finding each other in the dark. A fetus's cells dividing inside of her sleeping mother's body. Waking up to a flood of sunshine. Walking in the woods. When you set out to write *The Dreamers,* what did you want to reflect about this everyday strangeness? What came to seem especially bizarre to you about the "ordinary" rhythms of our lives on the planet?

KTW: This preoccupation might be the biggest carryover from my first book. I'm perpetually fascinated, and terrified, by the fragility of our experience of the world, and by the way the ordinary can be upended. But I'm also fascinated by the sheer beauty of ordinary things. As a reader, I love the way writers like Virginia Woolf and Marilynne Robinson capture the moments of reverie that can surge into the most everyday acts. And I think what both of those writers manage to do is find a language for what children know intuitively, which is that our feeling and sensing bodies and the world they are a part of really are miraculous things. Children meet the world with the appropriate and commensurate sense of wonder. It gets trained out of us as we grow up. But it's not irrecoverable, and fiction can sometimes give it back to us.

KR: Karen, you were pregnant twice while you were simultaneously gestating *The Dreamers*. Congratulations on such a beautiful, uncanny accomplishment—bringing two new humans *and* a new novel into this world. Can you tell us how your pregnancies affected *The Dreamers*?

KTW: It has been a busy four years! *The Dreamers* would be a different book if I had written the whole thing before I had my daughters. When my first daughter was eleven days old, I added a newborn baby to the book. I had so many new thoughts on the world during those first weeks. Raising children is a state of almost perpetual surprise. Words like *parenting* really do not capture the daily weirdness of having a young child. People don't talk enough about how fascinating children are. They're cute, of course, and tiring, but also so fascinating to watch and study. That feeling starts in pregnancy, knowing that their brains are gradually forming, that, for example, at a certain point, the fetal brain begins to dream. What you're really doing when you watch a child grow up is watching a human mind emerge. There's something about young children that seems connected to every element of reality. It brings you face-to-face with how uncanny—and unexplained—reality is. They don't yet have any habitual responses to the world, and their notion of cause and effect isn't the same as ours, which is why you keep them away from a stove, but it's also why they seem to exist in a state that's almost like a perpetual, fantastical dreaming. In the book, Ben, a new father, is caring for a newborn alone during this frightening outbreak, but his experience is a close approximation of what it feels like to have a newborn in a more ordinary time—especially when it's your first child. The first weeks of my first daughter's life were marked by an intense fear and awe that I've never felt before or since, and which I tried to capture in the book.

Reading Group Questions and Topics for Discussion

1. A contagious disease, a quarantined town—the characters in *The Dreamers* are facing an extreme situation. Our culture is dominated by two opposing narratives about how people respond to disasters: Some believe they bring out the worst in people, others that they bring out the best. How do these possibilities play out in *The Dreamers*?

2. What do you think of Matthew's character? Are his actions heroic or heartless? Selfless or self-aggrandizing? Or some combination? Is it ethical to privilege the lives of one's loved ones over the lives of strangers?

3. How does *The Dreamers* differ from other books about disaster and dystopia? What does it have in common with those stories?

4. Some of the sick characters dream of extraordinarily vivid alternate lives. Consider Rebecca, who dreams an entire lifetime, including a son. Do you think her dreamed-of life is somehow real, or just a delusion? What about Nathaniel's extended dream of Henry?

5. Why do you think Karen Thompson Walker chose to feature a large cast of characters instead of focusing on just one person's experience? How did this choice affect your reading of the book? Did one character resonate with you more than the others?

6. One of the main characters is a college freshman named Mei. How would you describe her personality? How does she change over the course of the novel?

7. *The Dreamers* includes many parent/child relationships. What do you think of the book's portrayal of these bonds? How does the crisis affect these relationships?

8. *The Dreamers* involves a fictitious disease in a fictitious town, but what parallels do you see to today's real world? How do you think the government would respond to a situation like this if it happened today?

9. How do you feel about the ending of the book? How do you imagine the lives of the surviving characters will look five years in the future? How do you think their experiences during the outbreak will affect the rest of their lives?

10. What do you think you would do if faced with the same situation as the characters in *The Dreamers*? Which character's journey and actions would be most similar to yours?

KAREN THOMPSON WALKER is the author of the *New York Times* bestselling novel *The Age of Miracles,* which has been translated into twenty-seven languages and named one of the best books of the year by *People, O: The Oprah Magazine,* and *Financial Times,* among others. Born and raised in San Diego, she is a graduate of UCLA and the Columbia MFA program. Walker lives with her husband, the novelist Casey Walker, and their two daughters in Portland. She is an assistant professor of creative writing at the University of Oregon.

KarenThompsonWalker.com
Instagram: @karenthompsonwalker